FIGHTER'S SECOND CHANCE

A. RIVERS

Cover design by Steamy Designs

Beta reading by Romance Refined

Editing by Free Bird Editing

Proofreading by Paper Poppy Editorial

To Mum,
For reading every single
book I write and being an
awesome cheerleader.

SETH

I don't remember the last time I was this nervous. Not when I stepped into the cage for a championship bout. Not even when I got married. Smoothing my hands down my button-down shirt—something I haven't worn in forever—I catch a glimpse of myself in the reflection from the cafe window and wince. I should have shaved. A week's worth of scruff decorates my jaw, with far more silver amongst it than there was back when I was with her.

With Ashlin.

Wiping my sweaty palms on my dark jeans—the nicest pair I own—I glance inside and spot her immediately, at a table in the rear of the cafe, as though she wants to be as far from the other customers as possible. At the sight of her, everything inside me clenches. There was a time when that woman was my entire world. But that was before she sat me down with a homemade dinner and asked for a divorce.

I haul in a breath, straighten my spine, and shove the door open. Inside, the cafe smells of cinnamon buns and pastries. My stomach gurgles, but I dare not put anything in it. I don't know what she wants with me or why she asked me to meet her, but I'm hoping it's for a second chance. There's nothing I want more.

"Ashlin," I say as I stop at her table.

She meets my eyes, every bit as gorgeous as I remember, with delicate pixie features, dark silky hair, and porcelain skin. But where's her smile? Ashlin Isles has a smile for every occasion. At least, she used to. Now, she's cool and reserved as she appraises me. Curling my fingers into my fists, I resist the urge to fidget as I wonder what she sees. I've changed since we were together. I've grown rougher, because it was her influence that smoothed my jagged edges. These days, I rarely glance in a mirror, but I know the crinkles around my eyes have multiplied, and tattoos cover even more of my skin than before—not that she can see them, since the long sleeves and jeans hide the majority.

"Hi, Seth." Her voice is quiet but strong. "Thanks for coming."

"No problem." I pull out the seat opposite her and drop into it. "Want to tell me why we're here?"

A furrow forms between her brows. "Would you like to get coffee first? Something to eat?"

I shake my head. "No, thanks. I'm not hungry."

She nods, and her fingers venture over to the ring finger of her left hand, then pause, and she glances down, as though confused by them. "Do you mind if I do?"

I shrug. "Sure. Go right ahead."

If this is a "let's try again" conversation, I want her to be as comfortable as possible. At the moment, it's plain she's nervous. Ashlin is usually the essence of grace, but every time I catch her eyes, they hold for only a moment before darting away. She waves to a waitress, who comes over, and orders a decaf latte. I raise a brow. Decaf? The Ashlin I knew loved her coffee strong. But then, I haven't seen her for years, so how much do I really know about her these days?

2

"Good day at the gym?" she asks while we wait for her drink to arrive.

"Same as usual." I've been running Crown MMA Gym for eight years, since before we divorced—before we were married, as a matter of fact. But she was there in the very beginning, encouraging me to pursue my dream because we both knew that my time as a professional MMA fighter was limited. No matter how good I was, age catches up with everyone. Becoming head coach at my own gym was a retirement plan. Now here I am, with one of the best gyms in the country, but no wife to share my success.

"Devon is back at training?" she asks.

I nod. "Dangerous" Devon Green has recently returned to the gym after a brief stint away while I came to grips with his relationship with my baby sister. I was worried about them at first since they effectively had a workplace romance, but fortunately, it seems to be working out. I'll never hear the end of it for going overprotective big brother on their asses.

"Yeah. He is."

"How do you feel about that?"

"I wish they'd gone about things differently," I confess. It had taken them God knew how long to come clean with me. Am I really such a scary guy that my sister and one of my closest friends couldn't be honest from the beginning? "I'm not upset about them as a couple though. They'll be good for each other."

"I think so too," she says. Her drink is delivered, and she takes a sip, then clasps it between her hands as if to warm them, even though it's a balmy eighty degrees out. "Right." She takes a breath. "I suppose I should get to the point."

"That would be great. I've got no idea what I'm doing here."

She nods, then meets my eyes and holds the connection. "I want to have a baby."

"*What?*" I gasp for air as the metaphorical floor falls out from under me. No blow I've ever received from an opponent could knock me down the way she has with one statement.

I was there the last time she got pregnant. I witnessed the emotional aftermath of our miscarriage. Hell, I lived it. She fell apart, went through a period of depression, and I couldn't do anything to help. Why would she want to put herself through that again?

She continues to hold my gaze. For all that she's delicate and sweet, Ashlin is steely when it counts. "I still want children, and after all this time, I'm finally strong enough—body and mind—to have them."

I want to protest. She didn't see herself after we lost Cara. My thumb goes instinctively to the small tattoo inside my wrist. Our daughter's name. I rub it back and forth, soothing myself, trying to ward off a wave of helplessness brought on by the memories. Ashlin had vanished into herself, and I disappeared into work. Then everything I cared about came crumbling down. But on the heels of the old grief comes something else.

Jealousy.

"I didn't know you were seeing anyone." Why is she even telling me this? Some kind of misguided attempt to prevent me getting hurt if I were to learn about it later? Too late. I wanted to grow old with her. To raise a family. It was one thing when I thought she just didn't want that anymore because it was too much for her to handle, but to know she wants it with someone other than me is just cruel.

"I'm not." She sighs, and glances down for a second. Long enough for me to know she isn't comfortable with this conversation. "I'm going to do it by myself."

"Wait, what?" She remembers how pregnancy works, right? Man + Woman + Sex = Baby. I'm not sure how she intends to remove the male part of the equation.

She rolls her eyes. "IVF. I'll go through a fertility treatment and impregnation process. After the damage from our miscarriage, it's my best chance of success."

"No man involved?" I clarify.

"Well, actually…" She bites her lip. "I need a donor. I was going to choose one from a catalog, but none of them felt right."

My jaw drops. Choose a father for her baby from a goddamn catalog? Of all the crazy ideas. Of course it didn't feel right. It's stupid.

"You're the only man I can imagine as the father." She swallows, and her throat bobs. "I know it's a lot to ask, but will you consider it? Will you help me have a baby?"

ASHLIN

They can probably hear my heart beating the next county over. Shock is written across Seth's face, and etched in the clench of his jaw. A vein throbs at his temple. I fight the urge to yell "Punked!" and run for the exit. I knew he'd be surprised, but I've spent weeks dwelling on my choice, and haven't approached him lightly. Right now, securing his agreement is the single most important thing in my universe, so I don't flinch when he curses. I don't glance down, or give him any indication that I'm not a hundred percent sure of my decision.

I am unwavering.

"Do you really think getting pregnant is a good idea?" he asks, the grooves around his mouth deepening.

I inhale slowly to buy myself a moment of calm. I knew this question would come, and I'm prepared for it. "I can understand why you'd ask that, considering what I put us both through last time, but I've been in therapy and it's really helped." One of my hands trembles, so I rest the other on top of it. "I'm ready to try again."

"Ash…" That vein continues to throb at his temple. "Are you

sure? Perhaps your memory of the time after the miscarriage is fuzzy, but for me, it's crystal clear. You weren't okay. And I... I let you down. Wasn't there when you needed me. I'll always regret that, and I'm not sure if I can be part of something that puts you at risk again."

My stomach sinks, even though I understood this was a possibility. I force my shoulders to stay back. Time to preserve my dignity.

"If you don't want to be involved, that's fine, but you should know that I'm going ahead anyway."

His eyes widen, and he flinches almost imperceptibly. "Still so fucking stubborn," he mutters.

He looks down at his hands, turning them over and studying his palms. I follow his gaze, ignoring the flash of warmth that travels through me. They're large and rough, and even though it was years ago, I remember with perfect clarity how they felt on my naked body. He used to touch me as though I was precious, but the more he lost control, the less care he took, and I reveled in his wildness.

"Just tell me something." He squeezes his hands into fists and raises his eyes, anger flaring in their blue-green depths. "Why the fuck do you want to hurt yourself this way?" He starts to reach for me, but then stops and drags in a slow breath. When he continues, his voice is like sandpaper. "I don't want to see you in pain."

Oh, God. It's just like it used to be. He's a great, unsettled beast of a man that needs taming, and I want to stand behind him and soothe him with my hands the way I used to. Run them down his shoulders and back. Kiss the side of his neck. Watch the tension ease from him. My body clenches with the effort it takes not to go to him. I didn't realize that his magnetism would be so potent after all this time. I should have known better. Whatever our problems, Seth and I have always been attracted to each other to the point of insanity.

"It's okay," I reassure him. "I can handle whatever comes." I

6

might not enjoy it, but I can survive. Of this, I'm certain. "I want a family, and I'm strong enough to fight for one. Like I said, if you'd rather not be involved, that's fine, but I'm doing it anyway."

His eyes narrow. Oh, he doesn't like that. Of course he doesn't. There was a time when I'd cave in to nearly anything he wanted if he used that gruff, bossy tone of his. But I'm not budging on this. His jaw shifts as he resists the urge to spill out the first response that pops into his head. Despite the circumstances, I have to smile. Always a hothead.

"I can give you time to think about it," I say, beginning to rise from my chair. "I know it's a serious decision."

"No." He gestures for me to stop. "Sit." I do. He rolls his shoulders up to his ears and back down again. "I want to help. I can't fucking stand the idea of seeing you pregnant with another man's kid."

He knows there would be no touching involved, right?

Still, a thrill shoots through me at his possessiveness. We're not together anymore, and perhaps I need to have my head examined, but I always loved the way he made it clear who I belonged with and warned off anyone else. It made me feel cherished. Adored. Sternness aside, Seth Isles is capable of making a woman feel like a siren and a princess all in one.

I stay quiet, waiting.

"Okay." His shoulders heave as the word leaves him on a rush of air. Those gorgeous turquoise eyes meet mine, and my insides tumble over each other. "I'll do it."

"Thank you." It feels like I've been holding my breath forever, and finally released it. I meant it when I said I'd go ahead with or without his help, but it wouldn't have felt right. Choosing candidates from a list of physical attributes and places of employment seems cold. Distant. Especially when I've spent months picturing a perfect little baby with Seth's crystal eyes and my dark hair.

Discomfort worms its way into my gut. Part of me is afraid

that all of this is my subconscious's method of bringing him back into my life, but I shut that little voice down. I'm strong enough to stand on my own two feet. I've been doing it for three years now. I've proved to myself that I'm resilient and capable. So what if Seth makes my pulse climb and my heart soften? It doesn't mean anything.

"You won't regret it." I reach for my bag and extract a sheath of papers, then pass them to him. "This is a legal contract that sets out how everything will work."

He baulks, glancing from the papers to me, and back again, his distaste apparent. "Is that really necessary?"

"Yes." Of this, I'm certain. I won't allow any shades of gray. "Read it later. Have your lawyer look at it. Whatever you need."

"I'm sure it's fine." He sets the papers aside and props his chin on his hand. "Let me pay for the procedure. IVF is expensive, right?"

I shake my head. "I have enough in my savings. It's important to me that I pay myself."

"Are you sure?" I can tell he wants to argue. He thinks he's protecting me by taking on a financial burden, but I know the truth: I have to prove that I can stand on my own. I *need* it.

"Yes." I raise my chin, waiting to see how he reacts.

To my surprise, he nods. "If that's what you want."

2

SETH

I set the papers aside.

This is my chance to get her back.

I asked for one, and the universe gave it to me. Sure, it doesn't look like I expected it to, but I'm going to grab on with both hands and not let go. If Ashlin and I have a baby, she'll be back in my life for good. We'll have to spend time together, and presumably, we'll have to have sex. My body heats at the thought of touching her. Laying my ugly boxer's hands on her pretty pinkness and bringing her down to my level. She was always an angel. Too good for me. But in our lust, we were perfectly matched. I ached to manhandle her, and she was desperate for me to do so. You'd never know it to look at her, but behind her good girl exterior is a dirty little deviant who likes to be punished for tormenting her man. God, I hope no one other than me has ever seen her naughty side, but considering how fucking gorgeous she is, she won't have been hurting for male attention. Damn, I want to hunt down anyone who's so much as looked at her pert ass and make them regret it.

Taking another breath, I get my possessiveness under control. Maybe she liked that side of me when we were together, but we're not married anymore. I don't get to fuck her against the wall because some asshole looked at her in the way only I'm allowed to.

"I'll send them to my lawyer tonight," I tell her, making a point not to skim the details. I need to be sharp, and reading legalese isn't something I've ever found easy. That's why she used to do it for me, and summarize the basics. Ashlin wasn't just my wife; she was also my sounding board and my conscience. Until I let her down.

"How are you feeling?" she asks, knowing me too well to buy the calm facade I'm putting on for her benefit.

"Crazy." In a way, this is everything I've ever wanted. I used to dream of raising a family with Ashlin, but that was before everything fell apart. Leaning forward on my elbows, I reach over and grasp one of her hands. It twitches, as though her instinct is to yank it away, but she doesn't.

I frown. Her palm isn't as soft as it used to be. She has calluses, and her nails are short and bare. When we were together, she always sported a manicure, and I could tell by its color what mood she was in. I never mentioned that to her, but it was my barometer for when she might need more affection, or was feeling particularly spicy. My stomach drops an inch. The unfamiliar sensation of her roughened skin drives home the fact that I don't know her anymore. I used to be the keeper of her secrets, but other than what I've been able to glean on social media—not a lot—I'm completely in the dark about her life.

"Ash," I begin, concentrating on the shape of her fingers because at least that hasn't changed. "I promise you, if things go wrong this time, I will be there for you." I put my whole heart into the words, hoping she knows how much I mean them. "I'll do a better job of taking care of you. I won't let history repeat."

Her lips part, her eyes flickering with something dark, but then she clears her throat and withdraws her hand from mine.

"That's sweet, but I don't need you to do that for me. This time, I'm capable of doing it myself."

Fuck. If she kicked me in the balls, it wouldn't hurt this much. She knows I always prided myself on my ability to give her what she needed. Only, I failed in the end, and apparently, she hasn't forgotten.

"Seth..." She cringes. "I didn't mean that the way it sounded. It's just that I'm a whole lot stronger than I used to be."

I nod, noting her raised chin and defiant expression. It seems I'm not the only one with a lot of pride. "So, how are you keeping yourself busy these days?"

Up until I saw her over the weekend, I hadn't looked her up for years because it hurt too much. In the months after she left me, I checked her social media every damn day, looking for a sign she was doing okay—or that she missed me and was miserable without me. She didn't post anything for six months, but then she replaced her profile photo of us on our honeymoon with one of her and two other women I'd never met. That prompted me to deep dive into her new friends' accounts, but when I found myself getting unreasonably angry because one of them had a good-looking brother, I realized I needed to back the hell off and let it go. She wasn't my business anymore.

"I'm working at the kindergarten again."

"Whoa." I lean back to study her. The set of her mouth tells me she's expecting me to make a big deal of it. As well I should. She took months off after the miscarriage because she couldn't handle seeing the kids every day and remembering what we'd lost. Now she's back there? "Are you... enjoying it?"

"I am." She smiles, and the flash of her teeth renders me speechless. My throat constricts, and my fingers itch to reach for her. "Being around the children reminds me of how much I want my own, and maybe it's risky, but honestly, they're worth it."

"That's great." I wince when my tone is hoarser than I'd like it to be. "Really, Ash. I'm glad you're happy."

11

"Thank you."

"There's no man in your life who's going to be pissed that you're having a baby with your ex?" I've assumed there isn't, but I'd prefer to know for sure.

"There's not." She doesn't elaborate, and I can't help the barrage of questions I want to throw at her. Have there been others? Has she dated? Kissed? Fucked? *Loved*? It's the last possibility that gets me the worst, chilling my chest and robbing me of my ability to breathe. "How about you? Any girlfriend I should be aware of?"

A ragged laugh gusts from me. "Nope."

There's been no one since her. Anytime I get close to someone, it feels wrong. One time, I nearly kissed a woman, but I couldn't go through with it and ended up heaving my guts into a toilet a few moments later.

"Is Harley still living with you?" she asks.

Harley is my kid sister, and a friend of Ashlin's. We divorced while Harley was out of the country, and as far as I know, no one has ever explained the reason for our separation to her. No one has explained it to anyone. It hurt too much.

"Yeah, for now. She and Dev seem pretty hot and heavy, so she might move in with him soon. I'll miss her, but it'll be a relief not to worry about seeing him naked every time I come home. He's not shy about his body, that's for fucking sure."

She giggles, and the reluctant sound makes me feel like a king. It reminds me of who she used to be when she wasn't quite so contained. Not that there's anything wrong with her current level of reserve, and considering we're separated, it's probably appropriate, but that doesn't mean I like it.

"Do you, uh, live with anyone?" I ask.

"No." She steeples her fingers and studies me over them. "I'd drive a roommate crazy with all the—" She cuts herself off, and shakes her head self-consciously. "I don't need to bore you with the details. Suffice it to say, I live alone." She slides her chair back and stands up. "I'd better get going. Call me if you have any questions about the contract."

"I will." I watch, bemused, as she leaves cash on the table and walks away. What was that last hesitation about?

ASHLIN

That was close. I nearly told Seth more than I'm comfortable with him knowing at this point. Honestly, I expected to be flustered by being around him, but I underestimated how much he's still imprinted on my heart. We're always going to have a physical attraction—that's just chemistry—but he stirred emotions I'd prefer to remain dormant.

When I reach my car, I pause to look at my hands. They're trembling. I breathe in to the count of five, then out to the count of seven, and repeat the cycle until I've calmed enough to unlock the door and let myself in. Sliding into the seat, I close my eyes and then rest my forehead on the steering wheel. I'm filled with jittery energy, and it's just as well I know exactly how to work it off—one of the few positive things that came of my miscarriage. I fish my phone from my purse and open the group chat I have running with Paige and Jessica, two of my best friends.

Ashlin: *He said yes!*

Paige: *Holy shit. So it's a go?*

Ashlin: *Once he's signed the contract.*

Jessica: *Are you okay after seeing him again?*

Ashlin: *A bit shaky, but good overall.*

Paige: *We're on our way to your place with pregnancy-approved snacks.*

I smile. When I first masterminded my plan, I was worried how they'd react, considering I met them in a support group for women who'd miscarried or gone through a stillbirth. I was aware that by trying to get pregnant, I might trigger their grief

13

and poke at old wounds, but they've both been wonderful. Except for some initial misgivings about involving Seth— because they know he's the love of my life and time hasn't changed that—they've been behind me all the way. I couldn't ask for better.

Ashlin: *I'll be there soon. Just leaving Sugar.*

Jessica: *Drive safe. XO*

It doesn't take me long to reach the brick house I bought a couple of years ago. Typically, a house this size in this part of town would be outside my budget, but the interior was an absolute disaster zone, so I picked it up for a bargain. Paige's sporty BMW convertible is parked on the road, and I pull up the short drive, pressing the automatic garage door opener to let myself in. As I park and get out, the girls approach from behind. Paige bounces toward me, her glossy brown curls swinging over her shoulders, while Jessica follows at a more dignified pace. My friends are very different from each other, and from me, but somehow the three of us work well together.

Paige comes from money, but except for her flashy car and designer outfits, you wouldn't know it. She's all smiles and seems to find something she likes about everyone she encounters. Jessica, on the other hand, is a former professional beach volleyball player who looks like Malibu Barbie, but she worked her way up from nothing and keeps her cards close to her chest. At the moment, her tanned legs eat up the distance between us, while her movements remain graceful and unhurried.

Paige sweeps me into a hug and lifts me off the ground— not difficult, considering I can barely claim a height of five-two. "Gah, I'm so happy for you." She sets me on my feet and grabs me by the shoulders. "Everything is falling into place, and now you're going to have a little fighter baby with sexy genes."

"I hope so." I brush my bangs off my face, and turn to Jessica. "Now we cross our fingers he doesn't question the contract."

She raises a perfectly arched brow. "You think he will?"

"Yeah." I sigh. "Seth is a lot of things, but easy isn't one of them. I can think of at least one clause off the top of my head that he'll probably argue."

"Custody," she says, and I nod. The three of us talked it over extensively. Seth didn't have the best childhood, and he always made it clear that he intended to be a better father than his own absent one had been. Once he sees the clause where I've asked him to sign away all parental rights, I'm expecting a call. Honestly, a joint custody arrangement might be best for our future child, but it won't be comfortable for me, so I decided it was worth trying for sole custody and seeing whether he made a fuss.

Paige deflates, but pats my arm encouragingly. "It's okay, Ash. We've got a game plan. You're ready for whatever comes, and we'll be with you no matter what."

"Thanks." We meet eyes, then simultaneously reach for Jessica and tug her into a three-way hug, ignoring her grunts of protest. "I love you guys." I release them and gesture toward the entrance. "Come in. Hope you're in the mood to break things."

Paige winks. "Always."

We step inside and scoot around the debris on the floor. There was a time when I was ashamed to bring them here because of what a mess it was, but I got over that about the same time Jessica opened up and showed me photos of the trailer park where she grew up. These days, I hardly notice the broken parts. All I see is the changes I'm making. The pieces I'm putting back together, and turning into something beautiful. A home. I lead them into the living area—one of four rooms in the house that's in good shape. The other usable rooms are the bathroom, the main bedroom, and the kitchen— all of which I've worked on with my own hands. How's that for being a kickass woman?

"What was it like to see him again?" Jessica asks as she rounds the counter that separates the kitchen from the living room. She collects three glasses from a drawer and fills each with water, then grabs a lemon from a bowl and slices thin wedges. She's such a caretaker. Looking after others comes naturally to her. I feel a pang, once again, that she had to suffer through a stillbirth. She'd be a wonderful mother.

"Strange." I accept a glass of water when she offers it. "We were both very polite."

Her forehead crinkles. "Isn't that good?"

"Yeah, but it's weirdly formal when we used to have hot, crazy, monkey sex."

Paige laughs, and flops onto a beanbag. The living room doesn't have furniture yet because I'm funneling my money toward fixing the other rooms and saving for a baby. "You mean that talking like strangers weirded you out when he used to fuck you on a daily basis?"

"Yeah," I admit.

She waggles her brows. "Was the spark still there?"

I duck my head so they can't see the blush that creeps over my cheeks. "The attraction never disappeared. That's not the reason we divorced. In fact…" I trail off.

"What?" Paige demands, sitting upright.

"Nothing." My face flames. "It's just, I think he might have thought the meeting was going somewhere else. He dressed up for it." I swallow, recalling how his body affected me. "He looked good."

Paige's lips curl up. "Honey, I've seen the man. He always looks good."

"Looks aren't everything," Jessica chastens, and Paige snorts, giving her a once-over as if to remind her how stunning she is herself. "They're not," Jessica insists. "I'd be happy with an averagely attractive guy who doesn't go out past nine and pays his share of the bills."

"So romantic," I tease. Like me, Jessica's relationship broke up after her pregnancy went wrong. Paige is the only one of us who managed to pull through, and come out the other side as a tight unit with her partner.

Paige sighs. "There are literally thousands of men in Vegas who meet your criteria and would kill for a chance with you."

Jessica rolls her eyes. "Here we go again."

Before they rehash old ground, I set my drink down, stride over to a toolbox on the floor and grab a hammer. "The wall between the two spare bedrooms needs to come down. Want to help?"

Leaping to her feet, Paige exclaims, "Hell, yes!"

"Have you checked with an engineer that it's safe to demolish the wall?" Jessica asks.

"Yes." I flash a piece of paper at her. "Got the permit yesterday. We're officially allowed to knock it down."

A smile tugs at her lips. "I'm in."

3

SETH

Tyrell Stephens, my lawyer, raises his head and smirks as I approach his desk. "If it isn't Iron-Shin Seth Isles. My only client who's ballsy enough to charge into the office after hours, without an appointment, and expect me to drop everything to help him."

He stands, and I slap my hand into his. Teasing aside, I've worked with Tyrell since we were both nobodies, and he's as loyal to me as I am to him. "I need you to review a contract. Fast. You got time tonight or tomorrow?"

One of his dark brows shoots up. "I'm booked out months in advance, but you already know that. I can have a quick look and do you a solid if you get me tickets to Gabe Mendoza's next fight."

I drag a seat around his desk so we can talk without it between us. "You need to impress a new client?"

He laughs. "Potential father-in-law. I've been seeing this new girl, Tyesha. Real pretty. Works as an agent. Her daddy manages a hockey team."

"Wait." I hold up a hand. "Tyrell and Tyesha? Isn't that a little too cutesy for you?"

He shrugs. "Can't ask her to change her name. Not gonna change mine. So who gives a fuck? Anyway, what do you say?"

"You got it." I bump his fist, then hand over the contract.

He scans the heading. "Whoa, man. Hang on. You're going to knock up your ex?" He drops the papers on his desk and stares at me. "Have you gone completely crazy? This is the worst idea ever."

I square my shoulders and narrow my eyes, knowing that I'm a scary-looking fucker when I want to be. "I don't plan on her being my ex for much longer."

"Oh." The word is filled with meaning. "Are you sure? The divorce destroyed you. Do you really want to go another round with her? It might not turn out the way you hope."

I shrug. "Until the weekend, I hadn't seen her for years. Whatever happens, it can't be worse than that. Not seeing her, or knowing what's going on in her life... that's hell." I roll my neck from one side to the other, trying to loosen the stiffness. What Tyrell doesn't know, and I'm not prepared to tell him yet, is that I'll do everything in my power to make Ashlin my family again. If that means rolling with the emotional punches, I'll do it. If it means being her shoulder to cry on, I'm there. If I have to woo her the old-fashioned way, with dates and love letters and flowers, then just call me Mr. Romantic. "Will you look at it, or what?"

He sighs. "You know I will. But as your lawyer, it's my job to tell you that I think this is a mistake."

"Got it. Loud and clear." Doesn't mean I intend to listen to him. He's my friend, but he's never had a love like the one I shared with Ashlin so he doesn't know how it feels to lose it, or the lengths I'd go to in order to repair what we had.

"You're a stubborn bastard." He reaches for the contract and skims the first page. "This looks pretty standard. I'll read it in bed tonight and get back to you tomorrow. Sound good?"

I nod. "Thanks. I appreciate it, Ty."

"I hope you know what you're doing."

"I've got this." I stand up and drag the seat back to where I got it from. "Talk tomorrow?"

"Yeah." He waves the papers at me. "In the meantime, promise that you'll think about whether this is a mistake." His expression is utterly serious. "I love Ashlin as much as the next person. She's pretty irresistible. But you're my first priority."

"I'll think on it."

For a moment, he opens his mouth as though he wants to call me on my bullshit, but then he just shakes his head and gestures to the door. "Don't let it hit you on the way out."

"See you."

I take the elevator down to my car, which is parked in the basement, and keep an eye on the shadows of the artificially lit area as I cross the concrete floor. I slide inside the vehicle, lock the doors, and then recline the seat to stare at the ceiling. My brain is so full of everything that's happened in the past hour I feel like I need to get it all out. But who can I talk to? Am I even supposed to mention this to anyone? Ashlin didn't say, and discussing it behind her back feels wrong.

Jerking upright, I grin. I've just been handed the perfect reason to call her. I grab my phone and dial her number from memory. I deleted it from my contacts not long after the divorce so I wouldn't be tempted to reach out and beg her to take me back, but it's stamped in my mind anyway.

"Hi." She's breathless, and my imagination automatically conjures an image of her naked and sweaty. I wonder if her body still looks the same as it used to. "Did you have a question?"

"Uh, yeah." I clear my throat, and squeeze my eyes shut, trying to dispel the image. It won't go. My gut churns, and I ache to know exactly why she sounds that way. What has she been doing?

No, Seth. You don't deserve to know what's going on in her life.

So I don't ask. Instead, I focus on the reason I called. "Can I tell anyone what we're doing, or should I keep it secret?"

"Hmm." She hums in the back of her throat, and my sex-deprived body remembers how she used to do that while my cock was in her mouth.

Oh, fuck.

Keeping my cool around her is going to be even harder than I realized. Emphasis on "hard."

"I suppose it's only fair that you have someone to talk it over with," she says after thinking for a moment. "But I'd appreciate if you could limit it to one or two people. And only those you trust. I don't want word getting out in case it doesn't work."

"I hadn't even thought about that." One of the only things that made our miscarriage manageable in my eyes was that we hadn't told anyone we were pregnant yet, so we didn't have to deal with their sympathy afterward.

She laughs without humor. "I can hardly think of anything else. I'm just wishing and hoping and praying that things will be different."

"They will be." If I say it convincingly enough, we might both believe it. "But if they aren't, we'll survive. We've done it once, and we can do it again."

"We can," she agrees. "Is that all? Because I have some guests over, and I should get back to them."

Before I can demand to know who she's with, I force myself to shut up and rethink my word choice. "That's all for now. I'll call if there's anything else. Bye, Ash."

"Talk later."

———

*A*SHLIN

"Ms. Isles, look at my painting!"

Smiling, I head to five-year-old Sasha Grey and pause at her shoulder to ooh and aah over her picture of what I presume is meant to be a cat. It has three legs and its whiskers are almost as long as its body, but her pride is evident and honestly, with her pink cheeks and darling curls, I don't have to fake my enthusiasm.

I love my job.

Yes, it was hard for me to be around children constantly when I'd recently miscarried, but eventually I decided that being around these kids was better than nothing at all, and now I only ever experience the faintest of twinges.

"Very good, Sasha. What's her name?"

"His name is Milo," she replies, adding a blue stripe to Milo's face.

Beside her, Bethany Yu bounces on the spot, desperate to receive attention. I turn to her. "What have you painted, Bethany?"

She points her brush at the paper. "It's Mrs. Chou's dog, Flossy. She lives next door. Mom says Flossy is a rat."

Her innocent statement startles a snort from me, and I cover my face to hide the reaction. "Do you like Flossy?"

She shrugs. "She's okay, I guess."

Something catches my attention in the corner of my eye, and I glance around just in time to see Benjamin Potts go bottom-up over a table and land in a heap on the other side. Fortunately, the table is only a foot or two high. Unfortunately, Benjamin is the king of drama. His lip wobbles, and I rush over, praying he'll hold it together, but just before I reach him, the waterworks start. He wails, scrunching his eyes and letting loose with a wave of sound an opera singer would envy.

"There now, Ben, you're okay," I soothe, checking him over to make sure he's uninjured.

"Not. Okay," he grumbles.

"There's barely a mark on you." Perhaps I sound unsympathetic, but I've found that with him, it's best to play things off and he'll come around. Act the slightest bit concerned and he'd have made such a fuss, his parents would be here within thirty minutes.

"Isn't there?" His lip wobbles again, and he glances down at himself as though expecting to be missing a limb. "Huh."

"So are you all good?" I ask. "Ready to get back to painting?"

He nods, and I help him clamber to his feet, then smooth my hands down my skirt. Dressing nicely isn't always the best idea as a kindergarten teacher but I enjoy the way it makes me feel, and it doesn't bother me if the kids mess me up. In fact, I kind of like it. It shows they're comfortable with me, and that I'm still capable of interacting with them despite what happened. Maybe I'll never be the kind of tough Seth was in the ring, but I have my own brand, and it's not any less valuable than his.

Seth.

I hope he'll say yes, even after he's had Tyrell read over the contract. I know he won't read it himself. The man doesn't have the patience for that. If he has concerns, I'm prepared to negotiate. A band constricts around my chest. I just want a baby, and for some reason I'd rather not delve into too deeply, I want it to be his.

What would our baby look like?

I spent plenty of time picturing Cara, the daughter we never had. We'd chosen a name before we even got pregnant. Perhaps that's what jinxed us. It's hard to break free of that image and try to build another child in her place. For a while, I felt like I was betraying her by wanting to try again. Not honoring her memory. But my therapist helped me see how misguided that was. After all, she'll always be a part of me, but she never even drew a breath. It hurts to think about losing her, but I want another chance.

At the back of the class, Ying Lee waves at me, and I smile. I want my own little girl more than I fear being devastated all over again.

4

I wipe sweat off my brow with a towel and toss it on the gym floor.

"Good job," I tell Jase, who's been working on pads with me for the past half hour. "Spend some more time practicing your fakes."

He nods, his slate gray eyes thoughtful. He knows that fancy footwork isn't a strength of his. He's more of a brawler, but he's getting to the point in his professional career where he can't afford to have weaknesses, which means we need to tighten up his flaws to the point where they won't provide a clever opponent with a way to beat him.

Jase starts to turn, but then pauses. "You okay, man? You seem a bit off this morning."

I'm struck by the urge to tell him everything. Jase may be more than a decade younger than me, but he's the little brother I never had. For some reason, I keep my mouth shut. Opening up isn't something I'm good at.

"Didn't sleep well."

"Damn." He pulls a sympathetic face. "Hope it's better tonight."

"Yeah." My phone rings, and I'm grateful for the reprieve. At least, I am until I check the screen and see it's Tyrell. I'm not sure I'm ready to hear whatever he has to tell me. Indicating to Jase that I have to take it, I head for my office and shut the door. The space is larger than I need because in my heart I'm still a kid born on the wrong side of the blanket in the kind of crappy town where people hold that shit against you, and this is my way of proving I've made something of myself. The office has been useful since the divorce though, because my condo doesn't feel like home. This space is familiar. Comforting. I know exactly who I am when I flop on the sofa and put my feet up: "Iron-Shin" Seth Isles, former UFC champion. Never been knocked out. The guy everyone wants to learn from.

"Hey, what's the deal with the contract?" I ask, in lieu of a greeting.

"Good morning to you, too."

"Good morning, Tyrell," I grind out, impatient for details.

"I'm good thanks," he replies, as though I'd asked. "The contract is nothing out of the ordinary. Basically, it's the best deal you could ask for. All you have to do is get your swimmers tested and then, if everything is fine with them, jerk off into a sample bottle. You'd have no ongoing responsibility to either Ashlin or any child that might result."

Wait, what?

"What the fuck?" I demand, shaking my head, trying to comprehend his words. "There's so much wrong with what you just said."

"What do you mean?"

"I have no rights to the kid?"

"No *responsibility* to provide for the kid," he clarifies, as though that should make all the difference.

"No. Hell, no." I put the phone on speaker and pace the length of the office, arms crossed over my chest. I can't believe Ashlin would even suggest that. Not when she knows how I grew up, never completely sure who my father was. I always vowed I'd take care of any kids we had. Even when we'd only just started dating, I let her know that if an accident happened, I was all in. To be fair, I was obsessed with Ashlin from the moment I saw her, looking completely out of place at a fight night. An innocent Snow White, with the sweetest smile and a habit of glancing down when she spoke as though she wasn't quite sure of her place in the world. I'd decided in that instant that her place was beside me. So, really, promising to take care of her had never been a hardship.

But I'd failed anyway.

"Buddy, this is a good thing. It means you're free and clear."

I don't want to be free. I want to be bound to Ashlin forever. "I need to talk to Ash. What was the other thing you said? Jack off into a cup? You mean there'd be no sex involved?"

"It's a hands-off process," he confirms. "IVF. Didn't she say?"

I frown. She did, but for some reason it never clicked. Damn. It hurts more than it should. I don't want to go through some impersonal laboratory process like our baby is a science experiment. Does she not trust me to touch her? To make her feel good? Because if she gave me the option, I'd make her feel better than she ever remembered. I may be out of practice, but I've never forgotten how it feels to strip off Ashlin Isles and help her block out everything except bliss.

"Okay, thanks for letting me know. I've gotta talk to her. I'll call later."

"You should sign it," he says before I hang up. "That's my official advice."

The more I think about it, the more I hate the idea, and I know that Ashlin must have expected this, which means she's waiting for me to call and argue. Excitement pings through me. She gave me an opening, and I'm not stupid enough to ignore it.

"I hear you. Talk later." I hang up, and sink back onto the sofa, my stomach churning with nerves and anticipation. My hands tremble more than they should as I bring up Ashlin's number. It rings for thirty seconds and no one answers. I try again, frustrated. With how much this means to her, shouldn't she be sitting by her phone and waiting to hear from me?

"Good morning," she answers, slightly breathless. "I'm in class. Can I call you back in twenty minutes?"

"Yeah, I guess—" A crash reverberates through the speaker, and then the sound dies.

The next twenty minutes feel like the longest of my life. I force myself to return to the gym floor and supervise some of the up-and-coming fighters, but my phone doesn't leave my hand, and the instant it buzzes, I beeline for my office, regardless of the fact I was halfway through telling Jimmy something.

"Sorry about that," she says. "The kids are working on art projects, and the collective mood is a bit destructive. What were you calling about?"

Hearing her voice cools my temper. I love the sound of her in my ear. Back before we lived together, I used to talk to her for hours on the phone at night, while I closed my eyes and pictured her beautiful face. I do that now, and feel the pressure in my chest ease.

"The contract."

"Do you… have questions?" The hesitation gives her away. She knew I'd want to make changes.

I decide to start with the easier thing, and get it out of the way first. "Would you really rather have the doctors shove a syringe up you than make love with me?"

Her short intake of breath tells me she didn't expect this question. "I, uh, thought it was better not to reopen old wounds. We broke up for a reason, and I don't think being intimate with each other is a good idea." She exhales shakily. "The fact you call it love-making rather than sex is a sign I'm right. Besides," she goes for the kill, "since I've miscarried before, a pregnancy is more likely to be successful that way. It makes sense."

I can't argue against science, so I don't try. Honestly, I'd have to be a messed up bastard to insist she have sex with me for any reason, but especially when it might put her at higher risk of failing to get pregnant or experiencing another miscarriage. She's vulnerable, and I'm not going to use that to twist her into a difficult position.

"Okay."

"Okay?" She seems surprised.

"Yeah." I rub my jawline. "Like you said, it makes sense." I just have to hope that those wounds she mentioned only exist because she still feels something for me, just as I still care for her. Love her.

Ashlin

Seth doesn't push the matter of IVF versus sex, for which I'm incredibly grateful. We never lacked a physical connection, but for me, it was always bound up in emotion, and I'm not sure I could handle him touching me the way he used to. I might cry. Or slap him. Or beg him to love me forever.

It's that last option I'm most afraid of. We were good partners to each other, but I was always the weaker link. I never had to stand on my own feet because he was right behind me, taking care of me, making sure I got what I wanted. I can't lie and say I didn't like it. The way he treated me made me feel cherished. Like I belonged with him. But it also meant I wasn't challenged to build my own internal strength—something I needed, and which I've been forced to do in the past three years.

"About the parental rights..." I begin, knowing this is what he wants to debate.

"You can't take them away from me," he states, drawing a line in the sand. "If you want me to be the father, I'm not signing away my rights. If we have a baby,"—his voice cracks on that last word, and I have the urge to smooth a hand over his big chest to soothe him the way I've done a thousand times before—"I want to be part of their life, and I want partial custody. Weekends at least, or maybe alternating weeks."

"How would you make that work?" I ask, wondering if he's thought about the logistics or whether he called the moment Tyrell told him what the contract said. Most likely the latter. "Harley says you're at the gym for twelve hours a day."

"Fucking Harley," he grumbles, and I cover my mouth so I don't laugh.

I rest my elbows on my desk and glance at the door, double-checking that no one has opened it. I'll only have my classroom to myself for another few minutes. In fact, I'm surprised no one has barged in to find out why I'm not on patrol.

"I know the baby would have to stay with you to begin with," he continues. "But I'd like to visit often, and once it's old enough to be away from you, I could have an assistant coach open in the mornings and close in the evenings so I could be home more."

"You need time to think about the options." Personally, I've thought of nothing else for weeks. "It's a big commitment, Seth. Are you sure that's the route you want to take?"

"Yeah. I'm not being an absentee dad."

"All right then." Even though he's adding a level of complication I'd hoped to avoid, I admire his principles. "I have an alternative contract with a partial custody arrangement outlined. I'll drop it off later so you can have a look at it."

"No need. I'll come and get it."

"No!"

Silence follows my exclamation. I know it sounded abrupt to the point of rudeness. The thing is, I'm not prepared to have him in my house. Not yet. I need to grow accustomed to the idea of having him in my life before inviting him into my sanctuary and letting him see what I've made of myself during our years apart. I also need to establish boundaries. Part of looking after myself means making it clear what I will and won't accept. Right now, despite desperately wanting him to say yes, I'm not willing to accept him marching into my life and taking over. Not that he'd mean to, that's just the kind of person he is. He takes charge.

"Ash…"

"I'll come to you," I say. "Would you rather I visit at the gym or drop by your place?" I have a reasonable idea of where he lives from Harley.

"My condo. It's number 302. You know the building I'm in?"

"Not exactly."

"I'll send you the address."

"Great, thanks. See you around five-thirty?"

"Sounds good."

"Bye." I hang up, my heart hammering harder than I'd like it to, and bury my face in my hands. I'd counted on myself not to let him have such an effect on me anymore, but it seems I miscalculated. I should have known nothing would ever be simple when it comes to Seth Isles.

But you did know, a voice in my mind whispers. *You knew he'd have a problem with the arrangement you initially proposed and you went ahead anyway.*

I try to turn my mind from this fact, but a sliver of doubt has lodged in my consciousness and I can't ignore it. Did I ask Seth to father my baby because I knew he'd fight to be involved for more than the couple of months it takes to conceive, and deep down, I want to keep a connection to him?

Please say that's not the case.

I want to deny it, one hundred percent, but I can't because, perhaps—just perhaps—there's a ring of truth to it.

5

SETH

After Ashlin hangs up, I do something that even if I had a gun to my head, I wouldn't admit to. It's too fucking embarrassing. I fire up my laptop, sit at my desk, and type into the Google search engine: how to make my ex fall back in love with me.

I know, it's humiliating. I'm bothered that it's come to this. But I'm not too proud to admit—to myself, at least—when I'm out of my depth. Ashlin seems to have erected barriers that will be difficult to breach. Hell, she doesn't even want me in her home. A bit insulting, when you consider the fact that the only reason we're talking is because she asked for my sperm.

A million links pop up, and I click on the top one. Frustration churns in my gut because I hate that I can't just sit down with her, put everything on the table, and see what she says. Unfortunately, if I do that, she'll probably run for the hills and find someone else to be her baby daddy. I'm not prepared to risk my shot for the slim chance she'd react positively.

My nostrils flare as I scan the blog post, which consists predominantly of photos of happy couples and pining singles.

Ugh. I'm halfway down the page before I find anything that looks remotely like advice.

Make sure you're well presented. Your ex found you attractive at some point in time, and if you want them back, you need to reignite that flame. Don't give in to the temptation to let yourself go in the face of post break-up blues.

I glance down at myself. My appearance isn't something I dwell on, except for when I know I'll be seeing Ashlin. Right now, I'm in shorts and a Crown MMA branded t-shirt that's faded from too many washes and has a hole near the waistband. My stubble is growing thick and I haven't been to a barber in years. Usually, I just deal with my hair using a trimmer to take most of it off. I study my palms. Callused. Scarred. Blunt fingers, short nails. Not fit to touch her. But then, they never were.

Grabbing a pen, I start a list.

1. Tidy myself the fuck up.

I scroll to the next item.

Remind her of positive memories. Don't be direct, but think of subtle ways to make her remember the good times you shared.

Rolling my eyes, I add to the list:

2. Remind her of the good times.

I'm not sure I can manage to be subtle. I'm more of a blunt instrument. But I have plenty of time to mull over how I could be different. I continue scrolling, but that's all the article has. God, I need more help than that. Returning to the search bar, I open another tab, which recommends acting like the guy she fell in love with so she remembers why she likes you. I can do that. I add it to the list. And then I add a fourth item: show her how I've changed for the better. I have no idea how I'll do that —or if I even have. All I know is that I was blindsided by her decision to leave last time and I didn't fight back. This time, I'm going to dig my heels in and stand strong.

Lowering the screen, I ponder how I can show her I'll be there for her this time around. I could accompany her to the medical appointments. Pregnancy comes with all kinds of appointments and meetings. Surely one that uses IVF will have even more than most, and I can be there with her every step of the way. I retrieve my phone from the desk and send her a message.

Seth: *When is your first appointment for the pregnancy stuff?*

She doesn't reply immediately, so I pocket the phone and return to the gym floor. Gabe, the most famous of my fighters, catches my eye and lifts a brow. He knows it's unlike me to disappear into my office while they're training. I shake my head, indicating I don't want to talk about it, and he shrugs. He's not the type to pry. It's nice to know he's interested though. Despite my position, I don't have a lot of people I'd actually consider friends. Many of the guys here are at a different stage of life than I am. I've done my partying and sleeping around. I'm not interested in those things. Haven't been in a long time. Fortunately, some of my longer-term fighters have found women and settled down, which gives us more common ground. But while I'm happy for them, seeing the way their girls look at them reminds me of how Ashlin used to gaze at me like she believed I could make all her dreams come true. It hurts, not gonna lie. But that's my problem.

I spend a few minutes watching Jimmy spar with Buster, who's a bull of a guy that hasn't figured out how important cardiovascular endurance is for success. Jimmy is much smaller, but he's agile and bobs and weaves easily around Buster's bulky form. The kid is a natural. Cocky, and with a lot to learn, but he could go far if he keeps his head on straight.

My phone buzzes, and I snatch it from my pocket.

Ashlin: *No appointments until after we have the results of your sperm count test. I'm taking prenatal vitamins and eating healthily. For now, that's enough.*

Shaking my head, I ward off disgust at the idea of having my swimmers tested. I'm sure they're fine. I'm a fit guy in his thirties—never mind that I'm at the dark end of the decade. What could possibly be wrong with them?

Ashlin: *Would you like me to come to the appointment with you? If you're in, that is.*

Would I like her to…? Hell, no.

My jaw clenches. It'll embarrass me enough to hand my spunk over to someone in a lab coat without having her there to make it weirder.

Seth: *No. I don't need to know you're in the waiting room while I jack off.*

Talk about making it stranger. Why did I even say that?

Her reply is immediate.

Ashlin: *They call it "providing a sample" :P*

Ashlin: *Should I book an appointment for you? I can let you know the details when I drop off the contract.*

She's far too amused for her own good. Little witch. I smile, loving that she's comfortable enough to tease me.

Seth: *Yeah.*

"Smooth," I mutter under my breath. All of my—admittedly limited—social skills go out the window where Ashlin is concerned. There was a time when I didn't need to worry about polishing my rough edges because being with her was as natural as breathing, but even then, it was a mystery to me why an angel like her would love me. I didn't know what she saw in me, I just counted myself a lucky son of a bitch that she saw something. How am I supposed to charm her into loving me again when I have no idea why she ever did to begin with?

ASHLIN

Jotting down the last part of tomorrow's lesson plan, I glance at the clock. It's a little past five, and I'm nearly due to drop off an alternative contract to Seth. Much as I tell myself it's none of my business and doesn't matter, I can't help but wonder whether he's leaving work early to meet with me. Toward the end of our relationship, he'd never been home before eight in the evening, and then he'd collapse onto the sofa and not move for the night. Meanwhile, I'd have spent the entire day lying listlessly in bed. I always suspected he'd been trying to avoid me and my grief rather than actually being busy enough to warrant such long hours. In hindsight, I can't blame him.

Don't think about it.

Instead, I stand, and stroll to the wall that's lined with photos of my students. I study their little faces, and emotion claws at my chest, stealing my breath. I want a child of my own so badly, and I fear it's never going to happen.

"Your time will come."

I jump and spin around, my hand flying to my chest. Margaret, one of the other teachers, is standing behind me, with sympathy and that emotion I hate more than anything, *pity*, written across her face. I try to speak, but my throat is clogged. I swallow, and try again.

"Thank you," I choke out. She means well, but all her statement serves to do is remind me that everyone on staff knows about my loss. That's what happens when you take a leave of absence and refuse to answer the phone for weeks. I'm just glad the administration felt sorry for me and allowed me to come back once I pulled myself together.

She smiles hesitantly. "You're still young."

Getting less so every day.

I don't say it. She doesn't need my bitterness.

"I suppose so." Striding away from the wall, I force myself to smile. "All done for the day?"

She nods, still watching me as though she expects me to break down at any moment. "Are you?"

"Yes." I grab my purse from the desk and slide the pregnancy contract under my arm, with the text facing inward so she can't see it. "Got a few errands to run tonight."

"See you tomorrow, Ashlin."

"Bye." I wave as I breeze into the corridor and beeline to the exit. I don't stop until I reach my car and slide into the driver's seat, where I slump forward and rest my head on the steering wheel, drawing in a long, slow breath. "You're fine, Ash. You're strong, you have a good support system, and you've got this." I raise my head and meet my eyes in the reflection from the rearview mirror. "You've got this."

I check the address Seth sent me earlier and plug it into my phone's GPS. I know the area, but not well, and I haven't visited Harley because it's Seth's turf and I'd hate to make him uncomfortable by encroaching. It wouldn't be fair. I start the engine and follow the directions to his apartment building. Twenty-five minutes later, I puff my way up two flights of stairs and count the doors until I arrive at the number he gave me. I pause, taking a moment to ask the universe to please let Harley be somewhere else. Then I knock.

When Seth opens the door, I nearly bite a hole in my lip.

Oh. My. God.

If I thought he'd looked good the other day, it's nothing compared to this. He's shaved, and it takes years off him. His t-shirt stretches tight over the muscles of his chest and strains against his broad shoulders. Based on the dampness of his hair —which has also been trimmed—and his clean, masculine scent, he's recently showered. I want to run my tongue all over his pulse points and breathe him in.

My fingers tighten on the contract, and I grit my teeth.

Be polite. Be professional. Don't jump him like a sex-deprived nymphomaniac.

I thrust the papers at him. "Here."

He glances down at them, and then at me. "This is an agreement with shared custody?"

"You'd have them every other week. Or is that too much?" I also have a contract with a one week per month option in my car, in case he realizes the magnitude of what he's getting himself into.

"It's not too much." His mouth firms. "I'll make it work."

"Seth." I lay a hand on his upper arm, guilt churning in my stomach that I've put him in a position where he feels like he has to change his life just because I want him to father my baby. "We don't have to do this. I hadn't really thought through how much it would impact you." I'd thought about custody, sure, but not how he'd have to reconfigure everything to make it work. I'd been too busy imagining gurgling babies with his beautiful eyes.

"If we didn't, you'd go ahead and do it yourself." He watches me steadily. "I know you, Ash. I want to do this."

His intensity makes me shiver. "Okay, then." I reach for my purse to get the appointment details I wrote down, and hand over the notepaper. "Here. This is where you need to be, and when."

He tucks it into his pocket, and tilts his head toward the inside of the condo. "Want to come in?"

I shouldn't. I really shouldn't. But I'm curious what his home looks like. "Sure, thanks."

Damn it, Ashlin.

He stands aside, and I brush past into his living room. It's largely empty. A sofa, armchair, coffee table, and television. A kitchen adjoins it, separated by a counter. Everything is weirdly tidy, as though he's in the process of moving in and hasn't taken his things out of storage yet.

"Nice place," I remark, to clear the tension in the air.

He grunts. "It does the job."

Yep, that tension isn't going anywhere. I turn to face him, and force a smile. "Was there anything in particular you wanted to talk about?"

He shakes his head and closes the door behind me. The click of the latch is magnified a thousand times in my head. I could swear it echoes around the room, reminding me that I'm in a private space with the only man to ever set me alight with lust.

"Shall I just sit here while you have a look over it, then?"

His brow furrows, and he strides to the sofa in about half as many steps as it would take me. Sinking onto it, he pats the cushion beside him. "Go through it with me."

It's not a question, so I join him, perching with one thigh crossed over the other and my hands clasped in my lap, a safe two inches of space between us. He leans closer, obliterating the gap. His freshly showered man scent washes over me as he moves, and I barely resist the urge to close my eyes and sniff him. He's not making this easy. The situation mirrors the past too closely. Us, side by side, as I walk him through the paper-work he always loathed to read. We go through the contract and I pause to explain the parts I think he'll actually care about.

When I finish, he nods. "Give me a pen. I'll sign."

My heart skips. "You should get Tyrell to review it first."

He shrugs. "You gonna pull the wool over my eyes, Ash? Take me for all I'm worth? We already went through a divorce and it was all I could do to make sure you left with enough money to get your life back together. I know you well enough to know you're not going to screw me." His words linger in the air between us, and his gaze darkens. "*Over*," he adds, looking uncomfortable. "Screw me *over*."

My lips twitch. I knew what he meant, but I'm tempted to clarify that there will be no screwing of any kind. I don't though, because some doors are best left unopened. "I want you to be fully informed."

He sighs, and runs a hand over the short ends of his hair. "Fine, I'll run it by Ty. He'll want a copy, anyway."

"Of course he will. It's his job to look out for you."

He rolls his eyes. "Funny. He seems to think his job is sticking his nose into my business."

This time, I can't hide my smile. He sees it, and one side of his mouth lifts. "He's being a friend."

"Yeah, yeah." He shuffles the papers into a neat pile and sets them on the floor. "So, once that's sorted out and the doctor has okayed my spunk, what next?"

Scooting back, I put space between us now that we're not both trying to read the contract. "I'll book an appointment to begin a course of fertility treatment."

A groove forms on his forehead, and he watches me in a way that could be unnerving if I weren't used to it. He's always studied me like a predator does its prey.

"I want to be there."

I nod. "Okay."

"Good." His expression relaxes. "How long does the treatment last?"

"A couple of weeks. The doctor will talk us both through it. I don't know all of the details yet."

He falls silent, and stays that way for long enough that I wonder whether I should excuse myself. Perhaps I've overstayed my welcome. But then he speaks. "Where are you living these days?"

"Huh?" That's not the direction I expected this conversation to take.

He cocks his head. "If you're going to be pregnant with my kid, I should know where you're living."

I wince. He has a point. "That's fair. I bought a house a couple of years ago, and I'm renovating it myself." I wait for laughter, but it doesn't come. I was never particularly handy, so I can't imagine what he thinks of the idea of me undertaking a project like that.

He hums in the back of his throat. "Good for you. How's your family doing? Have you thought about how you're going to tell them?"

I grit my teeth. Unintentionally or not, he's poking at all my sensitive spots today. "Not yet. I don't think there's any point mentioning it until everything is ready to go. No reason to upset them without good cause."

He lays a hand on my knee. My *bare* knee. My skirt has ridden up my thighs. Heat flares along my skin. "Whatever they say, I'll stand by you. We're in this together."

"We are?" I ask, before I have time to filter the thought.

"Yeah." He flashes me one of his incredibly rare smiles, and I can't help but wish it would last for longer because it's over almost as soon as it begins. "You, me, and the future kiddo."

"Thank you." My ovaries want to weep for joy. It's sexy how supportive he is.

"No problem. From here on out, I've got your back."

I catch his unspoken meaning. He thinks he didn't in the past. I'm not sure I agree. Yeah, he was distant when I needed him most, but I was too dependent on him for my own good. Perhaps learning to stand on my own was a painful lesson, but it was a necessary one, nonetheless.

Something tickles my nostrils, and I sniff. "Are you... cooking?"

"Yeah." He acts like it's no big deal, but the Seth I married didn't cook unless it was a matter of reheating something someone else had already made. "It's just baked vegetables." He ducks his head, self-deprecating. "Harley is teaching me a few things."

"That's great. It smells good."

His face lights up. "You want to stay for a meal?"

Uh-oh, I hope he doesn't think I was angling for an invitation. If so, he's going to be disappointed.

"I can't, sorry. I need to get home." I don't tell him that the only thing waiting for me there is leftover chicken parmigiana. The fact is, if I stayed here, things could go sideways quickly. It's best if we avoid the potential for awkwardness. After all, we're going to be seeing each other for the rest of our lives.

6

_____

SETH

Several days after seeing Ashlin at my condo, I find myself standing outside a nondescript gray building near the hospital. The time has come for what I've been terming my "spunk test" but what I've been informed is properly referred to as a "sperm analysis." I head inside, take an elevator to the third floor, and give my name to the receptionist at the fertility clinic.

"Doctor Wood will be out soon," she assures me. "Please take a seat."

"Doctor Wood?" I ask, to confirm I haven't misheard.

She winks. "That's right. Purely a coincidence, I promise."

Nodding dubiously, I head over to one of two empty chairs. While I wait, I check my emails on my phone. There's one from a promoter who wants Devon at his event in a couple of months, and another from Mom, which I skim over, a flare of guilt surfacing. She's met a man, and it seems like they're getting serious. She's mentioned him a few times, and hinted that she'd like Harley and me to meet him. I made it clear I'm happy to pay for flights any time she wants to visit, but so far she hasn't taken me up on it. Perhaps they're not as serious as I think. It's just unlike her to talk about a man at

all. Mae Isles rarely dates, and not because no one is interested. She was barely twenty when I was born, and now she's
not far off sixty but could easily be mistaken for being in her
forties.

Unfortunately, spending most of my childhood being called
the town whore was enough to put her off dating for years.
Not that she was ever a prostitute—or even promiscuous, as far
as I could tell—but she made the poor life choice of sleeping
with the town mayor. Neither his wife nor the residents of
Cedar Bend approved. Making it worse, his son by his wife is
only a few months older than me, and everyone always
suspected he and I share a father. Mom never confirmed or
denied it.

Yeah, we were *that* family. The messed up one. The one
nobody wanted anything to do with. Not that Mae ever
acknowledged the rumors, or the mayor ever acknowledged
me. Both facts were damning. If the stories were untrue, surely
one of them would have said something. Mom isn't big, but
she's scrappy.

"Mr. Isles?" A man's voice jerks me from my reverie, and I
pocket my phone and stand, offering him a hand. "I'm Doctor
Wood," he says, smiling wryly. "Call me Allan. Would you like
to come on through?"

I follow him into a wide corridor and then into a room that
looks like a cross between an office and a laboratory. He goes
to one of the cupboards and collects a small plastic container.

"Label this with your name and the date. There's a pen in
the room you'll be using." He moves toward a door I hadn't
noticed, and opens it to reveal a dimly lit chamber containing a
sofa, a TV, and a coffee table covered by a stack of magazines.
When I pause to read the titles, I see they're different editions
of *Escort*. Oh, God. I know what this room is. It's the jack-off
closet.

I eye the sofa suspiciously. How many guys have gotten
their rocks off on it? I bet this is one of those rooms that you'd

never want to see illuminated by a black light like on those crime shows.

The good doctor must mistake my horror for confusion, because he explains. "There are a range of DVDs for stimulation in addition to the magazines. Once you're done, bring me the sample."

Forcing myself to nod, I ask, "Is there a time limit or something?"

This is a really fucking weird situation and I'm worried my dick is going to have performance anxiety. I mean, shit, is this guy going to sit in the adjoining room in his lab coat while I get down to business?

It's for Ashlin, I remind myself.

"No." He smiles gently. "But the sooner, the better. There are other men with appointments today."

I grimace. "Got it."

Other poor guys have to wank off in this dark little hole after me.

"See you soon." Dr. Wood shows himself to the door, then pauses. "I'll be in my office. Ring the buzzer on the desk in the other room when you finish."

"Sure." Whatever the hell gets him out of here.

The door clicks shut, and I immediately lock it. I don't need anyone interrupting what's bound to be one of the most uncomfortable experiences of my life.

Going to the TV, I scan the DVD titles, but honestly, I can't handle the thought of watching porn when that's exactly what Dr. Woods probably expects me to be doing. It's just too strange. Picking up a magazine, I try not to wonder whether people ever miss the sample jar. I flip through the pages until I find a woman I like the look of. Petite. Brunette. Small tits, slim hips.

Seth Junior doesn't stir. Sighing, I scrape a hand over my jaw. I'm not sitting on the sofa—no fucking way—so I unzip my jeans, slide them down, and cup my balls. Still nothing.

Honestly, I was harder than this the moment Ashlin entered my condo the other night, and I wasn't even touching her.

Ashlin.

My blood heats at the thought of her. I close the magazine, place it on the table, and turn away, not wanting to see any other women. My eyes flutter shut, and I tilt my head back. Is it wrong to get off to memories of Ashlin? Most people would probably say yes, but considering I'm doing this for her, I think I can let it slide just one time. I allow a vision to form in my mind of Ashlin on our wedding night. In my mind, I peel lace down her shoulders and let it pool on the floor. My dick hardens, Seth Junior finally engaged, and I slip my hand inside my underwear and give it a slow tug.

I groan. *Shit.* I forgot how quickly she gets under my skin, even when she's not really here. My imaginary Ashlin turns to me, almost shyly, even though I've seen her body a thousand times before. Her nipples peak beneath the translucent white silk of her bra, and I lower my mouth to suck through the fabric. She arches into me, and moans. My fingers tremble as I try to rid her of the bra without breaking it, and she urges me on with breathless whimpers. I rip it from her body, and she shudders.

"Yes, Seth," she murmurs. "Yes."

My hand moves faster on my dick as I think about pinning her to the bed, mauling her mouth, and then feasting on her pussy. Hearing the vows she uttered earlier in the day turned me into a beast. I'd wanted to toss her over my shoulder and beat on my chest all day when she promised to be with me always.

There's a pang in my chest.

Always.

Turns out, "always" wasn't as long as I expected.

I shove the thought to the back of my mind and imagine Ashlin's thighs trembling as I make her come with my fingers and tongue, then how she grips me as I slide inside her and thrust over and over again. She screams my name, and release claims me. I barely remember to aim into the sample container. My thighs shudder and I gasp her name as I ruthlessly milk my cock, squeezing out every drop I can.

I put a hand on the wall to steady myself, still breathing heavily. Fuck, it's been ages since I allowed myself to indulge in a fantasy about my ex-wife. Usually I feel so guilty afterward that it doesn't seem worth it, but this time, I have nothing to feel ashamed of. I did my best to provide the biggest, strongest sample the doctor's ever seen.

Taking a deep breath, I straighten, then grab one of the tissues in a box on the table—trying not to think of all the other men who've done the same—and clean myself off. That done, I screw the lid on the container, find a pen, and scrawl my name and the date on the label. Then I eye my sample, oddly proud. They've got plenty to work with, that's for sure.

I wipe the container with a tissue and head into the room next door, where I hit the buzzer to summon Dr. Wood. When he comes, I pass over the sample and get the hell out of there as quickly as possible. Making chitchat when I've just gotten myself off doesn't rank high on the list of things I ever want to do again.

But for Ashlin, I'd endure it.

ASHLIN

Everything inside me tenses when my ring tone sounds and Seth's name flashes across the screen. I've been waiting to hear from him following his appointment for three days, and the fact he's calling means he's probably got the results. But is it good news or bad?

I excuse myself from the teachers' lounge and walk outside, keeping my distance from the groups of children who are eating lunch or playing.

"Hi," I say.

"Hey, ba—Ash." He catches himself before he calls me 'babe'. "The results are in."

"And?" I ask, scarcely daring to breathe. Honestly, thinking they'll be anything other than spectacular seems like an affront to his masculinity, but things aren't always what they appear.

"You're in luck. They counted 150 million swimmers per milliliter. Apparently that's on the high end of normal."

I smile. "You sound proud of yourself."

He chuckles. "Can you blame me? If my little guys were no good then you'd have to go back to the drawing board. That's a lot of pressure."

I shrug, then remember he can't see me. "I hadn't thought of it that way. I wouldn't have held it against you if things didn't work out."

"I know." He sighs. "But I've let you down enough. I don't want to do it again."

Oh, Seth.

When he says things like that, I want to wrap him in a giant hug and never let go. Yeah, I felt alone after the miscarriage, but we handled it equally badly in our own ways.

"You didn't let me down," I tell him.

He scoffs, dismissive. "Of course I fucking did. You needed me, and I wasn't there."

I wander over to the building, lean against the wall and let it take my weight. "How were you supposed to know that I needed you if I never said anything?"

"I should have instinctively known."

I can almost picture his bull-headed expression, the obstinate man.

"And I should have communicated better, or gotten help on my own and not expected you to fix things for me. It was as much on me as you. Neither of us was completely at fault."

"I'll always want to fix things for you."

46

His confession stirs something within me, which means it's time to steer this ship to safer waters.

"Thanks for letting me know about the test. There's a course of oral contraceptives that come before the fertility medication. I'll start them tomorrow."

"I want to—"

I grin, knowing exactly what he's about to say. "Don't worry, I'll tell you when I have my first appointment."

"Hmph," he grumbles. "Don't forget."

"I won't." It's endearing how much he wants to be involved. A bell rings, and I glance at the clock. "I have to get back to work."

"Wait." His command is fast and hints at an emotion I can't decipher. "Have dinner with me tomorrow."

My pulse ratchets up, and I cock my head. Am I leaping to conclusions, or did he just ask me on a date? "Um…"

"Not as a date," he hastens to add. "There's a lot for us to talk about. If we're going to have a baby together, we need to work out the details. I'd also like to hear what you've been doing for the last few years."

"Er…" I hesitate, my instincts screaming at me that this is a terrible idea. "Not a date? Purely for the sake of the baby?"

"Yeah."

Nibbling my lip, I have to admit I can see the sense in it. If we're going to co-parent, we need to get a better idea of what our approach is going to be. Besides, I kind of want to know what his life has looked like since I left. Will I admit that? Uh, no. But that doesn't make it any less true.

"Okay," I decide. "Let's do it."

"Great. My place, eight o'clock."

"Nope." Pushing off the wall, I walk back toward my class. "Eight o'clock is fine, but we'll eat at Callie's." Callie's is a restaurant that's opened in the past year. I'd rather not be alone with Seth in a private location where my inhibitions might vanish. Likewise, I don't want to revisit any of our old haunts and suffer through nostalgia.

"My place is more private," he argues, as though that's a positive.

"Exactly." I pause in the corridor outside my room. "Callie's at eight. I'll see you there." I hang up before he can disagree.

7

SETH

I've worn more button-down shirts this month than I have in the past three years combined, but if this is what it takes to win Ashlin, it's not a big ask. I'm keeping my list in the front of my mind: dress nice, remind her of good times and why she used to love me, show her I've changed for the better. To that end, I'm five minutes early and claim a table in the back corner of the trendy, modern restaurant as far from other patrons as possible. I want her all to myself.

While I wait, I look around. Callie's has a nice atmosphere. Warm and intimate, with dim lighting and the kind of waitstaff who call you sir or ma'am. There are a few people here, but not so many that I feel crowded, and none of them spare me a second glance. There was a time when I drew attention everywhere I went, but my years of fame have passed, and these days, it's my students who are worshiped by the masses. Strangely, I prefer it that way. If you'd told me ten years ago that I'd grow tired of hearing thousands of people scream my name, I'd have called you a liar. Yet here I am. Interesting how the world works.

"Excuse me, sir." A waiter approaches, smiling politely. "Can I get you something to drink?"

"Whatever beer you've got on tap, thanks." I hesitate for a moment, then add, "A cranberry juice too."

Are women allowed to drink alcohol when they're hoping to get pregnant? I can't remember for sure, but I have a fuzzy memory of Ashlin sticking to juice and soda while we were trying last time. I swear under my breath as a thought occurs to me. Does she even like cranberry anymore? As far as I know, her tastes could have changed.

The waiter returns with our drinks, and I sip my beer while keeping an eye on the door. Finally, a couple of minutes late, she enters. Everything inside me seizes. If I thought she was beautiful last time I saw her, it's nothing compared to this. She dazzles me. Her hair is sleek and silky, perfectly framing her delicate face, and a silver chain around her neck draws my attention to the expanse of skin visible above the V-neck of her dress.

And that dress.

It's a sheath that hugs the line of her body down her narrow waist and slightly curved hips, over legs that seem much longer than I know them to be considering she barely tops five feet. Worst of all, it's held up by a bow that's tied behind her neck. If I were to tug on the end of the ribbon, the whole thing would pool at her feet.

She meets my eyes, but doesn't smile, and I hate that. The Ashlin I knew was constantly on the verge of smiling—at least until the last few months. This reserved version of her is a stranger in many ways, and I'll have to earn her trust all over again when I'd rather just toss her over my shoulder and announce that she's mine. I stand as she approaches, and find myself leaning close to kiss her cheek, only to stop when I'm a couple of inches away.

"Sorry," I mutter. "Old habits."

Fuck man, why you gotta be so awkward?

"It's okay." She smooths over the moment by patting my cheek and giving me the smile I crave. God, this is what I miss about her. Always sandpapering over my rough exterior. "You got me a drink?"

"Cranberry. Wasn't sure what you like these days."

She sinks into a chair and slides the glass toward herself. "This is good, thanks." When she sips, she leaves a pink smudge on the rim of the glass from her lipstick. Then she draws a small notepad from her purse, along with a pen, and sets them beside her. "You wanted to talk about where we go from here?"

I hide my wince. Honestly, while I claimed this wasn't a date, I'd hoped it might be a little more casual. She's ready to get down to business. How am I supposed to woo her if she's taking notes? "Yeah. But maybe we can order first."

"Fair enough." She raises her hand, and the waiter returns in record time, his expression a whole lot friendlier than it was before. "Hi." She bestows her one-of-a-kind smile on him. "Could my friend and I trouble you for a menu, please?"

"Absolutely." The guy's eyes dart to her ring finger and find it empty. His grin broadens. Meanwhile, my fists clench in my lap. A good part of the reason I married Ashlin was to ward off opportunists like this little shit. Unfortunately, her rings are probably sitting in her dresser. I doubt she'd have pawned them. That's just not the kind of person she is.

He passes her a menu. "Shall I wait, or come back in a few minutes?"

"Give us a couple of minutes." She tucks her hair behind her ear, and his gaze lingers on the graceful line of her neck. My fingernails dig into my palms. He'd better remove his eyes from her body before I forget that she isn't mine anymore and do something I regret. I clear my throat, give him a meaningful look. He backs away.

Ashlin chuckles. "You were never good with people. Nice to see some things don't change."

"It's not all people that I have a problem with," I grumble. I don't explain myself, and she doesn't ask for more. Together, we scan the options, and when the waiter returns, I order a steak while Ashlin asks for quinoa salad.

"What happened to the girl who'd down a hamburger in three seconds flat?" I tease.

She sighs, and her breath stirs her bangs. "Thirty happened. My metabolism doesn't bounce back the way it used to. I still eat burgers sometimes, but I have to go for a run to work it off."

My gaze skims over her. She's always been petite, and honestly, I don't see why she thinks she has anything to worry about. "You look great."

Her lips quirk in acknowledgment, but she doesn't say anything. We sit there for several moments, watching each other without speaking. Eventually, she sits forward and props her chin on her hands. "So, have you thought about what will happen if the pregnancy is successful?"

"We'll have a baby," I say, partly because being around her turns me into an idiot and partly because I just like the way the words sound in my mouth.

"Yes, Seth," she says slowly, her expression asking if I've taken a blow to the head at training.

"And we'll share custody," I continue. Obviously I'd rather both her and the baby live with me, but if I say that right now, it'll freak her the hell out. I have enough control over myself to hold back. Thank God for small mercies. "You'll probably have him more often than me in the early days because he'll need to be fed. Once he's a bit older, we can have a more even custody split."

Ashlin cocks her head. "We're having a boy, are we?"

My thumb goes to the tattoo on the inside of my wrist. *Cara*. Somehow, it feels like less of a betrayal of our daughter if the next child is male. "It's a figure of speech."

She nods, but I can tell she wants to dig deeper into my

psyche and figure out what's going on in there. "Is your condo child-friendly?"

"Yeah. What about your place? You said you're renovating it. Does it have a nursery?" Yet another thing I hadn't expected. Ashlin working with her hands. While she wasn't afraid of hard work when we were together, she wasn't exactly hands-on either.

She visibly brightens. "It will soon. That's the room I'm currently doing up."

"Okay." I just hope she's not setting herself up for more hurt if she makes a home for a baby that might never come. I gulp a mouthful of beer, then add, "Are you sure it's a good idea to start working on it before we get pregnant?"

The excitement in her eyes dims. "I know I'm getting ahead of myself, but I need to stay positive. Besides, if I don't do something productive, I'll go out of my mind with all the waiting."

I'm glad she's at least thought it through. I'd hate for her to end up where she was last time. "I'd be happy to help with the renovations."

She glances away. "I've probably got all the help I need, but thanks for offering."

Ouch. That was definitely a rejection. I'd have thought she'd be happy for any help she could get. Renovations are time-consuming, and especially if you're working on them alone.

Unless she's not.

She told me she doesn't have a boyfriend, but what do I really know about her life? She could be seeing someone casually, or perhaps Paige Donovan's smarmy brother likes to make himself useful, although I can't imagine the trust funder brat from the photos I spent hours checking would go out of his way for anyone else.

Damn it. Now I desperately want to know whether she's dated in the past three years, and I don't have any right to ask. Perhaps I can frame it in a way that won't make her angry.

"Did you, uh, try to meet anyone to do this baby thing with the natural way?" Fuck, I sound like an ass. The "natural way." As if what we're doing is wrong. It's just giving nature a boost. Fortunately, she doesn't seem to take it badly.

"I dated a few guys, but no one I was really interested in. Besides, men don't generally want to be rushed into having kids, and I have a ticking clock." She raises a shoulder and lets it drop. "I've probably got a few good years left in me, but I know what I want and I don't see the sense in waiting."

"I get it." While many people have mistaken her for being easygoing, at her core she's as stubborn as me. It's just that there are few things she cares about enough to show her steely backbone. Ashlin doesn't lose her temper when challenged, she just quietly goes on and does the thing she always intended to.

"You'd be one of the few who does."

When she doesn't ask me for my dating history in response, it disappoints me. I'd like her to know there hasn't been anyone other than her. That the one time I got close to fucking another woman, I could barely look myself in the mirror.

"Who are the others who get it?" I ask, refusing to let the glimpse of insight into her life pass.

Ashlin

I breathe a sigh of relief when the waiter arrives with our food. He sets mine in front of me with a smile, then narrows his eyes at Seth as he passes the steak. I can't help smirking at my ex-husband across the table.

When the waiter leaves, I murmur, "I think you've made a friend."

He snorts, then does a double-take, as though the sound of his own laughter has shocked him. Sadness fills me. I hope that's not the case.

"So, who's your support system?" he asks.

"My therapist, and my friends, Jessica and Paige, who I met at a group for women who've miscarried or gone through a stillbirth."

His lips part, and he doesn't seem to know how to respond. Finally, he chokes out, "You joined a support group?"

"I did." Nerves churn in my stomach, but I need to put my cards on the table because it wouldn't be fair to keep things to myself when he's doing so much for me. "It's been amazing. I still go once a month to help out other women who've been through the same thing. Jessica and Paige do too."

"They miscarried?" he asks. "I didn't know that."

"You know who they are?"

He colors. "I looked them up not long after the divorce, when I saw them start appearing on your social media, but I never knew how you met."

I frown, disconcerted by the fact he'd kept an eye on my social media. "It was the support group. Paige miscarried like me, and Jessica had a stillbirth." My heart aches for her when I think about it. While a couple of years have passed, I know it's not often she makes it through a day without feeling the pain.

"That's hard."

I nod. I've personally railed at the universe on her behalf.

"And therapy?"

"Also amazing." I pause while I eat, wondering how much to tell him. I was in a dark place when we broke up and it's largely thanks to my therapist, Dr. Casey, that I'm in a better mental and emotional space now. "I worked through a lot of grief and anger, and learned to accept that it happened and it's part of what makes me who I am."

He shifts uncomfortably, and concentrates on cutting his steak. This is a tough topic for him. Partly because of our shared past, and partly because he's one of those stoic men who keep everything trapped inside and doesn't believe that talking helps. His attitude exacerbated our problems because he never opened up about what he viewed as taboo topics, and I was too emotionally dependent on him to force the matter when doing so might make him unhappy. These days, I know that challenging conversations are often necessary for healing. I wonder if he's made the same discovery, or if there are another three years' worth of repressed feelings simmering under his surface.

He clears his throat. "You're doing okay now?"

"Yeah." I smile. "I am." Then, because I'm on a roll, I continue, "Actually, the renovation is part of my therapy too. It's an outlet for pent-up energy and frustration, and it feels really good to take something damaged and make it better."

His gaze searches mine. I let him look his fill, and resist the urge to lose myself in eyes as turbulent as an ocean. "That's great, Ash. Are you..." He hesitates. "Are you sure it's a good idea to be doing renovations when you're trying to get pregnant?"

A laugh bursts through me, releasing the tension like a valve. Good old Seth. Always trying to take care of me, even when it means protecting me from myself. Shaking my head, I spoon more of the salad into my mouth and keep quiet.

"What?" he demands, his brows furrowing together.

"Nothing." I swallow and cover my mouth so he can't see me smile. "Yes, I've checked with a doctor and I'm being careful not to overdo anything."

He doesn't look appeased.

"It's fine. Really."

His lips press into a line, and the glint in his eye is the same one he used to have before he'd put me over his lap and swat my ass. All humor vanishes at the memory, and heat spirals downward. I focus on dinner, hoping my cheeks aren't as fiery as they feel. Knowing me, they probably are. It's near impossible to hide a blush with my fair complexion.

"Have you given any more thought to how you're going to tell your family?" he asks, changing the topic.

I lay my cutlery beside my plate. The nerves churning in my gut have migrated to my throat, and it's so constricted that I don't trust myself to swallow properly. "I'm going to set something up with them next weekend. Get them all in the room at one time so I don't have to say it more than once."

"Sounds like a solid plan." He finishes his steak, wipes his mouth on a napkin, and grants me his full attention. "I haven't seen Liam for ages. How's he doing?"

Something in my stomach squeezes. *Liam.* My older brother is the reason Seth and I met. Back before Seth ran his own gym, they trained together, but then Seth became a champion while Liam got married and went back to school to become a physical education teacher. They'd been close friends, but their friendship seemed to end along with my marriage—something I heartily regret.

"He's all right." My voice is soft. "He and Marisol have three children now. They had a son not long after we separated, and then another a few months ago. Marisol is run off her feet, and apparently the kids talk back a lot more than Liam would like."

Seth nods, then says something that catches me by surprise. "He never kicked my ass."

"Huh?" My brow crinkles. I'm not following this twist in the conversation.

Seth eyes his beer, but doesn't gulp it down even though it seems he'd like to. "He always said that if I hurt you, he'd kick my ass, but he never did."

"Oh." Emergency lights flash in my mind. *Unsafe waters, turn back.* "I told them I was the one who ended it. I never gave him any reason to blame you."

He looks at me as though I'm a complex math equation he's struggling to solve. "But I hurt you."

"You did," I agree. "And I hurt you too. But the important thing is that my family—Liam included—always loved you, and I never did anything to change that."

"Huh." He cocks his head, still frowning. "When he stopped

57

inviting me over, I thought you must have run to him with your problems."

I gasp, horrified he'd think me capable of such a thing. Seth didn't have any family living nearby, so for all intents and purposes, my family had been his. Of course I wouldn't intentionally ruin that.

"I didn't tell him anything other than that we'd been having trouble for a while, and nobody was unfaithful so he didn't have to bust any faces. If he stopped calling, it was probably because he thought it would be awkward if you and I accidentally ran into each other at his place. I'm sorry you lost touch. That wasn't what I wanted to happen."

Seth stares at me so intensely that I squirm, but I don't look away. Hopefully he can see whatever he needs to on my face. Eventually, he shakes his head and sighs. "You're too good for this world."

"I am not." I roll my eyes because I'm very much human with plenty of flaws to go around. I mean, if I hadn't given up, we'd probably still be married. We might even have tidied up the frayed ends of our lives.

"Agree to disagree."

Raising a hand, I summon the waiter and request a hot chocolate. Seth asks for an espresso, and I resist the urge to point out that it'll keep him awake for hours. His quality of sleep is none of my business. When we finish our drinks, I insist on splitting the bill, even when his nostrils flare with annoyance. And when he walks me back to my car to make sure I'm safe, I can't help ogling his broad shoulders as they strain against the fabric of a shirt he probably hasn't worn in years. One that I bought for him. A coincidence? Or is he trying to remind me of the way things used to be? Whatever the case, it works. My lips yearn for the press of his. But I force myself to step back and maintain the respectful space we need. There's a lot of history between us, but I've become a woman who stands on her own two feet, and giving Seth any hint that I want him would be inviting him to sweep me off them.

Dangerous.

"I'll see you soon, Seth."

"See you, Angel."

8

SETH

It's the day of Ashlin's first appointment at the fertility treatment center, and I meet her in front of the building, full of certainty that I'm ready for anything. She marches up to me with a military bearing—something her dad drilled into her at a young age, and which usually only shows when she's nervous. She comes to a stop a few feet in front of me, and I close the distance between us and smooth my hands over her shoulders. Fuck propriety. She needs support, and I want to give it to her.

"You've got this," I say, ducking to look her in the eye.

Her jaw firms, and she nods. "I've got this."

"I'm with you all the way." She nods again, and I brush a kiss over her forehead, then step back and take her by the hand. "Let's make it happen."

Ten minutes later, I'm less sure we've got this.

"She has to do what?" I demand of the doctor, who's just finished explaining how Ashlin needs to inject herself each day with some kind of hormone thing.

"It's fine, Seth." Ashlin's expression gives nothing away, and my heart aches because I know she's trying to keep her emotions from me. Most of the time, she's an open book, but she doesn't trust me with her innermost thoughts anymore. "I knew it was part of the process. No pain, no gain, right?"

"Maybe for my fighters," I mumble. "Not for you." I want to protect Ashlin from pain. To keep her safe. Despite all of her supposed growth over the past few years—everything she's learned from therapy and her support group—I'm gripped by the fear that history will repeat itself.

"It'll be worth it," she assures me, then adds, "I'm tougher than I look."

Fuck, I hope so. Because when you consider the fact she's only a little over five feet and ninety pounds, she looks breakable. Like I could snap her with one arm. Although I guess, in reality, she's the one who broke me.

The doctor clears her throat. Her lips curl in one corner as though we amuse her. "Thousands of women have been through this clinic and dealt with the injections," she says. "I have absolutely no doubt that Ashlin will too."

She weighs Ashlin to determine the correct dosage, then sits at her computer and starts typing. A thousand questions fly through my mind, and I try to sift through them. This may be one of my few chances to get the information I want before we hit the point of no return.

"What's the chance she'll actually get pregnant?" I ask.

The doctor glances up and adjusts her glasses on the bridge of her nose. "Approximately 30 percent per cycle, although the likelihood decreases each time it's unsuccessful."

"Shit." I flex my hands into fists, then shove them into my pockets so I don't freak anyone out. "There's a two in three chance it won't work?" That's not what I expected. I thought this was pretty much a done deal. Fertilize some eggs, stick them in the right place, nine months later there'd be a baby.

"In most cases." The doctor stacks her hands one on top of the other and cocks a brow at Ashlin. "You two haven't talked about the risks and possible outcomes?"

Ashlin flushes. "Uh, not really."

"Okay." The doctor returns her attention to me. "Of the women who conceive, about twenty percent will miscarry, which is a similar proportion when compared to women who conceive naturally."

"Wait, what?" I hold up a hand to indicate for her to stop talking, and turn to Ashlin. "So there's a three in ten chance you'll get pregnant, and then if you do, there's a one in five chance you'll miscarry? Baby, I don't like those odds."

Her chin juts stubbornly forward. "It's better than the zero percent chance I currently have."

"I'm not sure I can watch you go through that again." I close my eyes and rub my temples, remembering the days following the awful night when we lost Cara. Ashlin wouldn't get out of bed. She lay on her back and stared at the ceiling, or curled into a ball and cried silently. I wanted to be there for her. I tried to comfort her. To climb into bed and wrap myself around her, but that only seemed to make things worse. It was as if she didn't think she deserved to be held or treated with gentleness, and when she pushed me away, my invisible wound deepened. It tore out everything inside me and I couldn't figure out how to glue it back into place.

To my surprise, she reaches for my hand. It's the first time I've felt her touch since she announced that we should separate.

"It'll be okay," she murmurs, as though she's soothing an agitated beast. Maybe that's what I am. "However it goes, we'll get through this."

I clasp her hand tight, and inhale freely for the first time in three years. She needs this, and I need her. I give her one final squeeze and let her go. Raising my eyes, I focus on the doctor and try to even out my breathing.

Don't panic, Isles. You can survive anything if it brings Ashlin back into your life.

"What else do I need to know?"

The doctor stands, and crosses to a poster on the wall. My

gaze follows and I note that the poster sets out the risks and benefits of IVF alongside photos of babies and smiling parents. "There's a slightly increased risk of multiple births or of premature birth with a lower birth weight."

"So, we might have twins?" I clarify, pausing on a photo of a woman with a baby in each arm.

"Yes. There's also a chance that complications may arise during the egg-retrieval procedure."

My breath hitches. "Complications?"

Ashlin's arm hooks around me, and she scoots closer to my side. "The needle could poke something it's not supposed to."

"Oh." My hand lands on her hip and reflexively tightens.

"That's right," the doctor agrees. "In which case it could result in bleeding or damage to the bowel or bladder."

This plan is sounding worse and worse. Why do women go through this?

"Anything else?" My voice is taut.

"A small percentage of women suffer an ectopic pregnancy. The egg implants somewhere other than the uterus, and the pregnancy can't progress."

"Would that put Ashlin in danger?"

"It's a life-threatening condition."

My jaw clenches and the room seems to spin around me. I glance down at my girl. This all sounds too dangerous, especially considering we haven't even tried the old fashioned way. I know that's not what she wants, but if it's more likely to keep her safe, then surely it's worth any discomfort. "We need to talk in private."

She makes a face. "Dr. Slater probably has another appointment waiting."

"They can keep on waiting." I don't care about them, I care about Ashlin.

She looks at the doctor apologetically. "We'll be back in a second."

Dr. Slater shrugs. "No need to go anywhere. I'll step out for a moment." She leaves, and the door clicks shut behind her.

I turn to Ashlin and rest my hands on her shoulders. "Are you sure you want to do this? There are other ways."

She tilts her chin defiantly. "One hundred percent." Her voice doesn't waver. "I know what the risks are, and I also know they're unlikely to happen. The chance of something going wrong is slim. I'm willing to take the chance." She studies me carefully. "The question is: are you?"

I don't answer immediately, because honestly, I don't have the same degree of certainty as her. She's thought about this for months, but it's all new to me. Besides, when it comes down to it, she's the one who'll be risking her health, and she has control over her body. If she wanted to go ahead without me, she could. The only input I have is whether I father her baby and therefore get to be here for her. If I suggest trying via sex, I might frighten her off, and the prospect of losing her terrifies me. I'd rather do things her way and hope I come out the other side with both my girl and a baby as a prize.

The family I always wanted.

I swallow, my throat stiff, the motion uncomfortable. "Yes."

She beams, hugs me, and nuzzles my chest. "You won't regret it. Everything is going to be all right."

I close my eyes and soak up the feel of her, but when the embrace drags on for too long, I force myself to let her go. Clearing my throat, I blink up at the ceiling so she won't see the tears in my eyes. Holding her is so right. It's everything I thought I'd never have again.

That's when I know I'll do anything to keep her in my life again. And if things go wrong, I'll be there for her. Unlike last time, I won't let her down. I refuse to give up on us.

"You can call the doctor back in."

"It's okay," I tell myself as I apply mascara and put the finishing touches on my makeup. "People take their ex to dinner with their family all the time. No big deal."

Except it is. It's huge. I know it, he knows it, and within a few minutes of arriving, my family will know it too. I'm hoping they'll behave themselves because my nieces and nephews will be present, but honestly, Liam has the same temper as Seth, so who knows what will happen?

"Women choose to have children on their own terms every day," I continue, wiping off a bit of smudged lipstick. "We don't live in the dark ages."

"Who are you talking to?"

Squeaking, I spin around. Seth fills the doorway, watching me with the combination of affection and caution I'm starting to consider normal from him. Seeing him shouldn't surprise me—we're at his condo, after all—but I'm so used to having my own space that I tend to forget when others are around.

"Myself," I admit once my breathing has calmed. "Or perhaps I'm practicing for my parents."

It's Saturday evening and we're about to head over to the home I was raised in. I called earlier in the week and requested a family dinner. I'm sure everyone invited is dying to know the reason for it, especially considering I've kept to myself recently. I doubt any of them will expect the truth.

Seth nods. He's shaved tonight, and I can't help but be disappointed. While he more closely resembles the man I married, the roughness of his edges are beginning to grow on me. I find myself wanting to rub against him and purr. "I'm here for you," he promises. "Whatever they think."

"Thank you." I check myself once more in the mirror, stuff my makeup into my purse, and walk toward him. "It means a lot to have you on my side."

"Always." The rumble sends a shiver down my spine, and I try not to read too much into it. I begin to step past him, but he stops me with a hand on my upper arm. "How do you feel? Any side effects from the injections?"

If I didn't know him so well, I'd almost miss the pale tint of his skin. He really hates the idea of those needles. "My emotions are a little unbalanced and I'm tired, but everything is okay otherwise."

His ocean-colored eyes search mine. "You'll tell me if that changes?"

"I will." Checking my watch, I see we're due for dinner in twenty minutes. "We'd better go."

We take one car even though I argued for going separately, because Seth convinced me of the benefits of having someone else to drive me home in case I'm not in a good headspace after dinner. We arrive at the two-story home and make our way up the stairs. My heart flutters like a hummingbird. I'm wound tight. So is Seth, but he's also stoic. Determined. There's no putting him off, and I'm glad to have his support. When we knock, the door swings open and we're greeted by my father's smiling face. When he realizes there are two of us, his smile widens.

"What's this?" he asks. "I haven't seen the two of you together since... well, since the divorce."

"It's good to see you, sir." Seth offers him a hand. Dad shakes it and steps aside to let us in.

"I'll explain soon," I tell him. "Once we're all together."

"Of course." He looks intrigued, but doesn't push.

"Hello, beautiful!" Mom calls from the kitchen.

"Hi, Mom." I sweep through the dining room and into the kitchen, where I plant a kiss on her cheek.

"You look different," she says, her gaze raking over my features, probably noticing the makeup, which I don't usually bother to wear when I visit. "Have you been on a date?"

"Not tonight, sorry." I try not to laugh at her disappointment. Behind me, I sense Seth stiffen. Why? Because he doesn't like the idea of me going on dates?

"Oh." Seth's movement captures her attention, and her eyes widen with surprise, then flick back to me. "Are you two together?"

"Not in the sense you mean."

Her face falls. Much like the rest of my family, she never understood our divorce. Probably because we never explained it.

"It's lovely to have you in our home," she tells Seth, shooting me a strange look that I can't interpret. "Liam's family will be here soon. Why don't you take a seat at the table and we can catch up once dinner is ready?"

"Too late." My brother's voice sounds from behind Seth. "We're already here."

Seth and I pivot. Liam stands in the doorway between the kitchen and dining room, his arms folded over his chest, eyes narrow and shifting between us. My brother used to have a similar build to Seth, although he never matched my ex for height, but these days he's slimmed down. Being a father of three means he doesn't have as much time to hit the gym and maintain the muscle mass he used to carry. His wife, Marisol, doesn't seem to think any less of him for it. Every time he carries one of their children on his shoulders, she practically has hearts in her eyes.

"Hey, man." Seth nods to him, but otherwise doesn't make a move, obviously waiting to see how Liam will react to his presence.

"Well, look what the cat dragged in." A smile breaks over Liam's face and he steps forward and slaps Seth on the shoulder, then holds out a fist for him to bump. "Long time, no see, Bill. Missed your ugly face."

I roll my eyes. There he goes. My corny brother. When Seth and I married, he took to calling him "Bill"—short for brother-in-law. While Seth always pretended to hate the moniker, I know he secretly enjoyed it because it made him feel like part of the family.

"Are you guys seeing each other again?" Liam barrels on, not waiting for a reply. "About damn time."

"We're not together," I say. "We'll explain everything once we're all seated. Where are the kids?"

Liam winks. "Left them at home with a babysitter. When you asked for a family dinner, we figured something interesting must be going on. Didn't want them here in case they stunted the conversation."

Shit. He must read the thought on my face, because he smirks. So much for the kids providing a buffer to smooth things over.

"Out of my kitchen." Mom ushers us to the door. "Tell your father we'll be ready to eat in a few minutes."

"Will do, Mrs. Walsh." Seth tilts his head deferentially. For a surly guy, he's always treated my parents with the utmost respect. Probably because no one ever did the same for his mother, and he hated them for it.

"Ash," Marisol exclaims as we enter the dining room. She throws her arms around me and squeezes. I relax into the embrace. Marisol gives the best hugs. She's built like an hourglass and radiates genuine warmth. She whispers in my ear, "Thanks for the night off. Joseph was starting to drive me crazy. He's teething."

"No problem." I hug her back, ignoring the twinge in my heart that says I'd happily swap places with her if it meant I got to have a baby.

She draws back, and her gaze skims down me, then one dark brow cocks up. She knows that while I always make an effort with my appearance for work, I rarely do with family. "What's the occasion?"

"I'll let you know soon." I kiss her cheek. Of all my family, I expect Marisol to be the only one who's remotely on board with my plan.

"Color me intrigued."

We sit, and Liam asks Seth how things are going at the gym.

They launch into one of the sports-rich conversations that dominated family events during our marriage, only pausing when Mom delivers dinner to the table. She's cooked a vegetable stew that smells amazing, and has a loaf of home-made bread to accompany it. I breathe in the yeasty scent—one of my favorite things ever.

"So." Mom sets her hands on the edge of the table and meets my eyes. "Not that I don't love seeing you, but are you ready to explain why we're all here?"

Reaching for my drink, I gather my thoughts. I sip, then prepare myself for the inevitable reaction. "I've decided that I want children and I'm not waiting around for a new man to come along and give them to me. I'm going to have IVF. Seth has agreed to be the father."

"What the fuck?" Liam explodes to his feet. "You want to be a single mom?" He swings to glare at Seth. "And you're helping her? What the hell, man. I'd have thought that you—out of everyone—wouldn't willingly help someone become a single mom."

"Liam Walsh, sit down and stop acting like a child," Mom snaps, her eyes glinting fire. I'm not fooled though, her anger is directed at me just as much as Liam. She turns. "Ashlin, why would you want to force this? You're only thirty. You have plenty of time to meet another man and do things naturally." She glances between Seth and I. "Honestly, I always thought you'd reconcile. Have you considered that? And have you stopped to think about what effect it could have on a child to be raised without two loving parents?"

Her words cut, and I shrink into my chair. "Plenty of people do it these days, and I know I could be everything the baby would need. Besides, I wouldn't be doing it alone." The last sentence is almost a whisper, and I instinctively seek Seth out as though I expect him to protect me. Realizing what I'm doing, I straighten my back and speak more assertively. "Seth will be the baby's father, and have partial custody. Our son or daughter will have two loving parents." I take a deep breath to ease the tightness in my chest. "Perhaps it's not how you would do it, but I've made up my mind."

"Good for you," Marisol declares, earning my eternal gratitude. My sister-in-law is one of my favorite people, and I've always secretly wondered whether she guessed the reason behind the breakdown of my relationship with Seth. She's remarkably astute.

"*Mari.*" Liam looks horrified.

She raises an eyebrow. "Don't be old-fashioned. God forbid something terrible were to happen to you, do you think I'd be incapable of raising happy and healthy children on my own?"

He pales. "That's different. They'd have had a father, and know that they started out life as—"

"Part of a normal, nuclear family?" Marisol finishes, her eyes glinting dangerously. "But is that what we really are? There are people who'd say that we're not a natural family because the color of our skin is different."

Liam scoffs. "Those people are racists. It's a completely different situation."

"What about a situation when a gay couple want to adopt?" I chime in, supporting Marisol in her defense of me. "Should they bring a child into a situation where they may face discrimination from bigots?"

"The child would have two loving parents."

"So would ours." Everyone falls silent when Seth speaks. He has the kind of deep, rough voice that commands attention. His hand lands on my knee, and he squeezes gently. "Whether you approve or not, Ash and I are going ahead with this, and I promise you, if she gets pregnant, she won't be left to raise our baby alone."

Liam's jaw firms, but he nods once. He may argue against me, but he knows better than to pick a fight against the King of Stubborn.

"Dad, what do you think?" I ask, noting he's the only person at the table who hasn't spoken up.

Dad smiles, affection gleaming in his eyes. "I think this might bring you back together." He shrugs. "Or maybe not. Either way, I look forward to meeting another grandchild soon."

"Thank you, sir," Seth replies, his thumb brushing over my kneecap. I resist the urge to melt into his touch, not wanting to fuel any speculation about us reconnecting. "Everything is going to work out fine."

9

After Ashlin's father says his piece, the mood around the table lifts. While he's a softly spoken man, no one seems willing to directly contradict him. No doubt he and Joanne, Ashlin's mother, will have words later, and Liam definitely isn't finished with his crusade to change Ashlin's mind, but for now, both of them let it go. I'm proud of Ashlin's determination, which doesn't waver in the face of their disapproval. She must have known this was how the night would go, but her back is straight and—except for in the initial aftermath of her revelation—she doesn't let her old habit of shrinking until she's invisible take over. Perhaps I should have paid more attention when she told me she was stronger than she used to be, because now I'm seeing evidence of it with my own eyes, and it's sexy as fuck.

I'm like any red-blooded alpha male. I like protecting what's mine, and Ashlin used to fall within that category—still does, not that I'd admit it to her—but seeing her stand up for herself drives me crazy in the best way.

Marisol launches into a story about her daughter's karate class, and I sense the tension ease from Ashlin as the focus is drawn away from her. I make a mental note to send Marisol a box of chocolates. It's nice to know she still has Ashlin's back. The two were always close, but after the miscarriage, Ashlin pushed Marisol away, unable to handle the fact that her sister-in-law had a healthy child and was pregnant with another while we'd lost ours. Somewhere along the way, she must have moved past that.

My attention shifts from Marisol to her husband, whose hard gaze is leveled directly at me. When I see him staring, he raises a brow in a silent challenge. My hand is still on Ashlin's knee—fuck, I love touching her—and I do my best to silently communicate to Liam that I intend to stand by his sister whatever may come. To be honest, his quiet doubt is better than the outright hostility I expected to be met with tonight. I'm not sure why Ashlin never opened up with her family about our relationship, but it's a relief not to have to overcome their negative opinions as well as her own reservations.

My body soaks up Ashlin's nearness like I'm a plant that hasn't seen sunlight in days, and just as I've begun to wilt, a solitary ray shines upon me to bring me back to life. Every time she moves, there's a shift in the energy field that I can't help responding to. If she weren't sitting beside me, I'd be drinking her up visually as well as with my other senses. She tilts her head, her hair tumbling to the side, and the floral scent of her perfume wafts toward me. My teeth grit. I want to expose her throat and suck her pulse point. My dick begins to wake, and I immediately turn to Russel, needing a distraction.

"How is the business going?" I ask. My former father-in-law runs an Irish pub.

"People always need beer and good company," he replies with a self-deprecating smile. We both know that there's far more to his success than that, but I let him play it cool. "And you? The gym is producing some top-notch fighters."

"I only take on the ones who are willing to put in the work."

I glance over at Liam, and smirk. "You sure you don't want to leave retirement behind, old man?"

His brows draw together in a scowl. "You've got a few years on me, grandpa. It wouldn't be right of me to come back and show those kids that their coach isn't the man he used to be. I'd crush their dreams."

"You keep telling yourself that."

"Mari." He turns to his wife. "I could take Seth, couldn't I?"

"Uh." Her eyes widen like a deer in the headlights, but her mouth twists with humor. "If I say yes, will you accept that and resist the urge to do something stupid to find out for sure?"

"Of course." He smiles easily. "You're my wife. You know all."

"Then, yes." She winks at me. "Sorry, big guy, but my scrappy Liam could definitely take you down."

A laugh rumbles up my throat, shocking me. How long has it been since I sat around a table with family and talked shit? Years. I wasn't sure I'd ever have this again.

"I'll take your word for it."

"You'd better."

"I'll keep him in line," Ashlin cuts in, catching my eyes and smiling. The expression winds me more effectively than a kick in the gut. She makes a karate-chopping motion with her hands. "I'll bust out these bad boys if he tries anything dodgy."

Affection wraps around my heart, and for some reason there's a pricking sensation in the backs of my eyes.

No. I will not tear up in front of the woman I want to impress.

"I'm terrified," I drawl. "Please don't hurt me, Ash." To my surprise, I actually mean what I say, even if it's not on the level everyone thinks. She may be half my size, but my little angel could crush me beneath her heel if she wanted. I'm hers to do with what she will. Not that she seems to have realized it yet. Joanne speaks at the end of the table, and the attention moves away from us.

I lean close and murmur in Ashlin's ear, "You're doing amazing."

"Thanks," she whispers back. "I appreciate you coming."

I'd be here every day for the rest of my life if you asked me.

"No problem," I grunt, far less articulate than I'd like. She turns to speak to Marisol, and I sip my drink.

"I didn't know you two had kept in touch," Russel says to me, voice low enough that it doesn't carry.

"We haven't. Other than this month, I haven't seen her for years." Not since I forced myself to stop checking her social media for any glimpse of her, or a hint of what her life had become.

"Well then, I hope this is the start of something." He glances at Ashlin, who's engaged in conversation with Marisol. "I never understood why you two broke up, but you belong together."

"Thank you." I swallow past the thickness of my throat. "Would you mind telling her that?"

He chuckles. "Can't tell that girl anything. She'll figure it out for herself, if it's meant to be."

I nod, and though I'm pleased to have his support, there's a heavy feeling in my gut because Ashlin won't be won over easily. The hurdles for me to leap are high. Hopefully not impossibly so.

An hour later, Ashlin's shoulders stoop with exhaustion. I whisk her out of there at the first sign that people are moving away from the table, knowing that both Liam and Joanne would take advantage of the opportunity to get her alone and pressure her into rethinking her decision if given the chance. Considering she doesn't argue when I thank Joanne for dinner and say our goodbyes, I assume her mind is traveling the same tracks. I steer her to the door and we drive to my place together. I park beside her car, half expecting her to get out the moment we come to a halt, but she doesn't.

She relaxes deeper into the seat. "Thank you for tonight."

I roll my eyes. "Stop thanking me. I told you I'm here for whatever you need."

"You did, didn't you?" she muses. "Why is that, when I divorced you? Many men would laugh in my face if I asked of them what I did of you."

My spirit rebels at the reminder of our separation, and I can't help but wonder if that's what she intended. Is she trying to force space between us because she can sense our closeness returning?

"Divorced or not, I care about you. And I want a kid. Always have. I just figured it wouldn't happen for me now."

She turns to me, features shaded by the dim artificial light. "Can I ask you something?"

"Sweetheart, you just did."

I hear her sigh in the quiet space between us. "Dad jokes already?"

"Sorry," I say. "Yeah. Of course you can."

She's silent for so long that I curse myself for putting her off, but then she speaks. "Does it still hurt?"

My thumb goes to the tattoo on my inner wrist and traces the letters. "Every day."

"Me too," she replies. "I thought it would go away eventually, but there's always this shadow hanging over me, and it descends at the most unexpected moments."

My heart goes out to her, and I wish with every fiber of my being that I could rewind the clock and somehow fix it. Be a better man. Do something to shield her from the loss. But I can't. All I can do is share the little wisdom I've collected.

"The grief is part of us now. It won't ever fully go away, but it will fade more every year."

Her tear-bright eyes shine when the light hits them, and the pain in them wrenches my gut. I want to gather her in my arms and promise to never let her be hurt again. To kiss her and soothe her and do whatever I can to take away the hurt. I restrict myself to reaching for her hand and squeezing it.

"We're going to be all right." It's the first time I've come close to admitting my hope that we'll find our way back to each other out loud.

She cocks her head, studying me from behind a veil of shadows. For once, it's my turn to drag her into the light. "Some days I think that too," she says. "Others, I don't even know what all right is."

ASHLIN

It's D-Day. Or should I say E-Day, for the eggs? As in, the day I have to lie back while a massive needle is inserted up me and used to pluck eggs from my ovaries. Sounds like fun, right? At least I'm not alone. As we pass through a set of sliding doors, I glance up at Seth, who hovers beside me as though he's expecting a sneak attack. He's been helicoptering ever since he picked me up from the street outside my house. I got into his car as quickly as I could so he wouldn't have much time to see where I live. He hasn't been inside yet and I'm reluctant to change that. Letting him see my home renovation project would mean making myself vulnerable, and I'm not ready for that level of exposure yet. Not when half the reason I started was to overcome the pain of my miscarriage and our marriage falling apart.

Seth's hand brushes mine, and I glance up. Tension is etched in the line of his jaw and he stares forward. I can't tell if the contact was intentional or not. Then it happens again. I press my lips together to mask a smile, and thread my fingers between his, aligning our palms. The big, tough man needs emotional support but doesn't want to show his weakness. Good thing I can read his cues.

"You sure you want to do this?" he asks, drawing circles on the back of my hand with his thumb.

"Positive," I confirm. "Are you?"

He nods. "I just wish I could stay with you while they… you know."

Guilt tears through me. The fact is, he could stay with me and do his part either before or after, but I specifically asked the clinic to book us simultaneously because of my insistent need to prove to myself that I'm not dependent on him for my strength and courage anymore.

"I'll be fine." I extract my hand from his as we approach the ward's reception desk. "Hi." I smile at the woman behind it. "Ashlin and Seth Isles."

Seth's quick intake of breath draws my attention, and when I glance up at him, an unusual sight greets me. He's beaming. But why? I mentally track back through the last few moments. Is it the fact I introduced us like a married couple? Does it mean something to him that I kept his name? Honestly, it seemed like too much paperwork to bother changing it. Although there's a possibility I wasn't ready to kiss my last connection to this man goodbye. Even when I was angry at him —which was often, near the end—I never stopped loving him. I asked for a divorce because I depended on him too much, and when I needed to grieve, he wasn't there. It felt like I was experiencing the loss on my own.

"Please, take a seat," the receptionist tells us. "Mr. Isles, someone will be here for you shortly. Mrs. Isles, the doctor is running a few minutes behind, but it shouldn't take too long."

"Thank you."

We sit, and within thirty seconds, someone has arrived to escort Seth to the room where he's expected to make himself come into a sample jar.

Ah, God.

Automatically, images fill my mind of Seth wrapping a hand around his dick and jerking. Of his eyes turning dark and focusing on me like he's a mountain lion with a deer in his sights. Imagining the growl he makes as he comes, and the way he'd lose control. Making him shudder and curse used to be my favorite activity. There's a sense of power that comes from having a man like Iron-Shin Seth Isles at my sensual mercy. I squirm, pressing my thighs together. This is not the time to get turned on. I'm about to have a doctor poking around in my privates.

Enough time passes that I'm concerned Seth may finish before I'm called in, but then Dr. Slater appears in the doorway and nods for me to follow her down the corridor. They explain what will happen and then sedate me. The next thing I know, I'm slowly coming to in a recovery room. Seth is lurking in the corner.

When he notices that I've woken, he strides over and kisses my forehead. "You okay, honey?"

"Mmhmm." I'm still not fully awake yet, so I lie back and close my eyes. After napping on and off for what feels like minutes but is probably longer, my thoughts grow less muddled. I'm able to have a short conversation with Seth and the doctor, during which she advises me to take it easy and not drive for the rest of the day. When she discharges me, I have to lean on Seth's chest for support since my muscles feel weak.

"I've got you," he murmurs.

Tears spring to my eyes, but I have no idea why. That seems to be the status quo lately. The hormone injections are making me temperamental, with a hair trigger when it comes to crying. I bury my face in his chest. I know I should pull away and try to stand on my own, but he's broad and strong, and resting my head on him is so tempting. I close my eyes, and snuggle closer. He smooths a hand over my hair and tucks me beneath his chin. Sometimes, there are benefits to being short. I breathe in his scent, which is spicy from the liniment he applies after working out. So familiar. In many ways, so damn good.

Finally, I force myself to draw back. "We should go."

A groove forms between his brows, and heat rushes through me. He looks concerned, and part of me wants to rub my thumb over the indent and reassure him that everything is fine. The rest of me knows to keep my distance.

"But you're upset."

"No, I'm not." I swipe at the moisture on my eyelashes and release a shaky breath. "I'm just emotional. It's the hormones." Plus I'm feeling raw. The procedure makes everything that's happening real, which means that my chance of getting pregnant is real, but so is the chance I won't, or that I'll miscarry again. I've been going forward with blind faith, but soon I'm going to have to look reality in the eye, and I'm not sure I'll like what I see.

Seth must read some of my tangled feelings in my expression, because his jaw firms and he adopts what I think of as his don't-mess-with-the-coach stance. "Nuh-uh. You and I are getting an ice cream, and we're going to talk."

"I'm eating healthy because it maximizes the likelihood of a successful pregnancy."

He huffs. "Frozen yogurt, then." He ushers me toward the exit, his hand on my back. "Don't bother arguing, Ash."

I don't, because when he gets this way, arguing with him is a waste of energy. Besides, I do like the sound of frozen yogurt. We leave together, and he drives me to a nearby fro-yo place. We both get strawberry, although I add fruit while he loads up with chocolate sprinkles and nuts. Once we have our food, we sit at the bar in the window and eat. It's nice. I don't keep company with many men these days, and I've forgotten how good it can feel to sit silently with one.

"Tell me what's going on," he says after a while. "Did something happen during your appointment?"

"No." I sigh. "It's just sinking in that this is really happening, and I'm going to have to face the fallout soon, whether it's good or not."

He looks up from his yogurt. There's a smear of pink on his upper lip and before I know what I'm doing, I've wiped it off with a napkin. We both freeze. His nostrils flare. And then I drop my hand away before I do something stupid like caress him. Stupid muscle memory. It's harder to resist old habits when I'm tired. A rumble sounds in his throat. I stare into my bowl, refusing to meet his eyes even though I know he's waiting for me to do so.

"Are you afraid it won't work?" he asks eventually.

"Yes," I confess. "Or that it will, and then..." I can't bring myself to finish.

"You'll survive."

Other people might mistake his words for being curt or flippant, but I know he means them to his very core, and believes them deeply. He knows I can make it through whatever happens, and that warms me even more effectively than his sexy rumble.

"I will," I agree. "I will, I will, I will." If I say it often enough, with conviction, I might believe it.

"Damn right you will." He polishes off his yogurt and licks the spoon. "You're going to be a kickass mom."

"Thank you." Maybe it's silly, but his statement, combined with the yogurt, leaves me feeling better than I was before.

It doesn't mean I depend on him, I assure myself as I finish eating. *Just that we know each other well and he's a pro at talking me off a ledge.*

Lord, I hope that's true.

10

Seth

The most important day of my recent life begins much the same way as any other: with a gym full of men—and two young women—grunting as they swing kettlebells, lift weights, and punch bags. I absorb myself in the repetition, and help Devon throw the switch kick he loves but hasn't quite mastered over and over again, then I spar with one of the women who moved here to train with Harley. She has a powerful punch and killer instinct but her foot work is all over the place and she possesses the grace of a lumbering bear. That's okay. A few months partnered with Harley and she'll be moving like a deadly ballerina. My baby sister isn't for the faint of heart.

Things take a turn when my alarm sounds over the speakers, reminding me that I'm due to pick up Ashlin and take her to the clinic. Despite having had her explain to me numerous times that the procedure is simple and she won't even be sedated, I refuse to let her drive there on her own. What if she feels shaky afterward? Or gets a blast of emotion like she did after our last visit to the clinic? I want to be there for her should the need arise. I park outside the kindergarten building at the school and head to reception, where I ask the man behind the desk where to find her.

"You her boyfriend?" He assesses me as though he's scoping out the competition. "Thought she was single."

"I'm her ex-husband." I cross my arms and resist the primal need to stake a claim by telling him she's about to bear my child. I'm not sure when she intends to let her colleagues know, or if she already has, but what she chooses to do is her business. My jealousy can suck it.

"Huh." He leans back. "In that case, I'm not sure I should tell you where she is. How do I know you're not a threat to her?"

"Oh, for fuck's sake." If I thought he actually wanted to protect her, I'd appreciate it, but the kid is a poser. I grab my phone from my pocket and dial her number. When she answers, I don't bother with a greeting. "What room are you in?"

"Seth?" Her breath hitches. "Where are you?"

"Reception." I glare at the little fuckwad who thinks he's a man. "The guy here is afraid I'll hurt you, so he won't tell me where you are." The kid's eyes widen, and he makes a slashing motion for me to end the call. I don't.

"Down the righthand corridor. Second door on the left."

My lips curl into a satisfied smirk. "Thanks, babe. See you in a moment."

"Happy now?" I demand, then pivot in the direction she told me to go and walk away. A few seconds later, she appears in one of the doorways and beams.

"I'm so excited," she whispers. "But really nervous too."

"There's a thirty percent chance you'll be pregnant after today," I say, hoping the reminder will buoy her.

"I know!" She clasps her hands in front of her chest in a praying motion. "God, I just hope I'm not disappointed."

A niggle runs along my nerves. I want to tell her it'll all be okay, but it might not. In fact, she's more likely to not get pregnant than to get pregnant, and while I want to support her, I won't blow smoke up her cute ass.

"If it fails, we can try again."

She sighs. "Let's not think about it." She starts walking, and I catch up in a few strides. "Bye, Harry." She waves to the reception guy as we pass. He gives me a shitty look, and I give it right back. She shakes her head, but doesn't comment.

I escort her to my car, and manage not to give in to the urge to hold her hand during the drive, but as soon as we enter the clinic, I slide an arm around her and adopt a protective stance. Come what may, I will do everything in my power to be here for her. The fact she doesn't tease me speaks to her level of anxiety. We wait for all of two minutes before she's invited into a back room. My woman is pale but determined. I crack my knuckles and pace restlessly, waiting for her to return.

Time seems to move through a layer of molasses. Finally, the doctor appears in the corridor and gestures for me to follow her. I hurry over and go to Ashlin's side. She's sitting on the edge of the bed, fully clothed. "How are you doing, baby?" I smooth the hair back from her face so I can see her properly.

"I'm good." Her mischievous smile tells me she's more amused than anything else. "I think you took it harder than I did."

I can't deny it. "Hey, if my discomfort makes you smile, it's worth it." I kiss her cheek, hoping she won't mind. Given the circumstances, I need to touch her. "Seriously, are you okay?"

She nods, and the edges of her smile climb higher. "I might be pregnant." Her eyes shine with emotion. "Our baby might be getting settled inside of me right now."

Possessiveness sweeps through me, catching me off guard in its intensity. Fuck, I forgot how her pregnancy affected me last time. Knowing that this woman could be growing our child robs me of my ability to breathe normally. Every instinct I have shouts at me to shut her away in a cozy room and refuse to let her leave.

She must stay safe. She must stay *mine*.

Closing my eyes, I remind myself she isn't mine. Not really. These urges are just the caveman part of my brain wanting me to ensure my lineage continues, or some bullshit like that.

Ashlin's dark eyes study me carefully. "Are you all right?"

"Yeah." I clear my throat. "I'm fine."

Dr. Slater clears her throat. "I've just got a few pointers before you go." She starts talking, and by the time we leave, my head is ready to explode. Who knew there was so much to know about getting pregnant? Last time we just had sex a few times and voila. Then, during the pregnancy, Ashlin took care of most things. I went with her to the scans and medical checks, but I didn't delve into the details. She did that all by herself. I was busy getting my gym up and running, recruiting fighters, and trying to carve out a space for myself on the coaching scene, so I was relieved to let her handle it.

I should have done more.

While I drive her home, I vow I'll be better this time. Now that the appointment is over, my nerves should have eased, but they've only morphed into something else because for the first time, I get to see where she lives. She's been secretive about it. Not downright evasive, but sketchy enough that I want to know what she's hiding and why. When we arrive outside, the reason for her behavior does not become any more obvious. Her house looks nice enough. Cream-walled, with a brown tile roof, in a decent neighborhood. It's cute, but classy. Very her.

"Nice place."

"It's home." She rubs her lips together. A nervous tick. "You can just leave me out here. You don't need to walk me in."

"Yeah, I do." It's time to address the elephant in the room. "What is it you don't want me to see?"

"Nothing." She climbs from the car and waves a hand at me. "Come in, then. You may as well." Her tone is flat.

"What's wrong, Ash?"

"It's just…" She sniffles and turns to face me, swiping at her

85

eyes. "Sorry. Stupid hormones. I told you I've been doing some renovations. I'm a little sensitive about it because I've never been what you'd call handy, and I'm afraid it won't be what you're expecting." Her lips rub together again, but she raises her chin as if daring me to say the wrong thing.

"You're worried I'll criticize what you've done?"

"Maybe." She gives a tiny shrug of her shoulders. "I'm proud of myself, but you can see where I was learning as I worked on the bathroom and kitchen. It's not up to a professional standard."

"Sweetheart." I rest a hand on her shoulder. "The fact you renovated your bathroom and kitchen all on your own impresses the hell out of me. Why don't you give me the grand tour? I'm dying to see what a home looks like when you get to make all the design and decor choices."

She still seems dubious. "Well, okay then."

We walk to the door and she slots a key into the lock, her hand trembling. I can't say I understand exactly why this is such a big deal to her, but it is, and I respect that. The interior of the hall is dusty, and the wallpaper is faded floral and has been stripped away in places. There's no carpet. By the looks of it, she's ripped up whatever was there. She glances at me over her shoulder, expression cautious. I gesture for her to lead the way. She takes me into the living area.

"I finished this room most recently. When I first started, I focused on the bathroom, kitchen, and main bedroom because I figured those were the most important rooms to have done. I've, uh, just started on the spare bedroom. I'm planning to turn it into a nursery."

I force myself to breathe easier. I don't want to freak her out over how excited I am to see the nursery. The room where she'll raise our baby. Instead, I study the interior of the living room. It's pretty. Walls with a creamy yellow tint that gives the impression of warmth. A comfortable bean bag in the corner. Large windows that face the small back yard. On the windowsill there's a framed photo, and I cross to it. Smiling back at me are the faces of three women: Ashlin, and the two I know from online research are Paige Donovan and Jessica Leighton. Paige is a cute brunette, whereas Jessica is an icy blonde. Looking at the photo, you'd think Jessica was the one who came from money because of the way she holds herself aloof as Ashlin and Paige wrap her in an embrace from each side. However, it's Paige's family who are actually wealthy.

"You guys seem close," I say, as if I didn't dig deep into each of her friends' social media profiles for any hint they might mean her harm or be a negative influence.

"We are." She smiles softly at the picture. "I wouldn't be where I am today without them."

Is that a boxing glove stuck in my throat? Sure as hell feels like it.

While I'm glad she had friends who cared for her when I wasn't able to, I can't help resenting them for occupying a place in her heart that I no longer have access to.

"I'll show you the kitchen." She takes my hand and tugs. I follow her silently. "I wanted plenty of counter space," she tells me, waving her free hand at the length of counter that wraps around one wall. The kitchen is long and narrow, with cupboards on one side and the counter on the other. Like the living room, the walls are cream, but the cupboards are a dark blue. I wish I could pick her up, place her on the counter and make love to her until she screams. When we lived together, we christened every room in the house, and here, we could start over. Do it again.

"Seth?" she asks. "You're awfully quiet."

"Just taking it in." I study the line where the painted wall meets the tiles behind the counter, noting a couple of spots where the tiles don't quite line up. It's nearly impossible to see unless you're looking for it, but I have no doubt these are the imperfections she's so concerned about. "I can't believe you did all of this. It's incredible."

"Thanks." She ducks her head, suddenly shy. "I didn't do it alone. My friends helped."

"I'm glad you have them."

"So am I." She turns. "Through that door is the laundry. There's a functional washing machine, but I doubt I'll get around to redoing the room for a while yet. I want to finish the rest of the house first."

"You said you'd already done the bathroom," I prompt.

"I did." She seems pleased I remember. As if I don't store every tidbit I collect about her like a squirrel hoarding nuts. "Back this way."

The bathroom comes off the short hall that leads to the living room. It's small but elegant, with a deep tub and a wet floor shower. Perfectly designed for sex. I can't help but wonder how many other men have been here, and whether any of them have had the opportunity to take her against the wall the way I want to.

Get your mind out of the fucking gutter, Isles.

"It's great."

"Yeah, well, I don't have the resources you do, but I did the best I could."

My eyes narrow and my nostrils flare with annoyance. The only reason she doesn't have equal access to my resources is because she insisted I not pay her any alimony. I wanted to, and at first, I sent her money anyway, but she always returned it.

"You don't need to be defensive." I do my best to relax my features and show my sincerity, but displaying emotion has never come easily to me—one of the primary reasons for our breakup. "I meant it when I said it looks great. You've done well."

"Okay, thanks." She's on edge, and I don't know how to help. "I'll show you the room that will be the nursery."

She leads me down the hall, pulling the door to her bedroom shut as we pass. Before she does, I catch a glimpse of a bed with a baby blue comforter and an array of dark blue cushions. My eyes widen as she lets me into the nursery because it seems she removed a wall separating two smaller rooms, and I have to step over rubble on my way to the center of the space.

"Did you, uh, have a permit to demolish that wall?" I ask.

She rolls her eyes. "Yes, Captain Obvious. I'm not stupid enough to knock down what could be a load-bearing wall without having it checked out. I got the go-ahead. All of the boxes are ticked."

Of course they are. I shouldn't have questioned it. She's never been rash. I'm debating how to respond without stepping on another land mine when I hear a car outside.

"Are you expecting someone?"

"No." She frowns, but then her face lights up. "It's probably the girls." She starts toward the door, then glances at me and I can almost hear the cogs whirring in her brain. For whatever reason, she's reluctant to introduce me to her friends, but there's no chance of her spiriting me away without them noticing.

"They're waiting," I say before she can dream up a plot to get rid of me.

"You're right." She sighs, then looks me up and down. "Do you think you could tone down the broody hotness?" Her cheeks flush as she asks the question, but she doesn't stop. "I don't want them getting the wrong idea about us."

Uh, what?

My lips curl in a slow smile. "You think I'm hot?"

She rolls her eyes. "I married you. It's a given."

"You divorced me too," I point out.

She touches my arm. "We both know that had nothing to do with a lack of physical chemistry."

"We do," I agree. "But it's still nice to hear." Especially considering she's improved with age while I've gotten rougher. "I want to meet them."

She nods, apparently resigned. We backtrack into the hall,

and to the front door. Ashlin opens it, and I wait behind her. A cherub-cheeked face appears as the door opens, and the talking begins.

"Sorry for knocking. I wanted to come right in, but Jessica made me wait since we didn't recognize the car out front. She was afraid we'd interrupt—" Her eyes catch on me and widen. "Well crap, we did interrupt something, didn't we?"

"You must be Paige." I edge past Ashlin to offer her a hand, and her jaw drops.

"Holy shit, you're even better looking in person." She shakes my hand vigorously, then bounces inside, darting a look at Ashlin. "Sorry for turning up like this; we thought you might need support."

"I'm glad you did," Ashlin replies at the same time as I say, "Don't apologize."

We exchange glances, and I continue. "Thank you for being here when she needs you. We both appreciate your support."

"Both?" she squeaks, her eyes widening impossibly further. "You, uh, she…" She trails off.

A throat clears behind her, and when I raise my gaze, I find a statuesque blonde watching me with cold intensity.

"Good to meet you, Jessica." I hold my hand out to her too, but she doesn't take it.

"I don't care how many men you've knocked out, how rich you are, or how attractive most women find you," she tells me without inflection. "If you hurt Ashlin, I will make your life very difficult."

Despite the threat, I smile. "I'm pleased to know you've got her back."

She stares at me for a long moment, and I don't blink. I'm not sure what she's looking for, but this woman means a lot to Ashlin, and I'll earn her approval however I can, even if I feel my balls trying to climb up inside me. She looks at me like she's a cat and I'm a mouse. She's trying to decide if I'm worth toying with.

"I mean it," she warns, pursing her lips.

Built like a goddess, Jessica Leighton would drive most men out of their minds with lust. She's nearly six feet tall, with tousled blonde hair, golden skin, aquamarine eyes, and the kind of curves that rock a bikini. As a former professional beach volleyball player, I'm sure she's had plenty of people tell her so. But I prefer petite brunettes with big hearts.

"Tell you what," I say. "If I hurt her, I'll let you take a free shot."

"Deal." She still doesn't shake my hand, but she stops glaring and turns her attention to Ashlin instead. "How are you doing? Need a hug?"

"Yes, please."

Jessica and Paige sandwich Ashlin in the center of their three-person embrace, and I force myself to look away. They're sharing an intimate moment and don't need me staring at them. When I hear them break apart, I decide to beat a strategic retreat.

I grab Ashlin's hand and pull her aside. "If you're okay with them, I'll head out and let you catch up." Her bangs are mussed from the group hug and I itch to smooth them into place. "See you soon?"

"Yeah." She slides her hand from mine, and disappointment squeezes my heart. "Thanks for coming today. I'll call you when I have news."

"Okay." I back away from her. "Nice to meet you, ladies."

"You, too," Paige assures me.

Jessica just raises a hand. "Until we meet again."

11

"Oh. My. God." Paige fans her face as the door snicks shut behind Seth. "Are there pheromones in here, or what?"

I shake my head. "You're being ridiculous."

She flounces down the hall and into the living room. "Am not. That man is sexy, and the way he was looking at you? *Mm.* Potent."

Sighing, I ignore her. I know Seth is sexy. That's never been in doubt.

"I can tell why you want your baby to have his genes," she continues, regardless. "The two of you would make stunning children. Don't you think, Jess?" She flings herself onto the beanbag.

I hover in the doorway. "Can I get you a drink?"

"Nope." She points at a chair. "Sit."

"I'll make herbal tea," Jessica says, heading into the kitchen. "Put a pause on the conversation until I'm back."

We do, and when she carries a tray with three mugs of tea into the room and places it on the coffee table, she pauses before choosing her own and glancing over at me.

"Did I sense some sparks between you and your ex?"

"Sparks?" I repeat dumbly. "Uh, no." Except yes, she probably did, because they've been flying all day. Ever since he re-entered my life, if I'm being honest.

Jessica stares at me in a way that's enough to make me believe she can see into my soul. "I hope you're being careful not to put yourself in a position where you'll end up getting hurt."

"I am," I assure her. "Trust me. Seth and I have great chemistry, but in the end, there was a reason it didn't work out. I was too dependent on him for my happiness, and he didn't have the emotional capacity to deal with it. Or with his grief, I suspect." I always assumed that the death of our unborn baby affected me more than him, but based on what I've seen of him recently, I've begun to think he was as grief-stricken as me, but buried it deeper. Neither of us took a healthy approach to managing our loss.

"It can be easy to forget the parts that didn't work when reminiscing over better times." Jessica sits on the end of the sofa beside Paige's feet. "Be careful, is all I'm saying. You've got one of the kindest hearts I know, and I don't want to see it injured."

"I will be," I assure her, although honestly, I'm less certain of that than I'd like. Reconnecting with Seth has been intense, and several times I've caught him watching me in an unsettling way. It makes my nerves prickle and zap with restless energy. "Besides, he's been wonderful through this whole process."

"Because he's pining for you," Paige declares. We both stop and stare at her. She shimmies around into a seated position and shrugs. "What? It's true. You saw it, Jess. That big hunk of man is giving off lovesick tough-guy vibes."

"No." I immediately deny it and wait for Jessica to do the same. When she doesn't, I cock my head. "Right, Jess?"

"Umm." She sips her drink to buy herself time, and dread knots in my gut. "Actually, I'm with Paige on this one. He seems to have residual feelings for you."

The dread in my stomach intensifies, and a cold sweat breaks out on my forehead.

"That can't be right." If it is, it means that I'm the woman who manipulated those feelings to get what I want, and I'd rather not believe that. Is it still manipulation if you don't realize you're doing it? "He didn't even fight the divorce. I mean, he argued at first. Seemed shocked. Told me I was over-reacting and that he could fix things, but when I stood my ground, he just let it go. I figured that once he got over the blow to his pride, he was relieved he didn't have to deal with me anymore."

Eyes downcast, I nibble my lip, recalling how low I was at that time in my life. Initially, Seth tried to help, but nothing he did could shake me out of my funk, and eventually he gave up and started hiding away at the gym. When he seemed to throw in the towel, I figured our separation was best for everyone.

"Well, I don't know about that," Paige says. "But the man I just saw has it bad for you."

"Damn." Maybe I should have left Seth alone and never have brought him into this. I've been so worried about making sure he doesn't hurt me that I overlooked the potential for the reverse to occur. "Do you think I made a mistake?"

Jessica raises a brow. "If so, you're realizing it a bit late. You might already be pregnant."

She makes a good point, and wrong or not, I can't bring myself to regret my choices. I do want Seth to be the father of my child, and spending time with him has been nice. It seems like we've both worked through some of our issues and we've come out stronger for it.

"We'll be fine," I decide out loud.

"If you say so, babe."

Seth

94

When I leave Ashlin's place, I head to Devon's apartment rather than going home because I need to talk to Harley and she spends most of her time there. I pause in the corridor outside and knock. Things have been pretty good between us for the past few weeks, but it's still strange to think that they're in love with each other. For as long as I've known him, Devon has been a player. Not in a bad way—women always knew what they were getting into with him—but he was never a one-woman man. These days, he dotes on my baby sister. I don't doubt they're happy, but I can't help worrying he's going to break her heart one day. Harley may be able to show most men a thing or two about using their fists, but she's surprisingly sensitive.

Devon opens the door, and breaks into a grin, flashing white teeth against dark skin. "Hey, man. Long time, no see."

"It was this morning," I point out, but he just grins more broadly. "I need to talk to Harley."

He pretends to pout. "You mean you're not here to see more of me?"

I roll my eyes. "As if you need the ego boost."

He jerks his head toward the inside of the apartment and steps back to let me in. "I swear, now that Harley is here, you visit far more than you used to. What's that say about our friendship?"

I don't answer, because I'm too busy sniffing the air. Harley makes amazing curry, and the downside of her relationship with Devon is that he gets the benefit of her cooking skills while I'm left to fend for myself. I follow my nose to the kitchen.

"Smells good."

She stirs something in a frying pan, then spins around. "You left the gym early today."

I nod. "That's what I'm here about."

"Oh." She arches a brow. "Is everything okay?"

"I've gotta tell you something. Don't freak out."

Her hands go to her hips. "Nothing good ever starts with that phrase."

I'm hoping she'll change her mind. "Ash and I are trying to have a baby."

Her jaw drops.

"Holy shit," Devon breathes from somewhere behind me.

"You're... together?" Harley asks, eyes like saucers.

"No." With a substantial effort, I manage not to cringe. "She wants to have a baby and asked me to be the father. We're doing IVF. They implanted an embryo today."

"Wait." She holds up a hand, forehead crinkling. "You waited until after everything was done to mention it to me?"

Devon snorts. "Might not wanna cast shade, Harls."

She winces. He's referring to the fact they kept their relationship secret from me. "Fair call," she allows. "But still. I'm going to be an aunt."

"Maybe." My tone holds more warning than it ought, and I sigh, rubbing my temples. "Sorry, I just mean that IVF only has a thirty percent success rate, so it might not work, and I don't want you getting your hopes up in case it doesn't."

The glimmer in her eyes tells me that her hopes are well and truly raised. "Do you think you'll try to make it work with her? Wait—you are going to actually be the dad, right? This isn't like an anonymous donor type situation where the kid grows up having no idea who they are?" She exchanges a glance with Devon, and I frown. There's a story there.

"I'll be their dad," I confirm. "If there's a baby. It's still a big 'if.' As for Ash and me..." I rake my fingers over my scalp, embarrassed by what I'm about to say. "I'd do pretty much anything for another chance with her."

"Oh, Seth." Her expression is uncharacteristically gentle. "You two are so right together. She'd be stupid not to give you one, and we both know Ash is smarter than either of us."

"I hope so," I mutter, anxiety turning me inside out. "I miss her like crazy."

"Dude, you aren't doing this just to win her back, are you?" Devon asks. "'Cause if it doesn't work out, that's a lot of potential years of bitterness ahead."

"That's not the only reason," I assure him. "It's a factor, but I always wanted a kid, and however things end, I want Ash to be happy. It's the least she deserves."

"Okay, then." He nods, seeming satisfied.

"Pregnancy was actually the catalyst for our divorce," I admit, coming clean for the first time. "Ash miscarried. She got really down and I didn't handle it well. I buried myself in work and let her push me away. I wasn't there for her. But I will be this time."

"Oh, Seth." Harley's eyes shine with tears. "I never knew."

I shrug, uncomfortable. "No one did."

"I'm sorry you went through that," she said.

"Things will be different this time," Devon adds. "In fact, let's celebrate with champagne."

"How about a beer?" I suggest, pulling a face. I don't do the fancy stuff—a fact he's well aware of.

"Not for me." Harley checks dinner again and turns the stove off. "Stay and eat with us too."

The invitation warms me. I know I messed up by making such a big deal about her and Devon dating, and I thank my lucky stars that they're more understanding than some people might be. I don't mean to be a cynic, but when you've lost the love of your life, you spot all the potential pitfalls in relationships.

Later that night, I check in with Ashlin via text to make sure she's okay. I keep in touch that way for the rest of the week. It's rare for an hour to pass without me thinking of her, and half of my energy is expended worrying whether everything will work out. I want so badly for her dream to come true—even more badly than I want to have her back in my bed.

By the time Friday comes, I need to see her, to reassure myself she's in good health and not holed up in her living room in a state of constant anxiety. During my lunch break, I shut myself in the office and call her.

"Hi, Seth," she answers, a smile in her voice. "Everything is all right. I'm at work, supervising the children while they eat, and both my mental and physical states are A-okay."

"Have you eaten?" Even though I know she'll be taking every precaution, it's in my nature to worry about her.

"Of course I have." She huffs a slight laugh. "Is that all?"

"No." I pause, hoping like hell I'm not about to push for more than she's willing to give. "Will you visit tomorrow? I'd like to spend time with you. It might help with my nerves if I can see you for a while."

She's silent for so long that I start counting the seconds. Have I finally scared her off? But then she speaks. "I have a better idea. Why don't you come over and help me with the nursery?"

"Really?" I bark the word, shocked, and then mentally slap myself. "Are you sure?" I continue more softly.

"Yes." Thank God she sounds calm, because my thoughts are rioting and one of us needs to be in control of their faculties. Heat burns in the back of my eyes, and my throat thickens.

Don't cry, asshole.

I swallow hard and man the fuck up. "Yeah, that'd be great. When should I be there?"

"Can you be here at ten a.m.?" she asks. "Or does that interfere with your training schedule?"

"Fuck the schedule." I'll find someone else to fill in for me tomorrow. Devon has mentioned that he wouldn't mind learning to coach, so it'll give him the opportunity to jump in the deep end. "See you then, Ash."

"Dress dirty," she replies, then laughs at herself. "You know what I mean."

I do, but my dick perks up anyway.

Calm down, I tell it. *We have a long road home yet.*

12

SETH

"What are you envisioning?" I ask, standing in the room Ashlin has designated as the nursery. She's already moved the rubble from the demolition of the wall and is clad in yoga pants and a tank top with a toolbelt strapped around her waist. Fuck if she isn't the hottest thing I've ever seen.

"We need to smooth out the damage and add a new panel here." She gestures to the space where there's a hole that was previously occupied by a wall. "Once that's done, we can strip the wallpaper and sand the surface. I thought we'd paint it in the same shade of cream as the living room. I have enough of it left to do the job."

"Great."

Her hands go to her hips, and my gaze lingers on her belly, wondering if our baby is already growing inside her.

"Seth."

I glance up to find her smirking. It's an unusual expression on her, but one I remember well enough from the times she used to catch me checking her out and knew I liked what I saw. Once upon a time, she'd have sidled over, placed her hands on my chest, nibbled her lower lip and tempted me to give in to my craving for her. Images flash through my mind of my hands on her skin, my thumb and forefinger clasping her chin as I held her mouth still for a punishing kiss. The way her breath would come out in little pants as her eyes darkened with desire. I was an insatiable beast when it came to her, but she never had any control once the spark ignited either. Our need for each other eclipsed all else. The memory jolts me back a step, and I suck in a breath, the scent of wood and dust anchoring me in the present. I meet Ashlin's gaze, and find it burning back into mine. Neither of us speak.

Then she shakes her head ever so slightly and thrusts a sander into my hand. "Start over there."

Doing as she says, I mull over the moment we shared. After the brief intensity of that connection, I know there's something in her that hasn't let go of us yet. The question is, will she allow herself to ask for more from me than being a convenient sperm donor?

She switches on the radio and we listen while we work. I'm impressed by her competence, and even more so by how little she seems to notice it. She takes her own skills for granted, not realizing when she asks me to do things that are beyond my ability. Her easy self-assurance is new, and it hammers home how much she's changed since we were married.

Every now and then, I catch her watching me with something that resembles shyness, but on the whole there's a confidence about her that didn't used to exist. While she's never been weak, she used to look to me for support and it's obvious she no longer needs to. I want to congratulate her and let her know that she blows me away, but there's also a twinge in my chest because if I'm honest with myself, I liked the way she depended on me. At least, I did before it became an albatross around my neck.

Did she have to be away from me to experience this growth? I've always regretted the way things ended between us, but for the first time I'm beginning to wonder if it wasn't for the best. The years apart have brought us to this place where we stand on a more even footing. We got together when she was young—maybe too young—and now she's proved to herself what she's capable of. Hope blossoms in my heart. Perhaps this is exactly how things are supposed to be, and this time around, we're ready for each other.

ASHLIN

It's strange how natural it feels to work side by side with my ex-husband. As though we've done this dozens of times before. He holds a board in place and I secure it with a nail, brushing against him in the process. The scent of dusty man tickles my nostrils, appealing more than it should. There's just something about a guy who works with his hands. That's one of the things I always found incredibly sexy about Seth. He didn't earn his small fortune by sitting in an office or playing with other people's money. He earned it with his body. His blood and sweat.

My teeth sink into my lower lip and I ease away from him, ignoring the throb between my legs. It's been a long time since I had sex. About three years, as a matter of fact. During that time, my libido has been nonexistent, but all it takes is a moment of closeness with Seth—the smell of his skin and sound of his steady breathing—to reawaken a part of me I'd long thought dead. Squeezing my thighs together, I mentally berate myself. I can't let myself get turned on by the man who's going to be the father of my baby. Talk about complicated.

"What next?" he asks, straightening. His shoulders strain against his t-shirt, and heat spirals downward through my body. God, his arms are so bulky. He could hold me up with one hand, pin me against the wall...

Get yourself together, girl.

"Um." He stretches, revealing a band of firmly muscled stomach, and my capacity for thought flees. "Uh."

"Yeah?" He lowers his arms, and I manage to raise my gaze, only to find him smirking. Ugh. He always did know what effect he had on me.

I check my phone. "How about I make us some lunch?"

"I don't expect you to feed me," he replies with a frown.

I smile. "I want to. It's the least I can do in exchange for free labor."

"It's only right for me to be helping." He shifts his weight forward, and even though the movement is tiny, I suddenly feel suffocated. "The nursery is as much for my benefit as yours. If everything goes the way we want it to, I'd like my child to have the best possible place to live."

It occurs to me that he could provide a far more upscale living situation than I can. I wonder if he'll stay in his condo or move to a family-friendly home. I never expected him to make any dramatic life changes for my sake, but considering how dedicated he seems, maybe he'll want to set up somewhere better suited to raising the baby.

"Whatever the case, thanks. Does a sandwich work for you?"

He nods, and follows me to the bathroom, where I wash my hands. When I turn to exit, he's right there, in my face, far too close for comfort. I nearly walk into his chest.

That broad chest.

My mouth waters, and it isn't craving food. I'm tempted to burrow into him and lick the pulse point at the juncture of his neck and shoulder. He looks so manly standing in a space that's never housed a male I'm not related to. He has this way of man-spreading to occupy any area he's in. Not in an annoying way, but in a way that makes him impossible to ignore.

Swallowing, I step back, and then circle around him. "I'll be in the kitchen."

Knowing I have all of a minute before he enters, I take

advantage of the time to get a grip, closing my eyes and resting my forehead on the refrigerator. I inhale slowly to the count of six, then exhale to the count of eight. Hearing footsteps, I straighten and open the fridge, studying its contents.

"Do you mind a vegetarian sandwich? I haven't been keeping much meat in the house because there are a bunch of foods that are off-limits for me at the moment."

He makes a face but nods. "Whatever you've got."

I grab a pair of bread rolls from the pantry and slice them open, adding salad to mine. He gets a few slices of cheese to make up for the lack of meat, and then we sit at the coffee table and eat.

"Not bad," he says around a mouthful.

"Hard work makes it taste better."

"Can't argue with that." He polishes off his sandwich in a matter of minutes. "Is this how you usually spend your weekends?"

"Pretty much. Sometimes my friends help. Sometimes my family do. Every now and then I'll take a break and relax instead, but it's far more satisfying to accomplish something."

He nods, and I know he gets it. He's the sort of person who'd practice a kick ten thousand times purely for the satisfaction of being able to execute it perfectly once.

"Is it—" He cuts himself off, shaking his head.

"Is what?" I ask, curious.

"Doesn't matter."

I finish my sandwich and wipe my fingers on a napkin. "If it matters to you, it matters to me."

He sighs, and gives me a pointed look. "You might regret asking."

"Or I might not." I smile sweetly. "Don't assume you know how I'll respond."

He grunts. From years of interpreting Seth's grunts, I can tell it's dubious. "Is it bad that I'm glad you're busy with this on the weekends because it means you aren't dating?"

My mouth goes dry, and the sandwich becomes a lead weight in my stomach, giving me that weird sensation like when you drive over a dip in the road too fast and your innards can't keep up.

"Um."

I can't think of a single intelligent thing to say. Part of me wants to break into song. His possessiveness always turned me on. But the bigger part of me knows I shouldn't encourage him because it won't lead anywhere good.

"Fuck," he mutters. "Should've kept my mouth shut."

Reaching over, I grab his hand. Screw 'shouldn't'. Emotion doesn't always play by the rules. "There's nothing wrong with that."

13

ASHLIN

On Monday, Seth accompanies me to get a blood sample taken. Nerves crowd my stomach, and I can't tell whether the anxiety or excitement is strongest. He slips his hand into mine as we're led into a room by a smiling nurse.

"There's absolutely no need to stress," she assures us as she guides me to a padded bench and waits for me to pull up my sleeve. "This won't hurt a bit, and you'll have an answer either later today or tomorrow." She wipes cleansing alcohol on my forearm. "Even if it's not the result you want, it's better to know than not, isn't it?"

I catch Seth's eyes and rub my lips together. I'm not sure I agree. If I don't know, then I can exist in a state of blissful ignorance.

"We'll be fine," he tells me.

We. I like that.

The nurse nods approvingly. "That's the attitude."

She straps a band around my arm. I feel a prick, and force myself not to look. While I'm not as squeamish as some people, I don't love getting my blood taken. Blood belongs inside the body.

"There." She withdraws the needle and presses cotton wool over the spot where it had been. "All done. Can you hold this down for a moment?"

I place a finger on the cotton wool, trying not to think about the blood beneath it. A moment later, she gestures for me to move my hand and slips a Band-Aid over the top.

"Thanks." I allow hope to fill my heart. In only a matter of hours, I might be receiving the news that I'm pregnant. God, I hope so.

"No problem." She makes a note on my paperwork and hands it over. "Take this to the administrator. Best of luck."

I stand, and Seth is at my side in an instant, wrapping an arm around me. I smile up at him, letting my optimism shine through. "We might be pregnant."

He kisses my nose, and my heart flutters. I tell myself it's just a gesture of affection—it doesn't mean anything—but I don't really believe it. There's something between us. There always has been.

"I hope we are," he says, and hugs me tighter. "But if we're not, we'll make it through."

We retrace our earlier steps back out to reception. "Thank you for coming with me."

He glances down. "I wouldn't miss it for the world. You'll call me when you hear from them?"

"Absolutely." I just pray it's good news.

Once we've handled the paperwork, Seth drops me off at work, with yet another promise to call him as soon as I hear anything.

A little before five in the afternoon, not long after I return home from work, I get a phone call.

"Mrs. Isles?"

"It's Ms. Isles, actually," I correct. "Can I help you?"

"This is Ansel Arnaud from the medical laboratory. I'm calling with regard to your pregnancy test."

My heart leaps to my throat, and I lower myself onto my bed. "Do you have the result?"

"We do." He clears his throat. "It's negative."

"Oh."

My world crashes down around me.

Again.

"Okay. Thank you for letting me know."

"Are you all right, Ms. Isles?"

"Fine." I press my fist to my mouth so I don't cry. "I'm fine." Then I hang up. I hug my knees to my chest and release a strangled sob. My heart hurts. There's a pressure in my chest that won't let up, and the same thought replays over and over again in my mind.

It didn't work. I'm not pregnant.

I won't get to feel a baby grow within me, or hear their first cry. My womb is empty. Barren. But why? What did I do wrong? I've been so careful to follow all the rules. Eat healthy, get plenty of sleep, stay active but don't overdo it. I took the right vitamins and avoided anything that might make me sick. Is there something defective in my body that prevents me from getting pregnant? The doctor told me my eggs were fine, but maybe something else is wrong.

Tears stream down my cheeks and drip onto my yoga pants. There will be no tiny fingers for me to count, and no gurgling infant to cradle in my arms. At least, not this time. How do I tell Seth? He's nearly as excited as I've been. How can I admit my body has let us down? That I've failed?

I get up and walk numbly to the kitchen, where I take two painkillers and grab a chocolate bar from the cupboard. Then I go to bed. I can feel myself spiraling into despair, and know I should call Seth like I said I would, but I'm not sure I can handle him right now. Not when I feel like slapping myself for failing. Instead, I curl up and cry.

A couple of hours into my pity party, my phone pings with a message from Seth, which only starts the waterworks again. I ignore it because I don't know what to say to him. He'll be wanting to know if everything is fine, and it's not. I'm not okay. Twenty minutes later, he calls. I watch it ring, and pick up just before it goes to voicemail.

"It didn't work," I choke out, and then hang up before he can reply. I burrow deeper into my bed and pull the blankets up over my head. I want to insulate myself from the world for a while. I'll come out eventually. However miserable I am, I can survive this. But for now, I need to have a moment to work through my grief.

When there's a knock on the front door, I frown. Then I hear the rattle of a key in the lock, and my nerves fly into high alert.

"Ash?"

I relax. The voice is Seth's. Not ideal, but at least it's not an intruder. I sit up to greet him.

There are footsteps in the hall. They pass by my bedroom door, then track back and pause outside. The door creaks open.

"Ash, are you okay?"

"Yeah," I reply as he comes into view, hating the fact he's seeing me this way. So much like I used to be in the days after we lost Cara. Bundled up in bed, crying. Pathetic. "How did you get a key?"

"You still keep the spare inside one of your shoes on the doorstep, just like you used to."

"Oh, yeah." I should probably change that. "You don't need to come in."

He stands above me, his expression filled with concern. "You're not pregnant?"

My face crumples. "No. I'm sorry."

His gaze softens, and he sinks onto the bed, far enough from me that he isn't in my personal space, although the very fact he's in the room at all feels like an intrusion. "Don't apologize." He releases a shuddering breath and pinches the bridge of his nose between his thumb and forefinger. "I'm the one who's sorry, sweetheart. I know how much you wanted it to work." He starts to reach for me, then pauses. "Can I hold you?"

"Please." I whisper the word because I know I shouldn't accept his comfort. I need to stand strong on my own two legs, but despite his gruff exterior, Seth has an enormous heart and being in his arms is one of the few things that might have the power to help, even for a while.

"Thank you." He kicks off his shoes and climbs under the blankets with me. One of his brawny arms wraps around my waist, and he pulls me close, then presses a kiss to the crown of my head. Resting my forehead on his chest, I let the tears flow.

"I've got you," he tells me. "Let it all out. I know you're disappointed. I am too."

At that, I cry harder, because I know he is, and it's my fault. He may not have had any plans to try for another baby, but during the past weeks it's obvious he's become emotionally invested. Why else would he be there every time I turn around?

"I'm sorry," I sob. "I don't know what I did wrong."

For a microsecond, his big body stiffens, but then the muscles ease. "You did nothing wrong, baby girl. Sometimes things just don't work out, but we can try again. They have more embryos, right?"

I wipe my eyes on the backs of my hands and blink up at him. "They do."

His brows knit together. "Then however many times you want to try, I'm here to support you. If you need help financially, I'm here for that too." He nuzzles my temple in a way that makes me melt into him. I don't have any willpower to resist, and I can't believe he's being so sweet and understanding when he's lost as much as I have. A chance at a future we both yearn for. I bury my face in his chest and snuggle into his warmth, drawing comfort from his strength. He smells like Deep Heat, with a faint undertone of sweat. He must have been at the gym before he came here.

"I'm sorry for pulling you away from work," I mutter.

"Don't be." His hand smooths up and down my side. "I'm exactly where I'm supposed to be."

"Okay." I don't say anything further, even though my subconscious is cataloging the differences between now and the weeks after I miscarried, when he buried himself at the gym because he didn't know what to do or how to support me. This quiet companionship is something different. The Seth I knew was never any good with problems he couldn't fix. He didn't have the emotional capacity to deal with them. "Thank you for being here."

"Any time." His voice is a deep rumble. Soft and gentle, but firm enough that I feel like I can lean on him—at least for a while. "If you need me, all you have to do is call."

But I shouldn't. Depending on him too much is what got me into a bad place last time.

Still, as he sits with me and provides a safe space for me to let go, I can't help but wish he was mine.

After a while, he stirs. "Where's your phone?"

I gesture to the nightstand. "Why?"

"I'm going to call your friends. You need them right now."

Panic flares within me. "You shouldn't do that."

He hesitates. "They're women, Ash. They can be there for you in a way I can't."

"Please don't leave me alone." God, I hate my desperation.

"Never." His ocean eyes flash. "Never again, I promise."

———

SETH

The way she clings to me tears my fucking heart out. The sight of tears glistening on her cheeks flays me. My chest compresses more with each second that passes, and the fact I don't know how best to help her is the worst kind of torture, but I don't move from her side. I may not have any clue what to do, but I know that leaving is the wrong option. Losing myself in work after she miscarried was the worst mistake of my life, and I'm not about to repeat it. As before, my own heart is also cracking because I've grown to depend on the visions of myself with Ashlin and a little cherub-cheeked boy that encroach on my dreams every night. The future I've been eager for is drifting further away, but it's not out of reach. I'll try for it as many times as Ashlin wants to.

Reaching over, I grab her phone and scroll through the contact list until I hit the P's. Selecting Paige's number, I call it and raise the phone to my ear.

"Hi, pumpkin," Paige greets me cheerfully. "What's my best girl up to?"

I clear my throat. "It's Seth here."

"Oh." She trills with laughter. "Sorry about that. Why are you calling from Ashlin's phone?"

Glancing at the woman in question, I wonder whether I should have left the bed to make this call, so she wouldn't feel like we were discussing her right under her nose. But no, I refuse to leave her for even a minute.

"The test was negative." I let that sink in, then add, "She needs you."

For the first time, it occurs to me that Ashlin's friends might actually be busy, but if they love her half as much as I do, they'll make time. If not, they don't deserve her, and I'll let them know it.

"Oh, no. Poor Ash." She hums in thought. "You were right to call. I'll be there soon."

"Thanks, Paige."

"No problem."

I hang up.

"She's coming?" Ashlin asks.

"Yeah." I place the phone back on the nightstand, then turn and wrap my free arm around her so she's fully enveloped in an embrace. "She wants to be here for you, just like I do."

She nods. We remain that way—wrapped around each

other—for another half hour, until there's a knock. Ashlin starts to move, but I stop her.

"I'll get it." I swing my legs out of the bed and stride to the door. My fingers have grasped the handle when she speaks.

"Thanks, Seth. I appreciate you being here."

I huff. "No big deal." I'm just doing what I should have years ago, and sucking up my own discomfort to give her what she needs.

"No, it is," she insists.

"I'll get the girls." I yank the door open and step into the hall. A moment later, I let both Paige and Jessica into the house. Paige bustles right past me like I'm not there and hurries to Ashlin's room, while Jessica stops to appraise me with wary eyes.

"How is she?" she asks.

"Not great," I admit. "If I hadn't called her, she might have moped all night without letting me know."

She rolls her eyes. "That's Ash for you. Independent to a fault. Doesn't like to burden anyone."

"Huh." Back when we'd been together, Ashlin was certainly a strong woman, but I wouldn't have thought of her as overly independent. It goes to show how little I know of the person she's become. Besides, how could she ever think of herself as a burden? She has the most loving heart of anyone I know and it needs to be safeguarded.

When I don't say anything further, Jessica's stare intensifies. "Thanks for calling. When Ash told us about her plan to approach you, I thought she was out of her mind, but maybe she knew what she was doing. You're not quite the asshole I expected you to be."

How am I supposed to respond to that? And what the hell did Ashlin tell her to make her think I'd be an asshole? "Thanks, I guess."

Her lips press together. "My impression of you has improved. Don't fuck it up."

"I'll try not to." She starts to brush past me, but I stop her with a hand on her arm. "Thanks for having Ash's back. It takes a lot of balls to say what you just did to a guy like me."

She shrugs. "I have a vagina of steel. You don't scare me."

I sputter, but she doesn't give any indication that she's made a joke. In fact, she's deadly serious. "Got it."

I release her, and she continues to the bedroom, sparing me a final glance before vanishing through the doorway. I shiver. Fuck, that girl is intimidating. Dithering in the hall, I wonder whether to join them, but decide not to. They need time to talk without having me around. Instead, I go to the living room, collapse onto the sofa, and call Harley. Her phone rings and rings, and it occurs to me that she might not answer. I'm about to give up when the call connects.

"Hey," she says.

"Ash isn't pregnant," I blurt out with no tact at all, like a goddamn moron.

"Damn." She curses, and there's a muffled sound down the line, as though she's moving. "Hang on a sec." Devon's voice sounds in the background. "I'm back. Is she okay?"

"She's hanging in there. She's with a couple of her friends now."

"Fuck." Exactly my thought. "Poor Ash."

"I know." I drag a hand down my face, then press the heel of my palm into my eye socket. "What should I do? I can't stand to see her so upset." Which was half of the reason I vanished on her after our miscarriage. Seeing her but knowing I couldn't remove her pain was a nightmare.

"Just be there for her," my sister advises. "I'm not exactly the kind of woman who knows what it's like to want a baby, but if you stay with her and let her know you're there for whatever she needs, then I think that's the best you can do. Oh, and chocolate. You know how much she loves that stuff. Get her all the fancy-schmancy truffles and bonbons she can possibly eat."

"Good thinking." I make a mental note to do that. Ashlin

was always addicted to sweet things—not that she allowed herself to indulge often. "Thanks, Harley."

"No problem." There's a question in her voice, but I don't have to wait long for her to ask it. "Should I come over? I want to give her a massive hug."

I consider her suggestion. "Maybe tomorrow? I get the feeling she's maxed out on people for today. I'm going to give her a bit of time with her friends because they can be there for her in a way I can't, but I'm sure she'd be happy to see you soon."

"All right." She pauses, then adds, "I'm sorry it didn't work out. I know how much you wanted it to."

My breath catches, and it takes a moment for me to recover enough to breathe normally, but even then, my heart is hammering. "We're not giving up."

I say it for myself as much as for her. This isn't the end. Not for our journey to a family, and not for our love story.

"You'd better not. I want my sister back."

"I'll get her for you," I promise. "Thanks, Harls."

She snorts. "Oh, please. Not you too."

My lips curl ever so slightly. "Devon usually gets his way. The nickname is going to catch on. It'd be easier to embrace it."

"We'll never hear the end of it."

"Just the way you like," I shoot back.

"Maybe." I can hear her smile. "Let me know if there's anything I can do."

"Will do. See you tomorrow."

"Bye."

I shove the phone back in my pocket and knock lightly on the bedroom door. Paige emerges, her eyes bright with tears. Damn. Another emotional woman. At least it isn't my job to reassure this one. "Are you guys okay if I leave for a while?"

She nods, visibly curious, but I don't explain, just nod as I go. Twenty minutes later, I return laden with bags and boxes from the nearest chocolatier. I let myself in and drop them in the kitchen, all but one bag, then edge into Ashlin's bedroom. She's sandwiched between Paige and Jessica, who don't look like they're going anywhere soon. I'm torn between relief that they're here for her and frustration that I don't have her all to myself. The relief wins out. I'm grateful Ashlin has people in her life who would drop everything to support her at a time like this.

I hand the remaining paper bag to Ashlin and then sink to the floor and lean against the wall, legs sprawled in front of me. Perhaps the girls are here to stay, but so am I.

"What's this?" she asks, not opening it.

Nerves occupy every chamber of my heart. She's experienced a massive disappointment and all I can do is offer chocolate and company. I feel so fucking useless, all over again.

"Have a look."

She does, and to my horror, tears begin anew. "Oh, Seth, you didn't have to. That's so sweet." She sniffs. "Thank you." She withdraws a bonbon from the bag and pops it into her mouth.

Paige leans over and peers inside. "The good stuff. Nice work." Then she selects one and bites into it.

Jessica doesn't join them. She just strokes a hand up and down Ashlin's back and murmurs something in her ear. Hopefully it's not about me.

We stay in our positions for what feels like hours. Eventually, Paige and Jessica leave, although Jessica warns me not to upset her. I discover frozen casserole and cook it for dinner. Ashlin drags herself out of bed for long enough to eat, and then goes back to her hiding place. I join her, even when she protests. I'm going to be here with her all night. All day tomorrow. However long it takes until she no longer needs me. I let her push me away once before, and I won't let it happen again. Not this time.

14

ASHLIN

When I wake, I'm cocooned in a strong embrace, and for the first time since the divorce, I'm not alone. I squeeze my eyes more tightly shut because opening them would mean acknowledging that I'm in Seth's arms, and as soon as I do that, I need to reestablish the internal strength I've fought so hard for. Today, I feel well enough to get back on my feet, but I like being held and feeling as though I'm connected to him. Important to him. Cherished and adored. So many times I woke like this in the past, and I'd turn to face him, cup his jaw between my palms, and kiss him as though we had all the time in the world. We never realized how limited our years together would be.

Although lately, I'm beginning to wonder. We've both changed since we separated. I've grown confidence, and based on how he behaved yesterday, he's stopped running from his emotions. My heart beats in an irregular pattern. Perhaps there's hope for us yet. Maybe—just maybe—this is our second chance.

But do I want it to be?

Truth be told, no man has ever appealed to me the way Seth

does. After the first time I met him, no one else could measure up. He was sexier and more masculine than any of the boys I'd previously dated. Since the divorce, nothing has changed. I've been out a few times, but nobody has made my body zing with awareness the way he does, and after experiencing how intense that physical chemistry can be, I refuse to settle for anything less.

My eyelashes flutter open, and I roll over and study his face in the dim morning light. Sleep softens the line of his jaw, which is scruffy with reddish blond stubble. I ache to run my palm along it and feel the rasp against my skin. Breath eases between his slightly parted lips. With a flash of heat, I recall what that mouth is capable of. The pleasure it's brought me in the past. My gaze travels up, cataloging the faint scar on his brow bone where a knee once split the skin open during a fight. Even the memory makes my stomach churn but it's nothing compared to the panic I felt when I saw it happen. He acted as if it was no big deal, and perhaps to him it wasn't, but no woman likes to see her man bleed.

I catch a hint of blue in the corner of my awareness, and my eyes cut to his. He's awake, and watching me with an intensity that sends a shiver down my spine. Unconsciously, I press closer, my hand on his chest. He's so gorgeous, and there's potent desire in his eyes. But also more than that. A riot of emotion I can't begin to interpret. He never could mask his feelings first thing in the morning. Or perhaps he didn't want to. Whatever the case, it's clear that our position is stirring all kinds of buried memories for him, too.

"Ash..." he murmurs, his voice raspy with sleep. So sexy. And the way he's looking at me...

I can't help it. I kiss him.

My lips brush his. Softly at first. A kiss of gratitude and remembrance. But then he growls deep in his throat, and I'm done for. Every part of me wants him. I need him to help me forget everything that happened yesterday and get lost in sensation. I wriggle closer, desperate for the graze of his skin against mine, but the blankets get in the way and he's still clothed. Our tongues touch, and he groans. His entire body shudders, and I thrill in the revelation that he wants me as badly as I want him.

"Fuck," he mutters. "Ash."

He claims my mouth, sliding on top of me and pinning my body beneath him. Covering me on all angles with his delicious weight. His taste is so familiar, and his scent calls forth past pleasure. But then he tears his lips from mine and buries his face in the crook of my neck, breathing heavily. I writhe, silently asking for more.

"We can't." He slips off me, and scoots over until a foot of space separates us. "Not now." The yearning in his expression says differently, and I reach for him, but he wards me off. "No, Ash. You're vulnerable, and I don't want to take advantage."

"Excuse me?" My mouth drops open. If anything, I was the one taking advantage. "Did you just imply that I'm not capable of deciding what I want?"

"No," he denies, although he totally did. When I scowl, he inclines his head. "Okay, maybe. Sorry. I'm still learning not to be so overbearing."

My eyes widen. Did I just hear an apology from Seth Isles, king of bullheadedness?

Humor flashes in his eyes when he sees my surprise. "Things have changed. We're not the same people we were, and when our relationship escalates—and it will—it's going to be because we like and are attracted to the people we've turned into, not because shit went wrong and we want comfort."

I stare at him. I want to be pissed. The self-righteous feminist inside me declares that I should be allowed meaningless comfort sex if that's what I want, but on the other hand, it could never be meaningless between us. Besides, he has as much right to decide whether we have sex as I do, and he's saying no.

Oh, God.

My chin dips, and tears of humiliation prickle my eyes. He's saying *no*.

Ugh, why did I have to go and make this awkward? He's been amazing, and he's doing me a massive favor. I should be going out of my way not to scare him off.

"Hey." He touches my chin and gently levers it up. His gaze is tender and turns everything inside me upside down. "I want you, sweetheart. Don't doubt that. Just not like this."

"Okay." I nod jerkily. "I'm sorry for… whatever this is."

"I'm not." He draws me close, and I burrow into that safe space in front of his chest. "It proves that there's still something between us." His arms tighten around me, and his cheek touches the top of my head. "And that makes me brave enough to fight for you."

My breathing is choppy. He's going to fight for me. What does that mean? Is he saying he wants us to get back together? Thoughts swirl in my mind. Excitement, doubt, lust, fear. A cocktail of emotions I could get drunk on.

"What next?" he asks, and for a moment, I don't know what he means. "With trying to get pregnant—we are trying again, yeah?"

"Yes." I wet my lips. "If you're willing to. We'll need to wait for at least a month."

"I'm definitely willing." He sighs, and the tension eases from him. "Don't you know I'd walk through fire for you? I'm here for whatever you need. However you want me."

I fight the urge to cry at his sweet words. I want so badly for them to be true.

SETH

For the rest of the week, I make it my job to become Ashlin's rock. Whatever she needs, I get it. I call in sick for her at work and stay with her morning and night, occupying her bed without pushing for more. Sleeping with her in my arms is the best damn thing I've done in years, and I won't fuck it up by asking for more than she's ready to give. Yeah, I wake up with a hard-on wedged between her butt cheeks several times, but she doesn't mention it, and I convince myself that when she wiggles that sweet ass against me, it's completely innocent. It's not her fault I fantasize about her every time I close my eyes or that I have to go home every day after leaving her place to jack off before heading to the gym, and return to do it again before going to her in the evening. My sexual frustration is something I can take care of. Been doing it for years.

On Saturday, I spend most of the day at the gym, working with Devon. The guy has a lot of potential and now that he's taken down Karson Hayes—a former title contender—I've got the chance to set him up with a title shot of his own. We're just waiting for the right opportunity to come along. One that doesn't involve him facing off against Jase Rawlins, another of my fighters, who currently holds the title for the weight grade that Devon usually competes in. After leaving him to spar with Jase, I excuse myself to my condo and fuck my hand until I come, calling Ashlin's name, and then I drive to her place. When I arrive, the door is unlocked. I let myself in and wander through the house, but she's nowhere in sight.

"Seth?" Her voice comes from the bedroom.

"Yeah?" My feet glue themselves to the floor. I'm not entering that room unless invited, in case she's undressed. While I've had to deal with seeing the outlines of her nipples against her pajamas over the past few days, I've managed to avoid catching glimpses of anything more than that. I don't think I could resist the urge to touch her if I got an eyeful of her stunning body.

"Come in."

I push the door open, and step tentatively inside. Then stop. "Oh, fuck."

She's sprawled on the bed, wearing a scarlet corset and thigh-high stockings.

"Fuck, Ash. What are you doing?" If I sound desperate, it's because I am.

She shrugs one delicate shoulder, drawing my attention to the plumpness of her tits where they threaten to escape the corset. Her waist is so fucking tiny. Her pussy bare. *Fuck, fuck, fuck.* Despite its recent workout, my cock surges to life.

"I'm not in such a vulnerable place anymore, and I want you." She slides her legs off the edge of the bed and pads toward me on silent feet, stopping a scant inch from the flesh that's burning up for her. "Be with me, Seth. Make me feel good. It's been so long since I felt sexy."

"Aw, hell." A groan tears from me, and my hands twitch, eager to get a hold of the body she seems so willing to share. "Goddamn, you make it hard to be a good guy."

A smile curves lips that are as red as her corset. As though she's read my mind and knows every dirty Snow White fantasy I've ever had about her.

Oh, wait. She does. Because I've told her about them. Many, many times. This is what happens when a woman who knows you well decides to seduce you. She can make herself exactly what you desire.

"I don't want you to be a good guy," she whispers, settling her hands on my chest. I jerk beneath her touch, and shake because the desire to grab her and make her mine is that strong. "I want you to take me." She goes onto her tiptoes and smooths her hands up my chest. "Make me remember who I belong to." She glances down, suddenly shy, and rubs her lips together. "I haven't been with anyone in a long time. I think I'll go crazy if I don't have you."

"How long?" The question is rough. My breath ragged.

She raises her eyes, the truth shining in them. It's been as long for her as it has for me. "Three years."

"Hell." I give in to the impulse to grip her hips, and yank her close, letting her feel exactly what she does to me. "Are you sure you want this? Because if you give me a taste, I'll become a greedy bastard and want more. I can't..." I swallow, afraid to admit the truth, but I know she needs to hear it. "I can't do casual with you. It's already too late for that."

She nods. "I'm certain."

Thank fucking God.

15

ASHLIN

When Seth grabs me, I soften with relief. I'd been so worried he might reject me, and I don't know if I could take that. In fact, I've been more or less obsessing over the possibility of what could happen between us since the first night he spent with me, and today I realized that if I didn't want to always wonder, I needed to take action. Out of some misguided code of honor, he wasn't going to be the one to take the initiative.

His palms skim my skin, and it's the best sensation ever. They're calloused and large, nearly encircling my hips. I shiver, my body inherently knowing what pleasure those hands can bring. Then he lifts me, strides to the bed, and places me on the covers. I frown. The Seth of my memories would have dumped me on the comforter, then dragged me to the edge of the bed to bury his head in my thighs with no mercy. His gentleness makes me feel fragile, and I don't like it. Perhaps he needs reminding of how we used to be. Sitting up, I get to work on his jeans, dragging down the fly then trying to shove them over his hips.

"What's the hurry?" he asks, lips twitching.

I scowl, hating how calm he seems while I've been teetering on the edge of reason for days. "Off."

He nods, losing the smile. Beneath the jeans are a pair of boxer briefs. I pause, suddenly struck by the possibility that I'm not the only woman to see these briefs. How many has he been with since me?

Get out of your head.

Shaking myself, I reach around to grip his meaty ass, then peel down the waistband of his briefs, revealing the appendage I've missed like one of my own limbs. I eye his cock. It's engorged and stands at attention. His balls are full, and sprinkled with hair. My lips part, and breath eases between them as I stare, captivated. To this day, Seth is the only man I've seen naked in the flesh. I cup his balls and massage them gently, watching his cock bob.

"Ash…"

"Shh." I wrap a hand around the base of his shaft, needing him not to treat me as though I'm breakable. "Let me."

I moisten my lips and wrap them around him, then sink forward as far as I can, his salty taste blossoming in my mouth. He nudges the back of my throat, and I press my legs together, squirming. There's something about being in this position that really lights me up, and I don't know if it's because I feel power*ful* or power*less*. This man could grab my head and fuck my mouth. Use me for his pleasure. But then, he's also at my mercy. I'm the instrument of his demise, and I love it.

"Please," he whispers, and it's all the encouragement I need. I work his cock, sucking, humming each time I take him deeper, doing everything I can to bring him to the brink. He buries his hands in my hair and his blunt fingernails rake over my scalp, doing delicious things to me. I level up the enthusiasm, needing him to see that I'm not fragile. He can treat me the way he used to and it won't scare me off. His hips rock, and he groans—a combination of pleasure and misery. I pull back.

"Do it," I say, looking up. "You know I like it."

"You deserve better."

I hold his gaze, unflinching. "But that's not what I want."

He tries to palm himself, but I swat his hand away. This only works if I'm the place he comes to for relief. His shoulders roll, and something about the fact he's still clothed adds to the naughtiness of the moment.

"You're sure?" he asks.

"I want it."

"Fuck, you don't even know what you're asking for." But he shoves himself against my lips, and I eagerly part them, taking him in. He gives a tentative thrust, fucking my mouth the way I've always loved.

"Harder," I murmur around his length.

"Fuck," he repeats, his hips working more forcefully. My eyes swim with tears when he jams himself even deeper, but wetness rushes to my core and I moan. "Aw, hell." He falls into a rhythm that has me panting and writhing. His harsh grunts fuel my fire as he uses me to take his pleasure. "Such a sweet little mouth." Thrust. "Didn't know what you were asking for." Thrust. "It's been three fucking years since I was sucked off, Ash. Do you know what that does to a guy? How desperate it makes him?"

Yes, yes, yes.

This is what I want. What I need. Him talking to me like this. Touching me without finesse. Doing things that show he trusts me to give him what he needs and let him know what I want in return.

"Ah, God." He stops, and draws away. I follow, not letting him go, and he shudders, his thighs trembling. "Need to stop. If you want this cock inside you, you've gotta stop right now."

Reluctantly, I let him slide from my mouth. My disappointment doesn't last long because he grabs my hips and drags me to the edge of the bed, then drops to his knees in front of me, exactly as I imagined earlier.

"I've missed this." He raises his eyes to mine, and their

intensity scorches me to the soul. Blue-green fire encompasses me, warming and cooling at the same time. "Missed us."

"So have I," I admit, the confession stripping me bare and making me feel even more naked.

"Tell me this isn't a one-time thing. I need to hear it."

My heart swells in my chest. I'm simultaneously excited for this unexpected second chance and terrified we'll mess it up. There are so many things that could go wrong, but this isn't just sex, and we both need to recognize that.

"It's not a one-time thing."

"Good." He strokes a hand over my mound and up the soft skin of my belly, then lowers his gaze to the point between my legs. "I would worship at the altar of this pussy."

His mouth descends on me, and I cry out. The first lick is long and gentle, but the taste of me seems to rock him, because after that he can't lift himself off. His every groan rumbles against me, the vibrations winding me higher. His stubble rasps between my thighs, and I tighten my legs around his face, loving the sensation. I'll have beard burn to show for it later. I want to see the evidence of our lovemaking for days. His tongue bats my clit, and I gasp, my body tight and shaking. Only the softest of touches would put me over the edge, but he eases off. I try to press closer, but the most friction I can get is from his breath blowing across my damp flesh.

"You only come when I say you can," he tells me. The declaration should piss me off, but it only makes me feel safer. More desired. Because I know I can trust him to bring me maximum pleasure. There's nothing he loves more than to hear me scream. In this department, at least, he won't let me down. He strokes me, his fingers barely there. "Good girl. I've got you."

"I know," I whisper, locking eyes with him as my hips shift restlessly. My teeth sink into my lower lip. "I need you."

"You'll have me," he promises. "After I take care of this pretty pussy."

With that, he presses a thick finger inside me and curls it.

My hips raise from the bed, and when his mouth settles on me again, I scream as I come.

"That's it," he soothes, pinning my hips down with an arm across my belly. "Take what you need."

Shudders wrack me, but I force my eyes to stay open, blearily focused on him, until they finally stop. I flop back against the mattress, breathless. He stands over me, still wearing a shirt, with his jeans around his knees.

"Get the corset off. I want to see all of you."

"Okay." I hurry to oblige, waiting to see if he'll do the same. "Take your shirt off."

He hesitates. "I've had a few changes since last time."

If the moment wasn't so intense, I'd laugh at his concern. What does he have to be worried about? His biceps are big enough to wrangle a wild animal, and he's obviously still good with his tongue.

"Please?" I ask, because I feel like I've stripped myself off for him, and I'd hate to be the only one standing out on a ledge. With a swift nod, he grabs the hem of his shirt and whips it off.

My jaw drops. "You're so sexy."

Seth always had tattoos, but they've multiplied in my absence, and they now spread from his arms to his shoulders and across his chest, dipping all the way to the slabs of muscles that comprise his abdomen. And there, right in the middle, is a winged dagger with my name written on the blade. It skewers down the center of his ribcage, about 10 inches long. He didn't have this tattoo when we divorced. But why would he choose to ink my name on his body after we separated?

"Is that—"

"Your name?" He nods, and a flush works up his neck but he doesn't look away. "You're the love of my life. I knew there'd never be anyone else for me, so it seemed right to do it. Felt like I had you close even when years passed without seeing your beautiful face." He pauses, studying me, expression inscrutable. "Does it make you uncomfortable?"

My heart squeezes. "Um, maybe. I mean, how were you going to explain that if you got together with another woman?"

He rolls his eyes. "What part of 'you're it for me' don't you understand? There was never gonna be another woman."

"What?" Panic creeps up on me. I'm starting to feel the pressure. "You would've just never been with anyone ever again?"

"Yeah." He shrugs. "No point being with someone for the sake of it."

"Well, okay then." I'm not sure quite what to do with that, but then his cock shifts, and so does my attention. My core muscles clench, reminding me of how empty I am. "I want you now."

"Lie down," he instructs, and I comply. "I know how much you love it when I do you hard from behind, but this first time, I need to see you so I believe it's really happening."

"I'd like that."

I lie down, and he climbs between my legs, then kisses me. His tongue tangles with mine, and he butts against my entrance, and then notches inside. He eases in, inch by inch.

"You're tight."

I laugh breathlessly. "It's been three years."

"Fuck." He groans. "So good." He starts to move, and delicious friction melts me. He hits me on the best angles. Long and slow, filling me completely. My eyelids flicker shut, and he grips me by the jaw. "Open. Show me everything."

I do as he asks, locking my gaze on his. I love his dominant streak, and even if he's going to be gentle this time, seeing his rough edges stokes a fire in me. Rocking onto him, I bite my lip as pleasure crescendos inside me. Up and up it goes, and he slows, his movements becoming harder and more purposeful. The set of his jaw tells me he's not far from exploding. He grinds his hips into me once, twice, and then a bright light bursts behind my eyes as I crash into bliss. He fucks me right through the orgasm with a look of dogged determination that drives me crazy. He's battling his instincts to make sure I'm taken care of, and it's the sexiest thing ever. A moment later, he buries his face in the crook of my neck and gives a muffled shout, his cock throbbing as he empties himself into me.

It's then that I realize: we didn't use a condom. A moment later, the truth barrels into me, and I nearly laugh. I'm trying to get pregnant with this man. What does it matter if we use a condom?

Seth rolls off me and flops onto the bed, then hauls me to his side and holds me close. "You're incredible."

"So are you," I whisper, enjoying the moment even though I know we'll have to clean up soon. "Stay with me tonight?"

He kisses my cheek. "You couldn't get rid of me if you tried."

16

SETH

In the morning, I rouse a sleepy Ashlin for a round of slow lovemaking. Afterward, we shower together, and she cooks me breakfast before I head to the gym. When I get there, Harley and Devon are the only people present. Devon is holding pads for Harley, who punches with so much force I get the impression she's trying to work something out of her system. I don't offer any advice on her punching technique because my baby sister has had more fights than me and her movements are flawless. Jiu jitsu grappling is the only area where I can help her, other than being someone for her to talk tactics with. These days, she seems to do that with Devon more than me. I'm glad she's happy, but can't help feeling a little unnecessary.

Devon holds the pads to his side, and she kicks them, her shin thudding against the leather with a satisfying smack. At moments like this, I miss the days when I used to fight. Coaching is great, but you never get to test yourself against an opponent. These days, I could let myself go to seed and it wouldn't really matter. A beeper blares, ending the round, and Devon and Harley bump fists.

Harley turns to me. "I've been talking to Mom."

"Oh?"

"She wants us to take a trip to Cedar Bend to meet her new boyfriend."

My stomach drops. Subconsciously, I glance at my watch. "Things are busy right now. It'd be easier to fly them here."

Harley scowls and stalks toward me. She stops a foot in front of me and jabs a gloved fist into my chest. "It isn't always about what's easiest for you. Sometimes, you've got to make sacrifices for family."

I shrug. "Her weekends are usually free, and mine aren't. Seems like an obvious choice."

I pretend the thought of going to Cedar Bend doesn't have sweat breaking out on my upper lip and a lump of lead sitting in my gut. If I could never return to the town where I grew up, it'd be too soon.

Her scowl deepens, and she takes a breath as though she's gearing up to give me a prepared speech. "Look, you've clearly got some hang-ups about Cedar Bend, but you haven't been there for years, and if you want to have your own kid, perhaps you need to man up and address the problem so you don't pass some weird resentment toward their grandmother onto them."

Her words give me pause. Am I holding onto resentment toward Mom?

No, I don't think so. It's just that small-minded town I hate. "There's nothing for me in Cedar Bend. No reason to go. I can see Mom anywhere, and I've kept in touch with Don." Don is the man who taught Harley and me how to fight. I know he'd like me to visit in person the way Harley did a few weeks ago, but he understands why I don't. He knows how it was for me there.

Her eyes narrow.

"Come on, man, it's your mom," Devon says, approaching us. "She's the sweetest person ever. How can you say no to her?"

I don't reply. I've been telling Mom "no" for years. I might have bought her a house on the right side of town, but my preference would have been to move her to Las Vegas. It was only her strange attachment to a place that treated her like shit on the underside of their shoe that kept her there. If it had been someone else, I might have thought she stayed just to rub their noses in her newfound wealth, but she's not the vindictive sort. For some bizarre reason, she actually likes the place.

"I'm not going." I cross my arms over my chest and stare him down. "And I'm still your coach, Dev. You sure you want to push?"

He holds out his hands, palms up, and shrugs. "Not pushing. Just asking a question. Getting you to think it over."

"Don't bother," Harley snaps, fire flashing in her eyes. "It doesn't matter what we say, he's too scared to go."

Hang on. *Scared?* "Not true."

She shakes her head. "Clearly, it is. Otherwise you wouldn't be such big baby about it."

My nostrils flare, and my eyes widen in shock. "Jesus, you get your way once and now you think you're right about everything."

Her lips press into a firm line. "I'm right about this."

I don't answer, but hold her gaze. My temperature is rising, but the worst part is, she might be onto something. My heart is going crazy just thinking about stepping foot in that awful town. "I don't have anything to prove."

She smirks. "You're scared, and nothing you can say will make me think otherwise." More softly, she continues, "It's time, Seth. I know you can do it. I believe in you."

Damn. Just as I'm getting worked up, she has to go and say something like that.

I deflate. "Fine, I'll come."

She pumps a fist, and breaks into a grin.

"Just this once," I caution. "To prove I can."

To my surprise, she throws her arms around me and hugs me tight. "Thank you. I'm so proud of you."

My throat thickens with emotion and prevents me from replying so I squeeze her back and hope she knows how grateful I am to have her in my life.

ASHLIN

After Seth leaves for the gym, I get to work on the nursery. We've completed the major alterations, and now it's just a matter of painting and carpeting, which I've become reasonably comfortable with. I paint the ceiling first. It's a paler shade of white than the walls, and once it's dried, I can cover the edges with masking tape to stop myself from splashing anything else on it. I roller on the first layer, and then get down on my hands and knees to do the baseboards while it dries. The radio plays in the background, drowning out the silence. Sometimes I like the quiet, but other times I can't stand it because it reminds me too much of lying in bed for days on end, utterly alone for the hours between dawn and night when Seth was working. I'd stare into space and dwell on the future I sensed slipping away from me, feeling like a ship tossed on a stormy sea with no safe harbor in sight. Thank God those days are over.

By the time Seth arrives in the afternoon, I've finished the ceiling and the walls are ready to go whenever I get time. I answer the door in my paint-splattered clothes, momentarily self-conscious until he kisses my cheek and gives me the tender smile that's for my eyes only.

"You're adorable as hell." He touches a finger to the tip of my nose. "You've got a little something right here."

I laugh. "I've probably got it all over."

His lips curve in a knowing smile. "I'll investigate very thoroughly."

"I'm sure you will." I wink, and sashay inside.

He follows, coming to a stop in the nursery doorway.

133

"Looks perfect, Ash." He paces around the room, staring at the ceiling. "This could be a professional job and I'd never know the difference."

I glow with pride. "It's taken a lot of trial and error to get to that point."

He nods, and glances down at his hands.

"What is it?" I ask. I may not have spent much time with him over the last few years, but I can still tell when something is on his mind.

He walks to the window and gazes outside. "I'm going to Cedar Bend next weekend to meet Mom's new boyfriend."

Whoa.

I take a moment to formulate my reply. Seth and I were together for seven years, and during that time he never ventured back to his childhood home. At least, not to my knowledge. He hates that place. Hates how it treated him and his mother. Hates it for making him an outcast and the target of bullies. For being the kind of place where people lay the blame for an extramarital affair at the woman's feet, even though she wasn't the one breaking vows.

"That's... good." I keep my voice neutral, so it's a statement rather than a question. If he's facing his demons, it's positive. I just hope he won't have a meltdown while he's at it. Seth can be either stoic or a hothead depending on the situation, but very few people have witnessed him truly losing control.

"Come with me?"

My heart stutters. "Excuse me?"

He pivots, and closes the distance between us with a few strides, then cups my face between his palms. His turbulent eyes betray the emotion roiling inside. "Please, Ash." His thumb caresses my cheekbone. "I need you there."

Oh, God. How am I supposed to say no to that? He's turning me inside out. But we only just decided to take a chance on each other, and I'm not sure if I'm ready for his family to know.

"What made you decide to go?" I ask.

He swallows, and tucks me beneath his chin so I can no longer see his face. "If I'm going to be a father, I need to prove something to myself, and I'd really appreciate your support."

His heart beats steadily beneath my ear, and I wrap my arms around his waist and lose myself in the feel of him. This man may be larger and stronger than anyone else I know, but he needs me. Not to mention I'm the reason he's thinking of becoming a father in the first place. I nod. He's been there for me dozens of times, and I'd never turn down the option to do the same for him.

"I'll be there."

"Thank you." Something soft brushes the top of my head. His lips? "You're special, Ash. Couldn't do it without you."

A piece of my soul clicks into place, and I smile, recognizing it. I've been slowly putting myself back together for years, and I never know when two apparently disparate parts will suddenly fit. It means I'm doing the right thing.

I draw back and look him in the eye. "What are we going to tell them about us?"

He hesitates, searching my expression for something, but I'm not sure what. "Do you want to keep it secret?"

A quick intake of breath. Do I? It would be easier that way, but easier doesn't always mean better.

"We should be honest," I say. "Tell her that we're giving ourselves a second chance but taking it slow and seeing where things go."

"Perfect." He pulls me close again, and draws in a long inhale. "You make me want to be a better person."

"You're already a good person."

I feel a movement as he shakes his head. "A good person wouldn't have left you to deal with so much on your own."

"You can't put that on yourself. I fell apart, and it wasn't your job to put me back together. You were hurting too, just showing it in a different way." I kiss the shirt above his pectoral. "We were both at fault, or neither of us were. The blame doesn't lie with one person."

He huffs. "Try telling that to my heart. All I wanted to do was keep you safe, and I failed."

Tears fill my eyes. This beautiful, wounded man. He'd never have admitted this kind of thing to me before. He'd have shored it up inside and built a moat around it. "Nothing either of us did could have stopped what happened. But that's in the past. We can forge a new future."

"I hope so." His voice is gruff. "Come on, let's sit down with some coffee. I could use a break."

"Sure thing." I let him take my hand and lead me to the kitchen.

Ten minutes later, we're seated on the sofa in the living room when my phone buzzes with a message. I extract it from my pocket and check the screen. It's Harley.

Harley: *Did you and Seth get back together? He was glowing earlier.*

Laughing, I show Seth.

He scowls. "I do not glow."

"Of course not." I bite my lip to keep from giggling again. "You're okay if I'm honest with her?"

"May as well be." His arm, which has been resting on the top of the sofa behind me, sinks down to curve around my shoulders. "She's like a dog with a bone once she gets an idea in her head." He hesitates. "I told her about what we're doing. I hope that's okay."

I slide him a sidelong glance. "Of course. She's family. But I'd rather we don't tell too many people in case it doesn't work out."

He nods in acknowledgment while I type a reply.

Ashlin: *We're taking things day by day, but yeah, we're giving it a shot. Just don't make a big deal of it.*

Harley: *Have you slept together?*

Harley: *Ew, wait, no details please.*

Seth grunts beside me. I interpret it as annoyance tinged with amusement.

Ashlin: *I will neither confirm nor deny. But we're coming to Cedar Bend.*

Harley: *Best news ever. Can't wait to see you!*

I turn to Seth. "Is it strange for you that Harley and I are still close?"

"No." His jaw stiffens. "Although it did make it hard after she moved back, discovering that she kept in touch with you while I hadn't seen you for years. I was jealous."

"There's nothing to be jealous of." I caress the angle of his jaw. "Your relationship with me, and mine with her, are very different."

He snorts. "I know that, but for ages I couldn't think of you without hurting, and it always seemed like you walked away so easily."

I freeze in place, hardly daring to breathe. "It wasn't easy, Seth." I want to distance myself from him for this conversation, but if I try, he'll probably take it the wrong way. "Separating from you was the most difficult decision I ever made, but it was also an important one because it taught me to stand on my own."

"Why didn't you talk to me?" The raw pain in his voice slays me. Clearly this question has been weighing on him for some time. "Instead you just made a choice and I had to deal with it."

"I wasn't in a good head space." Reaching down, I twine my hand with his and raise it to my lips. "I'm sorry. I tried to talk to you, but never knew what to say. It seemed like you were handling things so much better than me, and I didn't want to drag you down."

"You should have tried harder."

My fingers reflexively tighten around his. "You didn't fight for me," I remind him.

"I didn't think you wanted me to."

Both of our bodies are rigid with tension. I breathe in

slowly through my nose and release the air through my mouth. "Honestly, I don't know what I wanted, but I thought you were relieved to be rid of me."

"Nothing could be further from the truth." He removes his arm from around my shoulder and we sit side by side, not looking at each other. "Although…"

"Although?"

"I didn't know how to help you," he admits. "I was struggling to keep my own head above water, and I couldn't seem to do or say the right thing. Everything made you cry."

A flush of embarrassment crawls up my cheeks, but I don't deny the accusation. I've come to terms with the depressive phase I went through following the miscarriage.

"I'm sorry for the impact my poor mental health had on you." Shimmying back a couple of inches, I face him again. "I know we have a lot to work through, but can we agree not to hold the past against each other?"

His expression softens. "You did nothing wrong, Ash. I just didn't know how to give you what you needed. Let's start fresh." One side of his mouth lifts in a wry smile. "Or, as fresh as possible. On that note, will you come for a meal with me? Official date status."

"Yes." I match his smile. "I'd really like that."

17

SETH

Nausea churns in my stomach, threatening to bring up everything I had for lunch. The day of our trip to Cedar Bend has rolled around, and the unshakable Seth Isles is officially shook. I can't even remember the last time I got sick, but I've battled this feeling all day, and I've already sweated through one shirt and had to change it. Perhaps I have the flu. When I say as much to Ashlin, who is packing an overnight bag to take to the airport, she stops what she's doing and touches my forehead.

"You're not hot."

"I feel fucking hot," I counter. "Are you sure I don't have a fever?"

She raises a brow. "I can take your temperature if you'd like, but you're probably just nervous."

I scoff. "Nerves don't make me feel this crap." Her lips twitch as she tries not to smile. I'm glad one of us can find humor in the situation. I might be gravely ill.

"Do you remember how worked up you used to get before a big fight?" she asks.

Shrugging, I don't answer, because I hate to admit she has a point. I once emptied my guts before a championship bout against a particularly brutal opponent. Fighting might be the only thing I've ever been good at, but I was well aware of what I stood to lose if I took a bad blow. I'd finally built myself a life worth having. Fortunately, that motivated me to win. Ashlin may not know it, but she was my lucky charm.

"We don't have to go," I mutter, pacing the length of the room as she zips her suitcase. I stride back, then wrap my arms around her from behind and thrust my hips forward so she knows what she does to me. "I can think of a much better way to get rid of this extra energy."

"No." She relaxes onto my chest. "Don't tempt me with your black magic. We need to do this."

"I need you," I whisper, dragging kisses up the length of her satiny neck.

"Nope." With a reluctant groan, she tears herself away from me. She pivots and places a gentle kiss on my cheek, then pats my upper arm. "No distraction tactics. It's time to go."

"Bossy." I don't remember her having such a spine of steel, but I can't deny I like it. There'd been a time when I would have been able to persuade her to get naked nearly anywhere. I hate to think I'm rusty enough that she can resist me now. I'd prefer to believe she's simply mastered the art of self-control.

I drive us to the airport, picking up Harley and Devon on the way. They squeeze into the back while Ashlin sits in front with me.

"I'm so glad you agreed to come," Harley says, leaning forward so she doesn't have to talk as loudly.

"I hope I don't regret it," I reply.

"You won't." She's far more certain than I am, but I take comfort in that. After all, she's visited our hometown more recently than me. Perhaps she knows what she's talking about.

"It was nice to talk to her the other day." Ashlin and I had called her together to explain that we'd both be coming, and that we were trying for a baby together and giving our relationship another chance. She'd been ecstatic.

"I can't wait to see her," Devon declares, and when I glance in the rearview mirror, he's practically bouncing in his seat.

"Keep it up and I'll be worried you're going to steal her from Rick," Harley teases.

"Rick?" I ask. "That's her boyfriend's name?" She hasn't mentioned much about him. All she's said is that the new man in her life is eager to meet me. She was more interested in discussing Ashlin and I than sharing her own gossip. What kind of grown-ass man goes by 'Rick'?

"Yeah." Harley pauses, and the car falls silent. "Hasn't she told you about him?"

"Not much." Although I haven't made it easy for her. The concept of Mom dating isn't one I'm comfortable with, even though I recognize she's a woman with a lot of life left to live. The thought of it dredges up old memories to do with the man who might be my father.

"Rick Snowdon," Harley tells me. "He's a real estate agent. Fifty. Has two daughters."

I grunt. "He's younger than Mom."

"Not by a lot." I can hear the eye-roll in Harley's voice. "A few years here and there doesn't make much difference. Don't be an asshole to him. He means a lot to Mom."

"I'll try not to. But I have questions."

"Uh-huh."

The flight goes smoothly—except for the fact Devon never stops an endless stream of conversation. A few hours later, we park a rental car on the gravel area in front of Mom's white stone house, which sits on a ridge above the river that divides the town in two. The place looks peaceful. From the outside, you'd never understand why being here gives me an overwhelming sensation of doom.

We grab our bags out of the trunk and walk to the front door. Dread creeps over me and I can't dislodge it. Devon pushes the doorbell with glee and we all wait for the sound of footsteps in the foyer behind. The door swings inward to reveal a woman so short she barely reaches my shoulders.

She squeals in excitement, and her mane of blonde hair bounces. "You're here!"

Her arms go around Devon first, since he's front and center, and then she hugs Harley. When it's my turn, I hold her tight and breathe in the familiar lavender scent that always reminds me of home.

She releases me, tips her head back, and smiles softly. "I'm so glad you came."

"Me, too." I love Mom, and seeing her is great. It's just that I'd rather do it anywhere but here.

"And you brought my daughter-in-law back." She steps toward Ashlin, who wraps her in an embrace. My heart warms at the sight. "How are you doing, honey?"

"I'm good." Ashlin smiles, and her gaze flicks to me. "Really good."

"Well, that's wonderful." She lays her hands on Ashlin's shoulders and squeezes. "Let me know if you need me to tune him up for you."

Ashlin snorts with amusement, her hand flying to her mouth, eyes sparkling. "I will. It's good to see you, Mae."

A movement behind Mom draws my attention, and I spot the man who must be Rick. He meets my eyes and smiles, wearing a self-deprecating expression that puts me on edge. He extends a suit-clad arm in my direction, perhaps sensing that I'll be the hardest to win over.

"I've heard a lot about you." His attention darts to Mom, then back to me. "Thank you for coming."

My lips purse. Listen to this guy, welcoming me to the house as if I wasn't the one who bought it. Mom's name is on the deed, but I provided it to her, and this asshat can't pretend to be a gracious host.

I bury my face in my palms. We're not even here two minutes and Seth is already looking at Mae's boyfriend like he wants to go three rounds with him in the cage. I lay a hand on his arm and will my calmness to seep through the fabric of his shirt and into his bloodstream. Soothing him has always been my superpower, although it's been a while since I exercised it. I shift closer to him and sense a fragment of his tension ease as he loops an arm around my waist.

"Hi," I say in greeting. The man beside Mae is a silver fox, although his silver is broken up by remnants of dark brown. The crinkles around his eyes deepen as he smiles, suggesting he does it often. "I'm Ashlin. It's lovely to meet you."

Rick shifts the hand that Seth left hanging and offers it to me. "You, too. I'm looking forward to getting to know you better."

At this, Seth blows air out of his nose like a temperamental bull. I reach behind him and pinch his butt. He startles, but it effectively knocks him out of the mood he was working himself into. I'm not sure why meeting his mother's boyfriend is so hard for him, but he has a lot of issues when it comes to his birth father, so maybe that plays into it. Or perhaps he's just protective of the woman who raised him.

"Hey." Harley pushes in beside us, and diverts Rick's attention. "I'm Harley, and this is Devon."

He shakes each of their hands in turn. "I'm Rick. Has Mae explained—"

"We know who you are," Seth cuts in, and I sigh from exasperation. I spent many years of my life loving this man, but he can be difficult at times, especially when he thinks someone he cares about is being taken advantage of. He's intensely loyal.

"Well, good." To Rick's credit, he chuckles. "That saves me

from using the term 'boyfriend.' It really isn't appropriate for anyone over thirty."

Harley nods and raises her bag. "Where should we put our stuff?"

"This way." Mae leads us into the house, across a tiled foyer, and down a long hall. She gestures at doors on each side of the hall. "Devon and Harley are in that one, and Seth and Ashlin are in the other." She stops, then flushes bright pink and stammers, "If you're, you know, together. We can put you in separate rooms if you'd prefer?"

"One is fine," I assure her, wanting to put her at ease because Seth sure isn't going to do it.

"Phew." She visibly relaxes. "Get yourselves set up, and I'll serve dinner in the dining room in five minutes."

"Perfect, Mrs. Isles." Devon kisses her cheek. "We'll be there soon."

I take Seth's hand and yank him into the bedroom, then close the door and spin to face him. "Behave yourself."

His jaw works and he presses his lips together in a man-pout. "That guy is too smooth. I don't like it."

"You've known him for two minutes," I point out. "Your mom cares about him, and it's the first time she's bothered trying to get you here to meet a man in person, so how about you respect her enough to reserve judgment?"

A furrow indents the space between his brows. He clearly didn't expect this. But then, he's been so wrapped up in his own angst over coming here that perhaps everything else has faded into the background.

I soften my tone. "I know it's hard for you to be here, and I'll do whatever I can to help, but please try not to take your stress out on others."

He sighs, and drops a kiss on my forehead. "You're right. I'm sorry. I just hate this fucking place." He opens his arms and hauls me close. I wriggle back a little so he doesn't squish my breasts, which are oddly tender today. "I'll try to rein it in. Feel free to pinch my ass anytime you need."

I roll my eyes. "There he is." I hug him. "Come on, slugger. Let's wash our hands for dinner."

We clean up, and head to the table. Devon and Harley are already there, and Harley's hair is disheveled in a way that makes me think Devon's had his hands all through it. I catch her gaze and wink. She blushes, yanks out her hair tie, and fixes it before Mae returns.

"Did Ash talk to you about playing nice?" Harley asks Seth.

"Yeah." He rubs his jaw. "I'll try to do better."

We all glance up as Mae and Rick enter, each carrying a platter. They set them down in the center of the table.

"Tacos?" Devon asks with a grin.

Mae smiles at him. "Assemble your own."

"Yes!" He fist pumps. "Exactly what I feel like."

I elbow Seth, and he nods. "Looks good."

Mae's smile broadens. "We weren't sure what to do that would work for everyone, but this way you can choose what you'd like to add. We have dessert too, but I know some of you won't eat any." She glances at Harley, who's notorious for not touching sweet food because she thinks it messes with her training.

"Thanks, Mom," Harley says.

Mae and Rick sit one at each end of the rectangular table. I sense Seth stiffen, and know what he's thinking. This guy is already at the head of the table. Because of the risk of the others overhearing, I can't point out the fact that we chose our seats, leaving those as the only options available. Instead, I drop my hand beneath the table and poke his side. He gives me a slight nod.

"What are you waiting for?" Mae asks. "We don't stand on ceremony."

Devon and I dive for the food, equally determined to make the meal pass as smoothly as possible. He winks at me across the table. Mae helps herself to a couple of soft taco shells, visibly amused by our efforts. At least she's not the kind of person to be put off by a little tension. I imagine raising two stubborn-as-hell Isles children was an exercise in patience and persistence. Seth and Harley join in, and Rick waits for us all to take our share before doing the same. He's just pouring sauce over his chicken when Seth asks his first question of the night.

"So, you're in real estate, Rick?"

Rick finishes assembling his tacos before responding. "That's right. I work with clients who want to buy or sell commercial spaces."

"Are you any good at it?"

I choke, eyes widening with surprise. Damn him. I know where this is going, and I shoot him a look. He raises a brow just enough that I notice but no one else will. All innocence.

Rick clears his throat. "Actually, I am." He smiles as though he's not unnerved to have Mae's son interrogate him over dinner. Her former MMA champion, built like a brick wall son. "If you're asking whether I'm financially stable, I can assure you that I earn a tidy living. In fact, my house, which I own outright, is only a couple of blocks away."

Seth nods. "Mom doesn't need someone to take care of her financially. Her business is doing great, which I'm sure you know. But she doesn't need someone who's going to be a drain on her resources either. I appreciate you being forthright with me."

Mae rolls her eyes, but underneath the surface, she's flushed with pleasure from her son's compliment. Not long after his first big win, he provided seed money for her to start an interior design business. She paid him back years ago, and has a nice nest egg she's earned by her own hard work.

"Any time." Rick pours himself a wine from the bottle on the table. "I mean that. If you have other burning questions, I'd rather you get them out in the open."

Respect flickers across Seth's face. Grudging, but present.

"You have daughters?"

"Two," he confirms. "They're the most important people in my world—other than your mother."

I bite into my taco, tasting chicken and a burst of sweet chili. So far, I don't think I need to intervene. Everyone here probably expected something along these lines, and the men seem to be handling it reasonably well.

"How old are they?" I ask, because he's a few years younger than Seth's mom, who had Seth when she was still very young herself, meaning there could be quite an age disparity between her children and his.

He sips his wine. "Fifteen and eighteen. Olivia, the eighteen-year-old, will be starting college soon, and Emma, the youngest, is a sophomore in high school. They live with me every second week."

"What's Olivia studying?" This question comes from Devon.

"Pre-med. She's very bright. Wants to be a gynecologist." He digs into his taco before anyone else has the chance to ask another question.

"We have a friend who's a surgical resident," Harley tells him. "Not in gynecology though."

He finishes his mouthful and nods. "Olivia would probably love to talk to her."

Harley and Devon exchange glances. "I think we could arrange that," Harley said

The rest of dinner passes without too many questions. We fall into a pattern of small talk. Rick doesn't ask about the strange relationship between Seth and me, for which I'm grateful. He'd be well within his rights to, considering how Seth grilled him, but perhaps Mae warned him not to pry. When we begin clearing off the table, Mae stands and goes to Seth, dipping her head to speak in his ear. He pushes his chair back and follows her out of the room. I watch them go, intrigued, but don't follow. They're long overdue for a private conversation, and hopefully Seth will feel better after.

18

SETH

Mom leads me to her upstairs office, which has a view over the river, and sinks gracefully into the executive chair behind the desk. The space is carefully curated. It has to be, given her profession. I know for a fact that I financed none of the high-end furniture, which further demonstrates her success. My heart swells. Perhaps I don't always show it, but I'm proud of how far she's come.

"Have a seat," she says, and I sit on the comfortable chair reserved for clients. "I think it's time for you and me to talk."

Uh-oh.

My stomach clenches. She didn't seem angry during dinner, but perhaps she just hid it well.

"About what?"

She runs a finger along the edge of her polished wooden desk and checks it for dust. "Everything." She leans forward, her chin resting on her palm. "I know you're only here because Harley pressured you into coming."

"Wait—" I start to protest, but she cuts me off.

"I don't care. I'm just grateful you came. I know how much

you hate Cedar Bend, and deep down, I think we both know you resent me too."

I stare at her, aghast. How can she think I resent her? She's the only parent I've ever had. She gave me everything. Enabled me to become the man I am. Supported me to make it big in Las Vegas even though it meant leaving her behind. Now she's watching me, calm as can be, as though she's stated a fact as simple as the sky being blue or grass being green. Those hazel eyes, nearly identical to Harley's, betray no hint of her emotion. For years, I hated my eyes for being different from theirs, and for reminding me of a man I wanted nothing to do with.

"I don't resent you."

Her expression grows challenging. "Are you sure about that?"

"Yeah." I want to shut this conversation down as fast as possible.

She shakes her head. "It's time to be honest with yourself. If you and Ashlin have a baby, you don't want to pass bitterness on to your child." Her fists clench, knuckles whitening. "I certainly don't want my first grandchild to avoid Cedar Bend. I want to be part of their life. So please, do me a favor and think really hard. Is there anything you'd like to clear up with me?"

I'd really fucking love to dismiss her concerns and stick to my guns, but she's my mom and she's clearly given this a lot of thought, so I give her the respect of doing the same.

And something hits home.

She's right. I do resent her. At least on one front.

"I can ask you anything?" I clarify, knowing that sometimes my idea of what's acceptable differs from other people's.

"Yes," she agrees with a determined thrust of her chin. "Anything."

"Why did you get pregnant with a married man?"

Her gulp is audible, but to her credit, she doesn't look away. "How long has that been simmering inside?"

"Too long," I admit.

She nods, and inspects her fingernails, remaining silent for so long that I wonder if she's regretting the invitation to be open. But then she raises her gaze and settles it on me. "Let me start at the beginning."

"Please don't try to explain it away."

Her shoulders square. "I was eighteen when I moved here, and I'd grown up very sheltered. It was my first time away from home, and I'd only been in town for a week when I met Harrison."

My breath freezes in my lungs. She's never come out and said his name before. Admitted who he is. There has only been hints and misdirection.

"He was older," she continues. "Mature. Very attractive." Her lips slant wryly. "I ran into him at a bar—I had a fake ID—and we flirted. He wasn't wearing a ring, and nobody mentioned his wife, so I assumed he was single."

"He hit on you?" In all the versions I've heard from others over the years, Mom was the seductress who lured a good man into sin. It didn't help that she never spoke out about what happened, either publicly or privately.

"He did. He asked to see me again, and we went to dinner a couple of nights later. He offered to drop me home, then asked me to invite him in for coffee. I was naive, so I did." She laughs without humor. "Harrison could be very persuasive. How do you think he managed to win five elections in a row?" She makes a sound of disgust in the back of her throat. "I was flattered by his attention, and went along with it. We had sex, and didn't use protection because he assured me it would feel much better that way, and that I couldn't possibly get pregnant from our first time."

"That fucker."

Her eyes flash. "Hindsight is twenty-twenty, honey. I'm not saying all of this to lay the blame at his feet, just to set the scene. I was foolish, and he was charming."

"He was a man with a pregnant wife at home who wanted to live large with a younger woman."

She tilts her head in acknowledgment. "I saw him another two times over the next week, but then I ran into him down the main street one day with his wife. She wasn't far along, but I could tell she was pregnant. When I approached him, he acted as though we'd never met. Treated me like a deluded little idiot." Her voice tightens with frustration. "Which I was, because I had no idea that I was the other woman. His wife knew though. I saw it on her face, and it was awful. You don't know how low you can feel until you have to watch a man's wife realize that her husband has been fucking you behind her back. That poor, poor lady. I never blamed her for what came next because I felt like I deserved it. I should have been smarter. Shouldn't have been at that bar with a fake ID in the first place."

I don't say anything, but my blood is heating with a level of fury I haven't experienced in a long time.

"He didn't call after that. When I realized I was pregnant, I went to his place but his wife answered the door and wouldn't let me in. I ended up writing him a letter, and the only response I got was an official request from his lawyer for a paternity test." Her eyes close, and emotions play across her face. For the first time, I can see how much she must have been hurting, and how difficult it must have been to navigate the strange playing field she found herself on as a teenager with no one to back her up.

"I did the test because I was in no financial position to have a baby, and I needed his help. I knew you were his because I hadn't been with anyone else." Her tone lacks inflection. If I were her, I'd be bitter as fuck. Her eyelids flutter open. "That's the truth of Cedar Bend's favorite harlot. I was a virgin before Harrison, and I wasn't with another man for years after. His wife spread vicious rumors about how I'd flaunted myself and led him down a path of treachery. Turned him into the dog he was. I understood. She was pregnant and afraid of being alone, so she needed to make me the bad guy to justify staying with him."

"But you let the stories continue for years," I cut in, finally unable to stay quiet. "Why didn't you speak up later?"

She shrugs, and the careless gesture drives me crazy. "No one would have believed me, and what would it have gained?" She reaches across the table and places her hand on mine. "I know the kids picked on you because of my reputation, but if I'd said anything, I'd only have made it worse because the other mothers would have rallied behind them, not us." She sighs. "People believe what fits their version of the narrative. Besides…" She squeezes my hand. "I had you. My little miracle. I could never regret the events that brought you to me."

"I love you, Mom."

Her eyes glimmer with unshed tears. "I love you too. You've always been what made everything worth it."

Guilt pricks my conscience. What am I supposed to do with that? For decades, I believed the stories about her—at least partially—because she never said anything to the contrary. I feel sick at the thought of how I behaved during my teenage years. I'd been a sullen little shit, and dozens of times, it would have been so easy for her to shout the truth, but she hadn't, because she'd just been happy to have me.

"I'm sorry." I swallow hard, feeling prickles in the back of my eyes that are not okay. "I didn't know."

"It's okay, honey." She smiles. "That's how I wanted it. If I'd told you what happened when you were younger, you might have wondered whether I even wanted you. At least the way they painted it, I intentionally got pregnant to try to coerce Harrison into leaving his family. Having an absent father was enough. You didn't need to question whether you'd ruined my life too. Because you didn't. You made it."

I lurch to my feet and round the desk. Mom remains seated, tilting her head to look up at me. Sometimes I forget how small she is. How fragile. Yet she managed to raise two children after being abandoned first by one man at the tender age of eighteen, and then another twelve years later. I offer her a hand and she takes it. I yank her into a hug. The tightest one I've ever given. My heart hurts for the girl she must have been. Alone, confused, and pregnant. But somehow she made it work.

"You could have told me," I murmur before releasing her. "Maybe not when I was a kid, but I've been a man for a long time."

She lifts one shoulder, then drops it. "The timing wasn't right. It is now." She rubs a hand over her heart. "I feel it in here."

"Thank you." I kiss her cheek. "I appreciate you being honest with me, and I'm sorry if I've ever said or done anything to make you feel bad about what happened."

"Oh, honey." Her smile softens. "You're already forgiven."

ASHLIN

When Seth returns to the living area after speaking privately with Mae, something is different. He's lost a little of the restless energy that radiated from him earlier. He glances at Mae, and his expression is gentle. But I don't get the chance to ask about it because Devon corrals us all into a card game. I sit on the sofa, my legs aligned with Seth's, nearly vibrating with the need to ask him about their conversation, but he seems determined to seduce me instead. His palm rests on my thigh, and his fingertips stroke the soft flesh on the inner side. When I sneak a look at him, he gives me a breathtaking smile that I haven't seen in an eternity. It's sweet and open. His eyes crinkle at the corners, and I long to climb onto his lap, cling to his chest, and stare at that ruggedly sexy face for hours.

Then he winks.

Winks.

The man I've been coming to know all over again doesn't wink. What did Mae do to him?

He dips his mouth near my ear and whispers, "You're so special to me, Ash."

I melt. What else is a girl supposed to do when the only man she's ever loved murmurs sweet nothings to her?

Finally, after hours of cards and conversation, we all head off to bed. Rick makes the comment that he'll see us in the morning, and I wait for Seth to react to the notion that the man will be spending the night with his mother, but other than a brief stiffening of his muscles, it doesn't come. He simply nods and shakes the guy's hand.

"Okay, I've got to know," I say the moment we're alone. "What did you and your mom talk about?"

He flops onto the bed and pats the space beside him. I lie alongside him, still fully clothed, and he places an arm over my waist.

"My dad."

"Really?" I didn't expect that. For as long as I can remember, Mae has been a locked vault when it comes to any questions about the man who donated his DNA to create Seth. He's filled in a lot of blanks himself, but I know it doesn't sit well with him. Nobody wants to think of their mother as a home-wrecker. That said, Mae was young when she had him. Barely more than a child herself. Everyone makes bad decisions at that age.

"It wasn't anything like I thought."

"I'm here if you want to talk, but no pressure." Despite my curiosity, I don't push, because all kinds of things are swirling behind his eyes and after nearly four decades of silence from the only person who could explain everything, I know he has a lot to process. It's okay if he needs to work it through for the night before he talks to me. Unless his temper is pricked, Seth is the type to mull things over.

But then he tells me everything. By the time he finishes, my

154

heart aches with pain at the thought of poor Mae and what she endured. For her to have knowingly entered into an affair with a married man would be one thing, but for him to intentionally mislead her because of her youth and naivety…. What an asshole. I've never met Seth's birth father, who served as mayor of this town for nearly twenty years, but I want to punch him in the nose. I could do some damage, too. Seth taught me to take an attacker down. He wanted me to be prepared in case he wasn't always around to protect me. But who has been protecting him?

I know Mae meant well in staying quiet all this time. Her logic makes a certain kind of sense. But she let bad feelings fester, and no matter how difficult it would have been to confess everything after decades of keeping it in, she should have tried sooner. At the very least, she should have said something the first time Seth made it clear he'd rather have a root canal than visit the town he grew up in.

"How are you feeling?" I ask, holding that blue-green gaze he's always hated because of the man he inherited it from. He showed me a photo once, and there was no denying that his eyes are a perfect copy of Harrison's.

"It's nice to know the truth." He pauses to collect his thoughts. "But I hate that it took so long, and that I let my issues get in the way of us having this conversation earlier. I never realized it, but Mom was right—I did resent her on some level for the way everyone in town treated me growing up." He sighs, and closes his eyes. "Mostly I feel guilty for assuming the worst of her, just like everyone else did. I should have known better."

I kiss the line of his jaw, and he shudders with suppressed emotion. "You know now. It's not too late for things to change."

His eyelashes flutter, and he looks down at me with a well of tenderness. "I don't know how I'd do this without you. Thank you for your support." He takes a breath. "And for being here with me."

"I always will be," I whisper back. It's about time I had the chance to be the one helping him stand strong through life's trials. Too many times in the past, I leaned on him. Now I can be an equal partner. Someone worthy of standing beside him.

He kisses my nose, then chuckles. "It seems like a lack of communication is a recurring theme for me, but I want to do better. Both with Mom and with you."

"You already are." He tucks me beneath his chin and I snuggle into the firm plane of his chest. "We had a good marriage, but I think we've been more honest with each other in the past month than we ever were back then."

"You might be right about that."

Deep down, I still have more to say to him, but this isn't the time. This is his night to work through things, and I won't steal it from him. My past problems can wait.

"Would you like to visit Mae more often?" I ask tentatively.

His hand slides down to the small of my back and draws me even closer. "Will you come with me?"

"Of course. As if you even have to ask."

Even though I can't see it, I sense him smile. "Then yeah, I'd like that."

19

ASHLIN

Wakefulness comes upon me slowly. First, I feel the softness of the blankets, and the warmth of my cocoon. Next, I hear the chirping of birds, and the sound of water whispering over stone. The river outside. I blink myself into full awareness and smile at the ceiling. Seth and I made love last night. There's no other phrase suitable. He took me the same way he did on our wedding night—as if he were afraid to believe I was really his, but determined to prove that no one else could ever satisfy me.

I'm so very satisfied.

The only thing that would make it better is if he were still in bed with me. But he's gone, and when I extend an arm into the space where he slept, it's cold enough to suggest he left some time ago. I sigh. This part of being with Seth I remember well. He'd always be exercising before dawn. Morning sex—one of my favorite things ever—was a rare occurrence. Something for special occasions. Slipping out of the bed, I scan the floor for my robe, then don it and head to the kitchen.

Mae glances up from the counter, where she's pouring a mug of coffee, and smiles. "Good morning, honey. I hope you slept well."

"I did, thank you." I infuse the words with a little too much enthusiasm and blush when she laughs.

She gestures to the mug. "Would you like one?"

"Yes, please." I wait for her to take a second mug from the cupboard since I don't know my way around. "Where'd Seth go?"

Mae pours my drink and hands it over. "He, Harley, and Devon went running." She raises a brow. "They assumed you wouldn't want to join them."

"Clever of them." Together, we take our mugs to the breakfast bar and sit side by side. "Sounds like you and Seth had a much-needed conversation last night."

Her eyes slide to mine. "How much did he tell you?"

"Everything, I think."

She nods, and blows on her coffee. "He was an angry kid. Got in a lot of fights, and most of them were because of me. His half-brother..." She shakes her head. "He was poisonous. I suppose it isn't easy seeing evidence in your classroom every day that your dad betrayed your mom, but he took it out on the wrong person. Seth never told me what the fights were about. He'd just sit there in the principal's office with a busted lip or a black eye and refuse to answer any questions. I knew though. A mother does."

"But you didn't tell him the truth?"

She sips her drink, then winces and sets it down. "I told myself I was doing him a favor by keeping quiet, but who knows?" She shrugs. "Perhaps it was just easier not to explain the full story." She levels her gaze at me. "Speaking of full stories. I know it's not any of my business, but I never understood your divorce. Seth said nobody was unfaithful, and the last time I saw you, you'd seemed as in love as ever. More, even."

I sigh. The last time she saw me, I'd just discovered I was pregnant, but we'd decided not to tell anyone until we were a bit further along in case something happened.

Just like it did.

I drink my coffee and appraise Mae. If Seth never told her, I don't want to overstep, but on the other hand, she's finally opened up about something that's been hard for her and deserves the truth in return. Especially if she wants to fully understand how finely balanced our emotions are likely to be for a while.

"I was pregnant," I tell her. Her eyes widen, and she touches her fingers to her lips as if to prevent herself from making a sound. "But before we were confident enough to tell anyone, I miscarried." I press my lips together, tears swelling behind my eyes at the memory. "It was still in the early stages, but we'd gotten carried away. Chosen a girl's name and a boy's name. It was hard to keep going after that."

Mae reaches for me and takes my hand. "I'm so sorry. I can't imagine what you went through."

My throat tightens to the point where I don't think words are possible, so I force myself to breathe in slowly and relax the muscles. "She was a girl," I whisper. "We found out after the miscarriage. Her name was Cara."

"Oh, Ashlin." Her voice is thick with sympathy.

I shake my head and get to the point. "The problem was that neither of us seemed to know how to communicate our grief. It felt like the future had been snatched away from us. I had a depressive period where I wouldn't leave the house for days. Seth went the other route and worked from dawn until late at night. I can see now that he was working through his grief in a different way, but at the time it seemed like he was fine while I was drowning."

A whimper escapes Mae. Her hazel eyes shimmer with emotion, and I can tell she's fighting back the urge to hug me until I've finished talking because she doesn't want to cut me off.

"It was my choice." The words are difficult to say because it means admitting the dark place I found myself in. "I didn't know what to do without him around, and I realized how dependent I'd let myself become on him for happiness. Days became weeks and nothing got better. I felt like my life was falling apart. Then, when I told him I wanted a divorce, he didn't fight me. Just let it happen. I figured he was relieved."

"Oh, Ash." Mae gets to her feet and hauls me into a hug. She holds on, refusing to let go, and I find comfort in her embrace. A tear trickles down my cheek, but I don't swipe it away. My therapist says it's better to let emotion out than try to repress it. Move through it, but don't wallow.

When Mae finally releases me, her cheeks are damp. "I wish I'd known."

I shake my head. "Don't do that to yourself. We've accepted it and we're moving on. Trying again. There's no point dwelling on the past."

She kisses my cheek. "When did you get so wise?"

Despite the tears, I smile. "Who the heck knows?" I sit, and indicate for her to do the same. "Anyway, perhaps you can see why trying to get pregnant again is such a big deal for us."

"I do." She taps the counter absent-mindedly. "I'm glad it's brought you back to us."

"So am I," I admit. "I feel like I'm ready to be the woman who can stand with Seth instead of depending on him."

"As it should be. Are you still planning another round of IVF now that you're together again or will you do it differently?"

"Yes, we're going for IVF but we haven't put a timeframe on it yet. The chances are just better, considering the damage done to my body the first time around."

"Fair enough." Her eyes search mine, and she hesitates, then takes the plunge. "Do you love him?"

I don't answer immediately, but pause to ponder the question. I feel so much for him, it's difficult to call it something so simple as love. We have nostalgia, deep caring, years of shared

160

memories. But then, we're not the same people we were and I adore the man I'm coming to know.

"I might," I say. "But I'm afraid to let myself love him fully because in my mind, I associate romantic love with dependency, and I don't want to end up in that situation again."

To my surprise, Mae smiles. "That won't happen. Not to the young woman I've been talking to for the past fifteen minutes. She's strong enough to manage anything, or haven't you been listening?" When I frown, she continues more gently. "Ash, you've got this. Maybe you needed some time apart, but you've grown as a person in the last few years and I already know that if, God forbid, you were to have another miscarriage, you'd survive. You're so much more self-possessed than you were. I can see the change in you from the outside looking in."

I'm speechless. I don't know what to say.

"Seth has changed, too," she adds. "Do you think I could have had the conversation I did with him yesterday when he was younger? He wasn't ready to hear it, and didn't have the communication skills to work it through. But now he does. He was forced to learn them, thanks to you."

"You think?"

She nods. "You're not the only one who's changed."

"I know." Hearing her say it, I feel foolish for not realizing sooner the extent to which we've both changed.

"Good." She drinks more of her coffee. "I'm glad to have you back in the family. If you ever need someone to talk to, or if you need a woman's ear, I'm only a phone call away. I hope you consider me family. I've always thought of you that way. Even after the divorce."

The tears start again, and I laugh self-consciously. "Now you've done it. Of course I think of you as family, Mae."

"I love you, honey." At the front end of the house, we hear a door open, and voices trip over the top of each other. "The cavalry has arrived."

When Seth enters, my heart fills at the sight of him. His

limbs move with unusual grace for someone his size, and perspiration dampens his short hair. He's wearing a tank top with a ragged neck, and as he wipes his face on the hem, I catch a glimpse of the dagger that bears my name. Flutters of anticipation stir in my lower half. He straightens, and catches me staring. His eyes fix on me, pupils dilating. Damn, he's so hot, and every part of me wants him.

I might be a little in love with him too.

SETH

Fuck, the way she's looking at me.

Like she's hungry and wants to eat me up. I'd gladly return the favor.

"Good run?" Mom asks, swiping her cheeks. Both her and Ashlin's eyes are suspiciously moist, but I don't mention it. If they've had a heart to heart, then good for them.

"Not bad," I reply, and jerk my thumb at Harley and Devon. "These two are out of shape though, if an old man like me can keep up with them."

"Hey!" Harley's protest comes right when I expect it. "We *intentionally* kept pace with you, and it's not as if you're that old. You spend every damn day at the gym."

"Yeah, standing around and holding pads. Hardly the same thing as training." I grin, my heart lighter than it's been in ages. Running through Cedar Bend in the dawn of a new day, following on the heels of my conversation with Mom, I can see it for what it is. Just a place. It's the people who made it seem so awful. People I don't have to see again if I don't want to now.

"You got us, old man." Devon flops onto the one spare seat left at the breakfast bar. "We'll have to up our game, or you'll replace us in no time." He looks at Mae. "You raised a hard-ass."

She smothers a smile. "I think he turned out all right." She

162

meets my eyes, a question in her own. I nod, to let her know we're all right.

"I need to shower," I announce, because despite all appearances to the contrary, I worked my ass off to keep up with those two, and I refuse to sit at the breakfast bar smelling of old gym shoes. I head to the bathroom and yank my top off, and I'm about to do the same with the bottoms when there's a knock on the door.

"I'm in here," I call.

The door handle turns, and a moment later, Ashlin slips inside. Her lips curve into a naughty smile when they settle on me. She locks the door, crosses to me, and rests her palms on my sweaty chest. Her gaze is fixed on me and she squeezes her thighs together. Fuck, my girl is turned on. She needs me. I recognize the signs. She traces the contours of my muscles with her hands, and then slips down my abdomen to the waistband of my shorts.

"Do you have any idea how sexy you are right now?" she asks.

"Me?" I scoff. "Look at yourself." Gripping her hips, I spin her to face the mirror, then position myself behind her. In the reflection, her eyes widen in shock. I slip a hand inside her robe and smooth it over her tits. A groan rips from deep in my throat, and I shove the fabric down her shoulders, baring her from the waist up. My fingers find her nipples, and the little buds are already tight from wanting my touch. The pad of my thumb grazes the top of one, and she shivers.

"Look at you," I repeat, snaking my other arm around her and drawing her back to my chest. Together, we look fucking indecent. I'm all sweaty ink and hulking muscle while she's delicate and porcelain-pale. Yet the flush of her cheeks and the short, sharp breaths she takes prove she wants me. I stroke her between her legs. "Fuck." Her pussy coats my fingers with sweetness. "You want it bad."

"I do," she whispers. "So, so bad." Her hips roll, begging me to give her what she needs.

I slide a finger into her folds and press my palm firmly over the mound of her sex. "Is this what you want? Me touching you like this while I'm worked up and unclean and you're fresh as a horny little daisy?"

She nods, and rests her head against my shoulder. "Yes."

God, how did I get so lucky?

My fingers continue to move, and she squirms against me. I should insist we wash first, rather than rubbing all over her with my dirty, sweaty self, but I can't bring myself to leave her unsatisfied for even a moment longer. We may have had problems near the end of our relationship, but never in bed.

I support her weight and press a blunt digit into her tight pussy, working it in and out, watching her flush deepen in the mirror until her entire body goes taught and she shudders in my arms. I kiss the side of her neck.

"I've got you, baby. I'm here." I don't stop until she grows limp, and then I nuzzle her temple. "Good?"

"Perfect." She turns in my arms. "Now you." She reaches behind me and starts the shower. The bathroom has one of those tiled floors where you can splash water as much as you like. She steps out of her robe, tosses it to the side, and kisses me. As our lips touch, I guide us into the stream of water. She shudders as it sluices over her, but I think it's from surprise rather than the temperature because the water is warm. My hands roam down her waist, over her hips, and around to her ass. She may be petite, but my wife—*ex*-wife—has plenty to tempt me with. Every part of her is perfectly made.

My fingers dig into her flesh, and I groan in her mouth. She stretches onto her toes, pressing closer. I never understood how someone who looked like an angel could let me touch her and make her mine. It doesn't add up, but I'm grateful for it. Taking her weight in my palms, I try to hoist her up, but she slips out of my grasp.

"No." She steps away from me. "Not like that."

"Then what?"

Her eyes light with wickedness, and I know I'm going to like what's coming. Slowly, she steps out of the water and drops to her knees.

"Hell."

Yeah, I'm gonna like what she has in mind. But before she gets started, I hurry to clean myself. When I'm done and the water has been shut off, she takes my dick in her tiny hands and places the tip against her lips. My hips jolt forward, shoving inside, and she moans around me. She tries to say something, to tell me what she wants, but her mouth is full of me. Thankfully, I'm adept at interpreting Ashlin's desires.

"You want me to fuck your mouth?" I ask.

She nods eagerly, granting me permission. When we first met, I worried that I'd be too rough for her, but that doubt vanished quickly. Ashlin has always been my equal in bed, taking what I give her and demanding more. She hums, and pleasure shoots through me. My sack tightens and draws up. Shit, I don't want this to end too soon. Carefully, I wind my hand around the nape of her neck and take a handful of her hair, baring her throat to me. The movement also dislodges her from my dick.

"You'll tell me if it's too much?" I ask.

"Yes." She eyes me longingly. "Please, Seth. I need this."

"Okay." I guide her back, and my entire body jerks when she fastens her mouth around me and sucks. Hard. "Fuck."

Keeping my hand in her hair, the way she likes it, I thrust my hips forward, sinking deeper into the wet heat of her mouth, bumping against the back of her throat. I growl as a spurt of liquid erupts from my overeager cock, and I tamp down the urge to come. I'd rather draw this out.

"Easy," I murmur—whether to myself or her, I'm not sure.

She waits for me to set the pace, because she's fucking perfect like that. I ease into a rhythm, slow enough to drag out

165

the pleasure but fast enough to satiate us both. In and out. She takes it like I knew she would. Happy to entrust me with care of her pleasure. Safe in the knowledge that I'd cut off my dick before hurting her. She tilts back her head, letting me see her blissed-out expression. She takes as much satisfaction from this act as I do, and I know if I were to stop and turn the tables, her pussy would be ready, even though she came only a few minutes ago. The memory of her breaking apart while I watched is enough to send me over the edge. I release her hair, giving her the option to pull back, but she grabs my ass and encourages me to keep going. White sears the fringes of my vision, and I bite into my palm to stop from shouting as I empty into her.

She swallows, and blinks up at me, her eyes glazed with need. In a few swift movements, I reverse our positions and bury my face in her pussy. She cries out, and I hope like hell that nobody else heard her or I might have to kill them.

I was right. She's wet on my tongue and tastes like she belongs to me. I growl against her and lick once, twice, then she whimpers and gives me a taste of what I've been missing.

I love you.

The words are right there on my tongue, but I don't say them. If I want her to know they're sincere, they need to come sometime that isn't on the heels of an epic orgasm.

I hold her until she's steady enough to stand on her own, then shift away and get to my feet. Instead of professing my love, I kiss her forehead and draw her close, hoping that my actions will tell her what my words don't.

20

SETH

After we dry off, Ashlin and I head into town while Harley and Devon borrow Mom's car and go to Cedar Bend Martial Arts to catch up with our former trainer, Don. I wouldn't mind dusting off the old gloves and getting back to my roots, but I'm mindful that this is Ashlin's first time in my hometown and there are places I'd like to show her. I'll drop by and see Don later.

"Are you sure you want to do this?" she asks as we climb into the rental car and buckle up. "You don't have to give me the grand tour."

"I want to," I assure her. "It's part of working out the negative energy from this place."

She giggles, hand flying to her mouth. "Seth Isles, did you just use the phrase 'negative energy' in a completely serious context?"

I roll my eyes. "Don't make too much of it."

We cruise across the river, into the other side of town. The poor side. Where I grew up. The houses nearest the river aren't too shabby, but the further we venture, the worse they get, until I stop outside a two-bedroom bungalow that hasn't seen a new coat of paint in fifty years. The small garden grows wild, and the letterbox has been knocked over—probably by vandals or a drunk driver.

"This is where we lived." I lower the window to have a better look, but I have no desire to get out. "It looked better then. The landlord—if he's still alive—has let it go to hell."

Ashlin gazes around, noting the row of mostly identical houses, and how this one, in its state of disrepair, fits in perfectly. "Did you like it?"

I grunt, not expecting the question. "It was okay. We had shelter. Food. It was freezing in winter, but on the worst days we'd make blanket forts and stay in there with our hot water bottles. We'd play games or Mom would tell stories. At least, that's what we did when I was young. I was a prick of a teenager. Thought I was too cool for that. So yeah, I guess I didn't mind it." I turn to her. "The problem was that it's on the wrong side of the river. Somehow—it must have been through a child support agreement—Mom managed to send me to a better school. She meant well, but the kids bullied me for being from bad stock. I'd rather have stuck to the public school over here. I think I'd have been happier."

Ashlin threads our fingers together. "You showed them though, didn't you? Look at you now. Half the country knows your name, and you could buy this entire street if you wanted." She leans forward and kisses my cheek. I hold her there, inhaling the scent of her. Like always, it brings comfort. It's hard to believe she's actually here with me. After staying away for so many years, I'm back in this godforsaken place, but it's not so terrible with her at my side. It's just a place, like any other.

She's right too. I may not dip into it often, but I have a small fortune in the bank. Crowds have screamed for me. So why do I let this shitty town bring me down?

"Where else would you like to see?" I ask.

She cocks her head. "What was your favorite place?"

"Other than the gym?" I don't even have to think about it. "The park by the river. I used to go there in the evenings for the peace and quiet."

"Then that's what I want to see."

I drive us there. The park has changed in the past twenty years. There's new playground equipment, and a water feature has been installed, which seems pointless to me when the river is right there. Several cars are parked in the lot, and we pull up beside a shiny black SUV. I get out and go around the car to take Ashlin's hand. Now that I've experienced the joy of being connected to her again, I'm never letting go. She seems fine with that because she gladly slips her hand into mine and walks alongside me, close enough that our bodies brush with each movement. I guide her to a picnic table beneath a tree that overlooks the river, and we sit.

"This is where I used to come when I needed space."

She looks around. "I can see why. It's beautiful."

It's nothing compared to her. She puts everything else to shame. I open my mouth to tell her so, but a shout interrupts me.

"Seth?" It's a man's voice, loud and obnoxious. "Seth Isles, is that you?"

Both Ashlin and I look in the direction of the sound, and I curse under my breath. Rapidly approaching, twenty years older but apparently no wiser, is the person responsible for making my school life hell: my half-brother.

Ashlin must notice me wince, because she squeezes my hand. "You okay?"

I nod almost imperceptibly. "That's Trip." Short for Harrison Yale the Third. Although I have no clue why the fuck he's smiling and waving as he approaches.

I stand, not wanting to be at a physical disadvantage, and prepare to defend Ashlin if needed. The change in position makes a couple of things clear. First, I have several inches on him, and second, the years have not been kind. The prom

169

king's muscular frame has gone to seed, leaving a beer gut in its place. His hair is thinning, and his eyes are rimmed with red.

"Long time, no see," Trip says, coming to a stop in front of us. His gaze lingers appreciatively on Ashlin, who fidgets with the hem of her skirt. If he ogles her for one more second, I'm going to have to hurt him.

"Trip," I reply, and don't introduce Ashlin.

"I didn't realize you were back in Cedar Bend," he continues, grinning as though I'm his long-lost friend. What the fuck is going on?

"I'm not. Just visiting Mom and her new boyfriend."

Something ugly flashes through his eyes, but he suppresses it quickly. "Never thought I'd see you again. You kicked ass in the UFC. Pity you retired when you did."

I stiffen, because plenty of people have opinions on me retiring from fighting at the top of my game, but I've never had regrets. I didn't want to be one of those old guys who insist on getting in the ring only to get knocked out over and over again. I wanted a full life with Ashlin.

I force myself to shrug. "It was my time."

He shakes his head, his fleshy chin wobbling. "You could've held onto your title for another year, easy."

"Didn't want to." My gaze wanders to Ashlin of its own accord. "My career wasn't the only thing in my life."

"Oh, yeah?" Trip's attention focuses on her in a way I don't like. My fists clench at my sides. "I heard you got divorced. Guess that freed you up to play the field with hot younger women." He holds up a hand as though he expects me to high-five it. "Am I right?"

"No." The word falls like a gunshot between us because this shit show of a conversation has gone on long enough. "This is Ashlin. My ex-wife. And if you speak another fucking disrespectful word about her, I'll introduce you to my famous right cross."

"Jesus, man." He holds up his hands and backs away. "Once a bastard, always a bastard."

Bastard.

I flinch. Fuck, I hate that word. Especially when it's spoken in the context in which he means it.

By-blow.

Accident.

I've heard them all. I take a step forward as though to lunge, but a hand on my shoulder stops me. Ashlin has moved from her spot at the table.

"Don't." Her voice is soft. "He's not worth it." She glares at Trip, who mutters something under his breath, and then shoves his hands in his pockets and walks away. "Seth. Look at me."

My gaze dips to her face, taking in lips that are puffy from sucking my dick, and an angular chin that's raised with determination.

"He's nothing," she says. "Just a pathetic little man who has to act like the big guy to feel important."

My breath rattles between my teeth. "You're right."

"He probably never left Cedar Bend and now he has a sad life where he tells people you're his brother because it makes him look famous. He's nothing, and you're everything, so please don't let him get to you."

I stare at my girl. How'd she get so smart? And what did I do to deserve her? I haul her against my chest and wrap my arms around her, resting my cheek on the top of her head. I'm a shadow engulfing her light, but she seems to like it that way. She sighs contentedly and goes languid, trusting me to support her. My heart expands.

"I'm not everything," I tell her, pulling back enough that I can see her face. "You are." I kiss her, gentle and sweet, pouring every bit of emotion I have into it. When I pull back, I summon my courage. "I love you, Ash." Her eyes widen, but I hold a finger to her lips. "I love you, and I don't want anything to be lost in communication. Don't say it back now because I don't want to wonder if you're only saying it because I did. Say it when it feels right." My lips brush over hers again, and for a brief moment, everything is good in the universe. "I love you."

ASHLIN

Hours later, as the family gathers for dinner, I'm still reeling from Seth's confession.

He loves me?

When I first approached him with my plan to have a baby, I'd never have guessed we'd end up here. I should have paid more attention when my friends warned me he still had feelings for me. But even though it wasn't part of the plan, I'm happy. He makes me believe we can have our happily ever after the second time around, whether it includes a baby or not. Of course, I'll be ecstatic if IVF works or if we get pregnant the old-fashioned way, but even just the idea of having Seth in my life makes me look forward to the future. Giving birth isn't everything. I want the full pregnancy experience, but if I can't have it, I'll settle for adopting a child in need.

I take my seat at the table, aware of Seth's big presence beside me. Harley has seated herself at the end nearest him, while Devon is at the other end, putting Mae and Rick opposite us. As we get settled, I can't help but wonder if this wonderful glowy feeling inside of me is why none of the sperm donors I checked out appealed. Maybe, on some level, I wanted Seth back, and knew I was emotionally ready to do it. My subconscious may have been leading me to this very moment.

"So, how did you spend your day?" Mae asks Seth as she digs a fork into the mound of spaghetti bolognese on her plate. Rick cooked for us all tonight, and if this meal is anything to go by, Mae is a lucky woman. It's better than any I've ever made. Still, my stomach rolls. It's been unsettled all day and I hope it doesn't get worse because I'd hate for Rick to think it's his bolognese that's made me unwell.

"I took Ash past our old place, and down to the park, then we dropped by the gym."

He leaves out the part where we parked at the local hookup point and made out like teenagers. I hide a smile at the thought. If not for another car arriving, I'd have been ready to ride him in the back seat.

"How's Don doing?" Rick asks. "I haven't seen him in a while."

I hold my breath, hoping Seth won't take this as another opportunity to start quizzing his mom's boyfriend.

Seth frowns. "You know Don?"

Rick raises an eyebrow. "This is Cedar Bend. Everyone knows everyone."

Seth inclines his head. "Fair point."

Then Rick breaks into a smile. "He taught me to box."

This time, everyone stops to stare at him.

"You box?" Harley's voice is heavy with disbelief, and I don't blame her. The guy wears a suit like he was born in it. But then, she should know better than to judge people by appearances.

He shrugs. "Only for a charity match. That's where I met your mother. She'd brought a pair of signed gloves to donate to the auction."

"I remember that," Seth murmurs. "She asked me to sign them, but I didn't know what they were for."

"To support local at-risk youth." Mae blushes as she speaks. "I didn't mention it because I wasn't sure how you'd feel about it." She raises her chin. "It's an important cause."

"It is."

I glance at Seth, worried by his tone. He's looking at her as though he's never seen her before. Beneath the table, I place my hand on his thigh. He glances at me, and gives me a slight nod as though to assure me everything is all right.

"I'm glad you did." He turns back to Rick. "Did you win?"

173

"Sure did." He grins proudly. "I've got no desire to go back for a second try though. Once was enough for me." He scans the table. "I don't know how all of you do it. I was exhausted by the end of the second round."

"It's our job," Harley says. "We have far more time to train than you probably did."

"Plus we're all crazy," Devon adds, and I laugh.

After that, the conversation settles into comfortable small talk. Finding out about Rick's charity boxing match seems to have broken the ice, as though Seth has finally got a read on what kind of man he is. When we finish eating, we adjourn to the living room and gather around the coffee table to play cards again. Devon and Harley are both terrible, but Seth and I have played together hundreds of times before and work effectively as a team. Rick isn't bad either, and Mae muddles through. By the end of the night, we're all laughing, and when we go to bed, we've already promised to visit again soon.

21

SETH

Ashlin and I strip off our clothes and collapse into bed. She snuggles into my side and rests her cheek over my heart—not far from where her name is written on my skin. I always knew she'd be the only one for me, and this weekend has confirmed it. Once upon a time, running into Trip would have ruined my entire day, but because of her, it was a blip on the radar. Instead, my memory wanders to the noises she made as we kissed in the backseat of the rental, and how her eyes lit up every time we won a hand of cards.

I love her. No fucking doubt about it. But I still don't know exactly what went wrong in the past. Obviously I wasn't there when she needed me to be, but when she announced that she was filing for divorce, it came as a motherfucker of a nasty shock. I'd thought she'd eventually start acting like herself again, and instead she left me. As I breathe in the scent of her hair, the last thing I want to do is disrupt what we've got going, but in order to move forward, we need to clear the air, the same way I did with Mom last night.

"Why did you ask for a divorce?"

Her breath catches. "Things weren't right between us. You know that."

Yeah, okay. So maybe I did. And perhaps I'd kept my head in the sand and hoped it would all come right rather than facing up to the truth.

"But why didn't you talk to me first?" I stroke a hand down her shoulder, hoping I won't drive her away with these questions. "I know I've asked before, but I really want to know. I could have tried to fix it."

"It wasn't something you could fix." She wriggles back so she can look me in the eye. "I felt like I was suffering alone because you buried yourself in work, and after that first week, it didn't seem to bother you that we lost..." She closes her eyes briefly. "Cara. God, we should never have named her. Not so early on in the pregnancy."

"I'm glad we did," I admit, the skin of my wrist tingling where our unborn baby's name is printed across it. "It makes it more real, and maybe that made it hurt more, but I don't regret it."

"You don't?" she whispers.

"No. I'm sorry I fucked up and made you feel like you were alone. I swear, I was hurting too."

"I know you were." She kisses my chin, her expression tender. "Just because I felt a particular way doesn't mean it was what actually happened. With therapy and hindsight, I can see that we each dealt with it differently. You got busy, and I wallowed. Neither of us experienced more grief than the other."

Some of the pressure on my chest eases, but not all of it. "I'm still sorry you felt that you had no choice but to leave. I hate that."

"It's not on you." She speaks gently, like I'm a wounded animal, and that feels a little too close for comfort. "I didn't try to explain what I was going through. I just gave up." She rubs her lips together and glances away before continuing. "Honestly, I felt like I'd become dependent on you for my happiness, and that scared me because suddenly you weren't there. I wish I'd been in a state of mind where I could have had a discussion with you like we're having now, but I was stuck in this cycle of grief. My instincts told me I had no choice but to get away and prove I could stand on my own." She finds one of my hands and grips it. "I'm sorry I hurt you in the process. That was selfish of me."

Everything inside of me is tight. I can't believe she felt that way, and I had no idea.

"It's not all your fault either. How about we agree that we both played a part and commit to communicating better in future?"

"That sounds perfect." She kisses me so sweetly that I feel it in my heart.

"I love you," I tell her, not wanting her to doubt it. "Any time you need something, you tell me what and I'll give it to you."

"Same here." She shifts closer again, cuddling to my side. "Thank you for telling me that, Seth. So, are we really doing this?"

"Yeah." I smile even though she can't see. "We are, and this time, we're going to get it right."

ASHLIN

Tonight is my second first date with Seth. He insisted we call it that and make it official, so I'm dressing to the nines. We're only doing dinner, but I want to wow him so badly he can't keep his hands off me. I always loved his possessive streak, and how tactile he was with me. He constantly touched my waist, hips, lower back, hair, neck, hands—whatever he could lay claim to in public without being arrested for indecency.

I wear a form-fitting red dress that accentuates my coloring

—fair skin and dark hair—and clings to every curve from my shoulders to my thighs. Seth has never seen this dress before, but it's a lot like the pencil skirts that used to drive him crazy. Checking my reflection in the mirror, I swipe red lipstick on— something I haven't worn in years, but goes so perfectly with the dress. I go to the dresser and scan the contents of my jewelry box, settling on a necklace he gave me for our third anniversary. Something else catches my eye. The plain black box that houses my wedding and engagement ring. I pop it open and study them. They sit nestled against the velvet, glimmering in the light. I never had the heart to get rid of them because giving them away felt like closing the door on that part of my life for good. Now, I roll them between my fingers. Slip them on, and admire the fit.

Perfect.

My phone rings, and I grab it off the bed and answer without checking the screen.

"Hi."

"Hey, Ash." It's Paige. "Getting ready for your big date?"

I confessed to my friends about Seth and me earlier in the week.

"Nearly there. Just deciding which jewelry to wear."

"What outfit have you gone with?"

I bite my lip. "The red dress."

She laughs. "Oh, girl. You are so gone on him."

"I just want to look good," I snap, then immediately shake my head, hating my tone. I never snap at my friends. "Sorry. Guess I'm a bit defensive, and my mood has been a bit all over the place today."

"I get that." Paige's tone is quieter. More circumspect. "Sorry if I upset you."

"It's fine." I glance in the mirror again, seeing how much effort I really have put in. I've never dressed up like this in the past three years. Never cared so much whether my outfit had the impact I desired. My fingers tremble, and I press them into my palm as a needle of fear pricks my conscious mind. My priority is to keep my heart safe, and I'm afraid I've already handed it into Seth's keeping.

"What else?" she asks. "Shoes? Jewelry?"

"Black heels, silver necklace."

She pauses for a beat. "The one he gave you?"

I sigh. "How do you remember every piece of my jewelry?"

"It's a gift." I can hear the smile in her voice. "Just like I also know you have your wedding ring box right where you can see it."

Discomfort churns in my gut, and I fall silent, staring at the rings on my hand, occupying the place they used to as though they never left, and the past three years didn't happen.

"Paige," I murmur, slipping them off and returning them to the box as quickly as possible. "I might be in trouble."

"Of course you are." She tuts, but not unsympathetically. "Seth could be a buff, tattooed Mr. January, and he adores you." She doesn't know the half of it. I don't mention the fact my name is tattooed on his chest because it feels oddly private. "If that doesn't spell trouble, I don't know what does. But whatever happens, I'm here for you. Got it?"

"Yes." I smile tremulously. "I need to finish getting ready. Call you after?"

"Talk then, babe. Unless," she adds slyly, "you're too busy getting busy. In which case, don't call. I don't need to hear all about the sex you're getting while I'm stuck here waiting for Daniel to get back from his work trip."

I laugh. "Deal."

I hang up and shut the jewelry box. I don't need to look at those rings for any longer or they'll give me all kinds of funny ideas. Instead, I opt for the simple look: the necklace and nothing else. It makes a statement while not being in his face.

When he arrives to pick me up, I take one look at him and laugh. A leather cord encircles his neck with a dog tag at the bottom. If I were to look closely, I know I'd see our names engraved on it, along with the date of our wedding. I gave it to him for a Valentine's gift the year after we married. He had the exact same idea with jewelry as I did. I hold up mine to show him what I'm laughing about, then, out of instinct, glance at his left hand and find the ring finger bare.

I'm afraid to wonder why I'm disappointed.

I think I've fallen back in love with my ex-husband.

SETH

The overhead lights in the locker room cast a white glow as I wrap Tempe Larson's hands. She's about to have her first professional MMA fight.

"You've got this," I tell her, carefully taping between her fingers. "You've wanted it for years, and this is your chance to show everyone what you're made of."

She nods, but doesn't speak. She's a reasonably new transfer to Crown MMA Gym, but she's been training since she was a kid and could never convince anyone to let her play in the big leagues. She came to me because of Harley, and I'm determined she won't regret the choice.

"Tell me about your opponent."

"Tara Wyatt," she says in a monotone, as though she's memorized the words. "Heavy hands, shitty kicks. Likes to roll."

"How are you going to beat her?"

At this, the corners of her mouth lift. I notice, even though I'm focused primarily on her hands. "By kicking the crap out of her and keeping her at a distance."

"Good girl." I finish her hands and sit back.

Tempe lifts her chin. The stark lighting illuminates every line and shadow of her face, and bleaches some of the color from her tawny skin. Grim determination gleams in her eye, along with something else: the invisible fire that prompted me to take her on as a fighter. This woman isn't afraid to be the underdog. She's put in every bit of work I've asked of her and more. Victory isn't a question tonight. Provided she approaches the fight with the same tenacity she has everything else, it's a certainty.

The back of my neck tingles, and I turn to find Ashlin watching me. Her gaze ignites a fire in me, and I try to communicate with my eyes exactly what I'll do once I get her alone. Our second first date was last night, and technically, it hasn't finished yet. It ended with us rushing to my condo so we could screw against the door, and over the back of the couch, and finally, in the bed. This morning, I persuaded her to come to the gym with me, and we couldn't handle the idea of dropping her at home for long enough to collect a change of clothes, so now she's wearing her heels and dress from last night with one of my "Iron-Shin Seth Isles" supporter shirts over top of it. Seeing my name on her does wicked things to me, but most of all, it lets everyone know who she belongs to. She looks sexy as fuck in that little red dress and while there may not be a ring on her finger, I don't want any men to think they have a chance. She's mine.

With a concerted effort, I turn back to Tempe. "Skip for five minutes, do some stretches, and then Harley will take you through pads. Don't go too hard. Save your energy for the fight. Just do enough to get warm."

"Got it." She leans closer and whispers, "Happy for you, boss."

A flush rises up my neck. "Am I that obvious?"

She winks. "I think we're both getting lucky tonight."

Jesus.

"Get to work," I mutter, afraid to face the room because of how red my face undoubtedly is. She gets up, grinning, and collects her skipping rope from the wall.

Time passes quickly after that, and before long, I'm following Tempe out to the ring with Harley and Devon bringing up the rear. Tempe glares straight ahead, her focus palpable, but as we pass the front row, I glance over and see Ashlin sandwiched between Jase's girlfriend Lena and Tempe's boyfriend. She meets my eyes and beams. My heart fills to overflowing. I'm not sure I can handle the emotion building inside of me without it spilling out my eyes and mouth. For the first time since she was pregnant with Cara, I feel whole. Completely and totally content.

"You're so whipped," Devon teases as we stop at our section of the cage, and I can't bring myself to care, because I am. Everything I have and am hinges on Ashlin. I just hope she feels the same way.

"Takes one to know one, bro."

22

ASHLIN

I'm late.

My period is late.

It's _never_ late.

And yet the day after Tempe Larson's big win, it's conspicuously absent. At first, I'm afraid to hope. It's not as though I'm the poster girl for fertility. The doctors told me IVF was my best shot. How likely is it that I'd get accidentally pregnant the natural way? So I ignore it, and pretend that I haven't also noticed the slight breast tenderness and the nausea that's been coming on sporadically.

The following day, my period still doesn't arrive, so during my lunch break, I drive to the local pharmacy and purchase a test. It hasn't been long since Seth and I first had unprotected sex, so even if I am pregnant, the test might not detect it. But then, there's also the possibility that the blood test could have been a false negative and the IVF worked after all, in which case I'd be further along. Sometimes a false negative can happen if a test is done in the early days. Excitement rises within me. What if I'm pregnant?

The box seems to burn a hole in my bag as I take it back to

work. I'm striding through the foyer toward the ladies' bathroom when Harry calls my name.

"Ashlin! Wait up." Footsteps sound behind me as he abandons his post at reception and chases me down. He puffs as he falls into step. I slow as we approach the bathroom door, wondering if he's going to make this awkward. I don't have time to talk right now if I want to do the test before I'm due back in class.

"How's everything with you?" he asks when I stop and face him.

"Good." I smile and tuck my hair behind my ear. His eyes track the motion, and he wears a puppy-dog expression I've seen too many times before. I like Harry, but he's ten years younger than me, and frankly, can't hold a candle to Seth. "Great, actually."

"That's good." He nods eagerly. "Are you, um, seeing that guy who was here with you a while ago?"

"You mean my ex-husband?"

"Yeah."

I nod. "Yes, and it's serious. Sorry, Harry, but I have to go."

"Oh, okay. I hope it works out for you." His tone says otherwise. I smile and hurry into the ladies' room, more concerned with the possibility of being pregnant than I am with Harry's hurt feelings. I shut myself in a cubicle, and retrieve the test from my purse. It's supposed to have super-early detection, and I read the instructions once, then twice, not wanting to screw it up. Finally, I pee on the stick, set it aside, and start the timer on my phone. I stare at the little display, willing it to do something. First one line appears. I stare, holding my breath, as the last minute ticks down. Twenty seconds from the end, a second line comes into focus.

Oh, my God. *I'm pregnant.*

The news takes a moment to settle in. I can scarcely believe it. A baby is forming inside me right now. Who knows whether it's a boy or a girl, or even twins, but it exists.

I'm pregnant.

Launching myself off the toilet seat where I've been sitting, I pump a fist in the air and whoop. We've actually done it. Created a new life. My cheeks feel wet and I realize I'm crying. I was so afraid we'd never get here, and there's still a lot that could go wrong, but we're on the way to becoming parents.

I can't wait to tell Seth. He's going to be so happy. Even better, I don't have to pay for another round of IVF, or suffer through the injections and hormone swings—although being pregnant comes with enough of those as it is. My hand falls to my belly, and I smile so widely my face hurts.

"I'm going to take good care of you, little one. Thank you." I send my gratitude out into the universe. *Thank you.*

Everything I went through to get here feels worth it. All the vitamins and healthy eating. Abstaining from alcohol. Taking a chance on Seth. It's all worth it because of the tiny human who's utterly dependent on me.

"I love you," I tell my baby. "I love you so much."

The squeal of the electronic bell drags me back to reality. I'm in a toilet cubicle, clutching a pregnancy test, and due in class two minutes ago. I shove the test back into the box and dump it in the rubbish bin, then wash my hands and rush out.

Hours later, I know I taught those kids something, but I can't for the life of me remember what. All I recall is making plans in my head and wondering how best to break the news to Seth. In the end, I opt for the direct approach, and head straight to Crown MMA Gym. It's off a busy street, and I swerve into the parking lot and circle twice before finding a space. Then I hurry inside, kicking off my shoes in the doorway because Seth has a weird thing about people training barefoot. He's standing beside the ring with his back to me, supervising a pair of guys as they spar. One of them I recognize as Jase, who lived with Seth and me briefly during the early days of our relationship until he got established as a professional fighter. He was a good kid, and it seems like he's grown

185

into a good man, with great taste in women. I met his girl-friend, Lena, the other night, and she reminds me of Harley in a lot of ways. Feisty, but more upper crust.

Pacing across the floor, I pay no attention to the men who check me out. Some will remember me from before. Many won't. But MMA gyms are testosterone-fueled environments and I'm used to the glances.

"Hi," I say as I arrive behind Seth. My instinct is to launch myself at him, but I don't want to shock him if he doesn't realize I'm here. Unexpected physical contact is dangerous in a place like this.

He turns, and his face creases in a smile. "Ash. What are you doing here?"

"Can I talk to you in private?"

His smile drops away. "Of course. Is something wrong?"

"The opposite." I take his hand and lead him to his office. Once inside, I study my surroundings while he closes the door. Near the back wall, there's a table that looks like the kind an executive would use. It's almost empty, except for a couple of framed photos. Curious, I circle it, and my breath catches in my chest. The largest photo is of us on our wedding day. He's handsome in a tux, and I'm leaning into him, gazing up as though he's the center of my universe.

He was.

I look up and find him watching me. "I can't believe you kept this here."

He shrugs. "In my heart, I always felt like I was still married to you. Getting divorced didn't change the promises I made that day. At least, not in here." He taps his chest.

I study the other photo. It's newer. One of him and Harley side by side, with his arm around her. She's in her fight gear, sweat glistening on her skin, and he's got a proud gleam in his eye.

"I love this."

"It's a good one," he agrees, placing his hands on his hips. "What's going on?"

Taking a deep breath, I circle back to him. My chest fizzes with excitement.

"I'm pregnant." The words burst from me more forcefully than intended. "We're having a baby."

His sharp intake of breath cracks through the air between us. "You sure?"

"Yes." I step closer and tilt my face up. "I took a test."

He shoves a hand through his hair, eyes fixed on me, breath growing erratic.

"Are you okay?" I ask.

"Fuck, yes." He grabs me by the waist and starts to lift me up, then stops and kisses me instead. His tongue invades my mouth, but the kiss doesn't last long. "That's the best news I've had all year." He caresses the flat of my stomach as though he can already sense the curve where my belly will expand. He kisses me again, swiftly, then buries his face in my shoulder. "What did I do to get so lucky?"

I press closer, loving the feel of him. "We're going to be parents."

"I know," he murmurs into my hair. "I love you, Ash. Fuck, I love you so much. Thank you for giving me this." He places a soft kiss on my neck. "I know you didn't plan for it to work out this way, but I hope you're as happy as I am." When he draws back, his eyes are shining, and the emotion in them matches my own.

"Thank *you* for agreeing," I counter. "If you'd called me crazy—which you'd have had every right to do—we'd never have gotten here." I clutch him close, snuggling into his broad chest. "I'm so happy." My eyes start leaking again, the moisture soaking into the fabric of his shirt. "You've made me so happy."

His arms loop around my lower back and secure me against him. "What do you need from me?"

I stiffen in surprise—although it's not unpleasant. "How do you mean?"

He releases me, and lowers himself onto the chair, then pats his lap, indicating I should sit there. I do, without hesitation.

"I want to give you what you need, but not be overbearing," he says, and his embrace feels like the safest place I've ever been. "Just tell me what that is. If it's food or help, I'm there. If you turn into a horn-dog again, I'll satisfy you as many times as it takes. But if space is what you need, I'm good with that too. You just tell me, and I'll make it happen."

That's when I know I love him again. If I ever stopped at all. He's taken what I told him about our past to heart and wants to move on in a healthy way.

I am here for it.

"Right now, I need another kiss."

A slow smile claims his mouth. "Anything you need."

Seth

Twenty-four hours after Ashlin tells me she's pregnant with our child, it still hasn't sunk in. Every part of me wants to grab her and hide her away, safe from the world, but I resist, even when it means getting out of bed at my usual time, kissing her on the cheek, and leaving. I know she'll be going to her own job, and she won't thank me for getting overprotective. Still, all of my instincts tell me that not having her nearby is wrong. All day, it eats at me that she's out there at work, while I'm here and anything could happen. By the time I can finally go home, my muscles are tense with the need to hold her.

She's a grown woman, I remind myself. *A tough, smart, too-good-for-you woman, and she needs you to keep your shit together.*

But when I leap out of the car at her house and she flings the door open, races down the path and hurls herself into my arms as though we haven't seen each other for months rather than hours, it's the best sensation ever. I hug her tighter and breathe in her delicate floral scent.

"I missed you," I say.

Our mouths crash together, and she practically climbs me. Hand cupping her ass, I stumble toward the house, determined not to put on any more of a show for the neighbors than we already have. Inside, we make love in a twist of limbs and desperation. Afterward, she runs her hand up and down my chest while we catch our breath. Catching her fingers, I bring them to my lips and kiss each one, lingering on the one that used to wear my ring. If I get my way, she'll be wearing it again soon. I'll hold off on asking for a while though. Wait until we're properly re-established. I don't want to push her into anything she's not ready for, and scare her away.

My phone rings, and I curse.

"You should get that," Ashlin says. "Might be important."

"Important enough to interrupt this?" I chuckle and run the back of my knuckles along her cheekbone. "Unlikely."

"Go on." She gives me a little push. "Get it."

I roll my eyes. "You're going to be stubborn. Got it." Reaching over, I grab the phone from the nightstand and check the screen, then frown. *Leo Delaney.* What the hell is he calling for? Leo is a fighter who trains at another gym. We've traveled in the same circles for years, but while we're friendly, I wouldn't say we're friends. I glance at Ashlin. I don't want to leave the magical bubble we've created for ourselves, but I'd better see what he wants.

"I've got to take this." I shuffle over to sit on the edge of the bed as I answer. "Leo, what's up?"

"You been listening to the grapevine today?" he asks in a Californian drawl I recognize well.

"Can't say I have." I scratch my chin. "Something happen?"

He whistles low. "You could say that. There's been a major drug bust at my gym. A bunch of guys were arrested, including Stan and Karson."

"Whoa." I stand up and pace the length of the room. Stan is the coach at Leo's gym, City Fight Center, and Karson is one of his two golden boys, with Leo being the other. While it doesn't surprise me that Karson is wrapped up in drugs, I'd never have expected Stan to be involved. "Sounds serious. What are you doing about it?" If I know Leo, he'll already have an exit plan. He's not the kind of guy who wants to be associated with cheaters.

"I've gathered a few fighters I know are clean. We'd like to move to Crown. You got room for us?"

Fuck. Leo is abandoning ship, and taking his friends with him. Knowing him like I do, I can guess who a couple of them are, and I'd be stupid not to welcome them with open arms.

"Always got room for you, man. Do you have stuff you need to store?"

"Only a few bits and pieces."

"Can you meet me at the gym in half an hour?" I glance at Ashlin, who's watching me with interest, not the slightest bit self-conscious in her nakedness. Exactly how I like her. Fuck, I wish I didn't have to leave.

"That'd be awesome. Thanks. I appreciate it."

"No problem. See you soon." I hang up and return to the bed. "There's been a drug bust. I've got to go help some guys shift their things to the gym. I'm not sure how long I'll be. Want to come with me?"

She shakes her head, and stretches her nude body. My mouth waters at the sight of her nipples, and the way her back arches as though I'm still inside her. Then she flops onto the mattress, relaxed. "No, I'll stay here and cook dinner. If you're out late, I don't want to miss any sleep." She smiles, but the brackets around her mouth speak of anxiety. "I need to take good care of us."

My heart fills with warmth. "Okay, you got it."

I bend and kiss her cheek. I'd much rather we stayed together, but I respect her boundaries and the reason behind them. She's trying to give our little guy his best shot at making it into the world.

"I love you."

Her lips quirk up. "I love you too."

My heart stops.

Holy fuck.

Now how am I supposed to leave?

"You do?"

"Yes." She rolls to the edge of the bed, gets to her feet, and then wraps her arms around me. "I love you."

I rock her from side to side, and press a tender kiss to her temple. "God, I wish I could stay with you."

She swats my butt and laughs. "Go." She moves away, making a shooing motion. "Be a boss man. I'll see you when you come home."

Home. I like the sound of that. "I will."

"Drive safe."

"See you, sweetheart."

I get dressed and head outside. The chill of the air refreshes me. By the time I reach the gym, I've achieved a second wind. The door is open because Devon and Harley were still here when I left, but a group of mostly men—with one woman—loiter outside. As I walk toward them, Leo breaks away from the group and approaches. He holds out a hand, and I grip it firmly.

"Thanks for coming," he says. "We stayed out here because we didn't want to overstep."

"No problem." I nod, appreciating his respect. Despite the fact he's fought against my top-ranked fighter, Gabe Mendoza, Leo and I maintain a good working relationship. He's a decent guy. He jerks his chin toward the others, and runs a hand through tousled blond hair that's longer than most fighters wear it. "I've brought Tony, Oman, Vic, and Enya with me. That okay?"

I run my gaze over the others, who have come up behind

him while we're speaking. Two of the three men are well-known and well-regarded. The third is an up-and-comer. But it's the woman, Enya, who captures my interest. She recently went up against Harley in the final of an eight-woman eliminator tournament, and lost. She meets my gaze and doesn't look away, proving she's no wilting violet. While she's slim and unassuming with a smattering of freckles across her nose, she's a tough girl who's had a bad run. America loves her, perhaps even more than they do Leo, but every time she gets a major bout, she can't seem to come away with the win. My palms itch with excitement as it occurs to me that I could be the one to change her losing streak.

"I'm glad you did," I tell Leo, then offer Enya a hand. "We haven't met properly." A ringside introduction when she was bathed in sweat and exhausted doesn't count. "I'm Seth Isles. Welcome to Crown MMA."

She nods once, as though I meet with her approval. "Enya." Her voice is as sweet as her exterior. It's only the steeliness of her eyes that gives away her true nature. "I hope we're not overstepping. Leo mentioned coming here, and considering how screwed up things are at our gym, it seemed like a good idea."

"Happy to have you." I thrust my chin at the other men, including them in the statement. "Why don't you come inside and we can talk?"

We head in, and I lead the five of them past Harley and Devon to my office. Harley is holding pads for her boyfriend, and her eyes track our movement, then narrow. I have no doubt she'll be joining us within a couple of minutes. I leave the office door ajar, and take the seat behind my desk. Leo sits in the one opposite and the others remain standing.

"So, are you looking for something temporary or permanent?" I ask, getting straight to business.

Leo glances behind him. "I can't speak for all of us, but I want a permanent change."

"Me, too," Enya adds, and the others echo their agreement.

I steeple my fingers and study them, my mind whirling. Taking on five new fighters—even if they know what they're doing—is a big ask. I absolutely want them here, but it's going to take a lot of adjustment on all our parts. They'll have habits and routines that will be shaken up, and I need to find the mental space to get up to date with their training regimens and make a game plan for each of them.

I face Leo, "You don't want to train with your dad?"

His father, Grant, owns Alpha MMA, a gym that produces topnotch fighters.

He scowls. "No."

I wait to see if he'll elaborate. Quiet moments tick by and he doesn't.

"Fine." I shrug one shoulder. "It's not going to be an easy transition since there are so many of you. Are you willing to put in extra time?"

They assure me they are.

The door opens, and everyone turns as Harley enters with Devon close behind her. She surveys the group, hands on hips.

"What's going on here?"

23

ASHLIN

Seth being called off for a work emergency should feel like a gut punch after how distant he became toward the end of our relationship, but I'm surprisingly okay with it. In fact, I'm glad he's confident in my ability to handle myself and feels safe to leave. I stay on the bed for a while, basking in a happy glow, but once my skin starts to cool, I get dressed and start a three-way video call with my friends. Jessica answers first, but I make her wait until Paige joins before saying anything.

"Guys." Their faces fill my screen, and I can't help smiling. I love these women so much. "I'm pregnant."

Jessica blinks. Paige's jaw drops. Then they both speak at once.

"Are you sure?" Jessica asks.

"Holy crap!" Paige exclaims.

They both roll their eyes.

I laugh. "Yes, Jess, I'm sure. And I know, right?" I drop onto the beanbag in the living room and rest my head on one arm, keeping the phone in front of me. "It's crazy, but I'm so happy."

"Congratulations!" they chorus.

Jessica's brows knit together. "I thought the IVF didn't work."

"The test was negative, but maybe it was too soon to tell. False negatives can happen." I blush. "Or it could be that Seth and I have been, uh, reconnecting. Either way, I guess it was meant to be."

Paige waggles her eyebrows. "Reconnecting." She giggles. "I need to remember that one. Babe, we're so happy for you."

Jessica's expression turns serious. "Are you sure it's a good idea to be telling people at this stage?" She pauses, as though considering her next words carefully. "It's just so early, and—"

"It's okay," I break in, not wanting her to finish a sentence that would be painful for all of us. "Other than Seth, you're the only ones I've told, and we'll probably keep it that way for a while. I just wanted you to know since you're both so important to me."

"Aww." Paige's expression softens, and her eyes sparkle with moisture. "You're important to us too, boo. How are we celebrating?"

My cheeks burn, and from the way Jessica squints at me, I'm sure they can see. "Well, I was going to start with another round of mind-blowing sex, but Seth got called away."

Paige pouts. "It better have been something important."

"Yes, it was urgent, and I'm okay," I say. "Better than okay. I'd love it if you guys could come over. No pressure if it's too difficult for either of you, but we could drink virgin cocktails and make an inspiration board for the nursery."

"I'm there," Paige declares. "Don't worry about us. If something is beyond what we can handle, we'll let you know. Won't we, Jess?"

"Of course." Jessica presses her lips together, but when she speaks again, I can hear the tears she's holding back and want to hug her so badly. "We're both happy for you, Ash. Our own pasts don't change that."

"Love you, Jess." I blow her a kiss since I can't wrap her in my arms. "I'll see you soon?"

"You bet."

Paige winks. "Couldn't keep us away if you wanted to."

We end the call, and I close my eyes while my heart swells with affection and love for my friends, Seth, and my new baby. I'm amazed it hasn't burst yet. I have no idea how I got so lucky, but I'll never take it for granted.

SETH

It's late by the time I get back to Ashlin's place. The street is dark and empty, and only a faint light glows inside. I let myself in and follow the light to the kitchen, where I discover a note on the counter that reads:

Seth

Dinner is in the warmer. I'm in bed. Had the girls over, but they've both gone home. Hope you fixed what you needed to at work.

Lots of love,

Ashlin XX

Smiling, I trace the tip of my finger over the word "love," then fold the note and slip it into my pocket. A wave of nostalgia rolls through me, shocking in its intensity. My breath catches in my throat, and emotion causes the backs of my eyes to burn. I blink rapidly, and shake myself. There's nothing to get worked up about. It's just that the note brings back memories of the best part of our marriage, before it all fell apart. Nights when I'd get home late, exhausted from a long day, and find a meal waiting, and know that the woman I loved would be in bed, ready to comfort me with her body and her kind words.

She's such a nurturer. Soft where I'm hard. Filling in the gaps to make me a better person. While I never understood why she wanted me in the first place, I always figured it must be the same for her. That I complemented the places she was weak. Now, as I open the warmer and find a pie that smells amazing, alongside a selection of vegetables, I can't help wondering if that perception led me to take over the reins too much in our relationship, and pushed her into feeling dependent. One thing is for sure: this time around, I won't let her feel helpless or alone. I'll be at her side the whole way, as her partner. Her equal.

I wolf down the pie, brush my teeth, check the locks, and switch off the lights. I pause outside her bedroom, listening to see if she's awake. When I don't hear anything, I inch the door open and step inside. Silently, I shuck off my clothes, then climb into the bed and cuddle up behind her. One of my arms rests on the dip of her waist, my hand caressing her lower stomach. She hums contentedly, and I kiss the side of her neck, then close my eyes, feeling like maybe everything is going to work out after all.

ASHLIN

For a week, life is bliss. I float through my days at work and spend my evenings making love with the man I adore. But then, with a rush of blood in my panties, it all comes crashing down. I stare at the red liquid coating my thighs and tremble.

This cannot be happening. Not again.

Not after everything has been so damn perfect. Squeezing my eyes shut, I will the blood away, but when I open them again, it's still there. A sob breaks from me, and I clap a hand over my mouth. I can't start crying in the ladies' room at the kindergarten. I need to do something. Get to a doctor. Find out whether my baby is all right.

But I'm so damn scared. I grab a wad of toilet paper and stuff it in my underwear, as if that could stop the bleeding, then fumble with my phone. Numbness makes my fingers clumsy, and I drop it on the floor. It slides beneath the cubicle door, and I swear. Without any finesse, I wipe my legs dry and exit the cubicle.

My phone lies on the floor, and I snatch it up and force my uncooperative hands to find Seth's number. I call, but he doesn't answer. It goes to voicemail. Panicking, I hang up and call again. Same thing. I leave a shaky message that I'm sure makes no sense, but I can't seem to find the right words to explain anything.

God, what am I going to do? I need a hospital. The blood is still coming. Sinking to the floor, I rest my forehead against the wall and think. I can't call Paige or Jessica. It would be too traumatic for them, given our histories.

Pull yourself together. You're an independent woman. You know what to do.

With a concerted effort, I stumble to my feet and use the wall to support myself while I dial another number. 911.

"Emergency services," a chirpy woman answers. "How can I help you?"

"I need an ambulance." My voice is stronger than I expect, and I draw comfort from the fact I sound like I have my shit together. "I'm pregnant, and I've started bleeding." I give her the school's address.

"An ambulance is on its way to you now," she says. "Stay with me. How far along are you?"

"Not long. A month or two, tops."

"Okay." I hear her tapping on a keyboard. "You're doing great. What's your name, darling?"

"Ashlin Isles." More tapping.

"Where are you?"

"I'm in the ladies' bathroom."

"Can you get yourself to the entrance?" she asks. "Or do you need them to come to you?"

My head spins at the thought of trying to cross the school grounds in my current state. "Can they come here? People

198

will ask questions if I leave alone, and I might scare the children."

"Then they'll come to you," she promises. "Have you called a friend? Is there someone who can be with you?"

Her question hits me like a slap, and I reel back. "N-no. I tried to call my hus—I mean, partner, but he didn't answer." The panic that's been slowly circling slams into me, and for a brief moment, I feel exactly like I did three years ago. As though I'm screaming for help and no one is listening. Seth is God knows where, not picking up his phone. My friends are not emotionally equipped to deal with this situation, even after all of their therapy. Helplessness batters at me like an accusation. *You're not strong enough. You can't do this.*

"I can," I whisper out loud. "I can do it."

"Uh, Ashlin?" The woman's tone turns questioning. "Do you have any family?"

Family. I almost cry with relief.

"Yes." It's on the tip of my tongue to give her Dad's name, but for some reason, I don't. "Harley. My sister-in-law."

"Okay. I'm going to put you on hold, and I want you to call Harley and ask her to meet you at Sunrise Hospital."

Part of me relaxes. She's giving me instructions. Right now, that's exactly what I need.

"If she doesn't answer, let me know, okay? I'm here for you, Ashlin."

"Thank you." She puts me on hold, and I find Harley's number, my fingers moving more surely now that I have a task to accomplish. When she answers, I clutch my chest against another wave of emotion.

"Harley, thank God."

"Ash, are you okay?"

"No." I whimper. "Something has happened. An ambulance is coming to get me. Where are you? Is Seth there?"

In the distance, I hear the murmur of another voice. Male. Seth?

"Shit, how bad is it? I'm at Dev's place," Harley replies. "We've just been for our run and were about to hit the gym, but we'll come to the hospital instead. Don't worry about Seth; I'll get a hold of him."

The bathroom door bursts open, and a paramedic hurries inside.

I swallow. "Gotta go. See you soon." I hang up. "I'm bleeding. Is my baby going to be okay?"

He hustles over to me, and another paramedic follows behind with a stretcher tucked under her arm.

"We'll do what we can, but you're our top priority," he says as his partner places the stretcher on the floor. "Let's take care of you first, and then we'll check on the baby. Can you lie down for us?"

"Oh, I can walk."

His expression tightens. "Please, we'd prefer you to lie down. It's safer that way."

That's all he needs to say to make me comply. Suddenly remembering the woman still on hold, I gesture to my phone.

"We'll deal with it," the female paramedic says. "You just hang in there."

"My purse," I said. "It's still in my classroom."

"I'll ask one of the other teachers to get it for you. Don't worry."

I close my eyes as they carry me out, ignoring the exclamations of surprise from my colleagues, and the interest from students as we pass by. I can't deal with them right now. I'm not even sure I can deal with myself. Forget being a strong woman. I was delusional. I'm frightened and alone, just like I always was.

24

SETH

"You and I both know Leo had nothing to do with drugs," I argue for the tenth time, furiously clicking the lid of my pen. I'm having a circular conversation with the promoter of the fight Leo is supposed to participate in this weekend. "He's taken a test and he's clean."

"I don't know what to say, Seth. It's going to take a while for the taint of the arrests to leave him. People will wonder."

"Let them fucking wonder." My pen snaps in two and I drop it in disgust. "It's not his fault he was training with cheaters."

"I can't help you. Not right now. Come back in a couple of months when everything has quietened down, and we can talk then."

"This is bullshit."

"It is what it is." His tone is final. Damn. I've wasted a fucking hour on this call with nothing to show for it.

"Thanks anyway. I've got to go." I hang up before I can say something I regret. As the call vanishes from the screen, a bunch of text fills it, and my blood freezes. A missed call from Ashlin, a voicemail, and two missed calls from Harley, along with a text.

Harley: *Ashlin at hospital. Come soon.*

Oh, fuck.

Something is wrong, and I've been so wrapped up in work that it's taken me forty minutes to see the message. I'd heard notifications while I'd been in the call, but I'd assumed they were nothing important. I mentally berate myself. Heart in my throat, I call Ashlin back.

Harley answers on the second ring. "About fucking time."

"What happened?"

"She started bleeding while she was at work. Called an ambulance. They're checking her out now. Where have you been?"

"On a call. Which hospital is it?" She gives me the name and address. "I'll be there soon. Text me if you learn anything." I rush out of the office into the gym and shove a set of keys at a startled Jimmy. "Lock up when you finish. I have to go."

He takes a look at me and blanches. "Everything okay?"

"No, but I don't have time to explain."

He nods. "Got it."

The trip to the hospital seems to take forever. Every set of traffic lights that turn red make me want to punch someone. Don't they know that time is vital? I can't lose our baby, or Ashlin, again. I park in the basement and take the elevator to the ground floor, where I'm forced to wait at reception for two other people to speak to the receptionist ahead of me. I glance at my watch. Time is ticking away. Is my girl okay? I haven't heard anything from Harley, and I'm not sure if that's a good sign or a bad sign.

When it's my turn, the words pour out of me in a rush. "I'm here for Ashlin Isles. I'm her husband."

The receptionist taps a few keys on the computer and checks the screen. "Your wife is in room 306."

"Thank you." I hurry away and take the stairs to the third floor, knowing I can get myself there faster than an elevator can. When I reach room 306, I spot Ashlin lying on a bed in a hospital gown with Harley standing beside her, holding her hand.

I shove the door open wider. "Ash, baby, are you okay?"

She glances up, but her eyes don't focus on me. Her pupils are pinpricks, which I know from experience usually indicates a shock reaction. Harley steps out of the way so I can approach her. I note Devon in the periphery of my vision, but all that matters is the pixie in the bed. Her cheeks are too damned pale for my peace of mind. I envelop her hand with mine, and kiss her forehead.

"Tell me you're all right," I plead.

She shakes her head, eyes still struggling to focus. "I don't know. There was blood. What if…" She bites her lip, tears welling in her eyes. "What if we lose the baby?"

"Don't even go there." I raise her hand to my mouth and kiss the back of it. "Everything is going to be okay."

The door swings open and a doctor enters. He glances at me. "You must be the daddy."

"That's right." I swallow. *Daddy*. I want badly for that to be true. *Please don't let anything have gone wrong*. Silently, I curse myself. I should have been with her. Regardless of her desire for independence, I should have been keeping an eye on her. Protecting her.

"Let's see how things look, shall we?" He pulls a curtain around us for privacy, blocking Harley and Devon out, then drapes a sheet over her lower body. I squeeze Ashlin's hand as he inserts a wand inside her, my gut clenching as tears streak quietly down her cheeks. Finally, the doctor has an image up on the screen. A little flashing star. He shows us both, and smiles. "Good news. Your baby is healthy. That's their heartbeat."

"Oh, my God," I exclaim, watching the faint pulse. Our baby is actually there. Knowing Ashlin is pregnant is one thing, but seeing the evidence of a new life… it's magical.

"They're okay?" Ashlin's voice is a whisper.

"And looking exactly as he or she ought to," the doctor assures her.

"Isn't it amazing?" I murmur, and drop a kiss on her forehead.

She stares at the screen in wonder. "I can hardly believe it." Her eyes meet mine, and they shine with emotion. "Our baby."

Pure joy flows through me, starting at my heart and traveling out from there. "Yeah, sweetheart. That's right."

The doctor clears his throat. "Take it slow over the next few days, but I don't think there's any cause to worry. Sometimes bleeding happens during pregnancy, and it doesn't necessarily mean anything bad. Given your history, I can see why it gave you such a scare, but everything seems to be in order." He gives her a kind smile and passes her a cloth to clean up. When she's finished, he helps cover her and takes off his gloves. "Your baby is fine. You might continue to get some spotting. If the bleeding becomes heavy again, come back, but in the meantime, you're free to go whenever you're ready."

"Thank you." Her eyes flutter shut in a moment of gratitude.

"We can't thank you enough, doctor." I offer him a hand, and he shakes it.

"Keep an eye on her," he adds softly. "Make sure she eats something tonight. I think the scare has been worse for her than the bleeding."

"I will," I promise. The doctor leaves, and I reclaim Ashlin's hand, expecting the worry to have faded from her expression, but while it's certainly reduced, it hasn't vanished. I raise her hand to my lips and kiss it. "Did you hear that, Ash? The baby is fine."

She tries to smile, but the edges of her mouth tremble and she can't hold the expression. "I was so scared."

"I know, sweetheart." I wrap her in a hug as best I can. "Let's get you home. We can cuddle it out. Okay?"

"Okay," she whispers.

Harley's face appears in the gap between the curtains. "Is everything okay?"

I haul her into an embrace. She squeaks in surprise. We're not generally an affectionate family. "Thank you for taking care of my girl."

"No problem," she gasps. "I love her too."

I release her and push through the curtains to hug Devon too.

"Anytime, bro," he says.

A sound behind me has us all turning. Ashlin has tugged on a skirt and is standing, but her legs are wobbly.

"Whoa." I place an arm around her. "I've got you."

She swats my shoulder. "I'm fine. I didn't lose that much blood."

"Maybe not." I keep my tone low and soothing since she seems to be veering into pissed-off territory. "But I want to help you. Please let me."

She sags. "Fine."

I hate how small and defeated she sounds. My girl is tough. Perhaps not in a stereotypical way, but tough nonetheless, and it pains me to see her like this.

"Do you mind driving us to her place in my car?" I ask Harley. "I want to sit with her."

"No problem. Devon can bring his car to drive me home in afterward."

I nod. We deal with the paperwork and make our way back to the basement. I insist on physically supporting Ashlin while Harley takes her purse. I keep my girl company in the back seat while Harley navigates the roads. When we're finally at Ashlin's place, and Harley and Devon have left, I settle her into the bed and climb in beside her.

"How are you doing?"

She draws her knees up to her chest, and her lower lip trembles. "I couldn't get a hold of you."

"I know." I'll never forgive myself for that. "I'm so sorry."

"I was terrified." She rests her forehead on her knees and her voice grows muffled. Her shoulders hunch, and I ache to remove the burden from them, but there's only so much I can do. "You know what scared me even more than losing the baby?"

Stroking a hand down her hair, I ask, "What's that?"

"How dependent I felt on you to rescue me." Her eyes gleam with tears. Slowly, they start to stream down her cheeks. "I thought I'd become stronger than that, but now I'm worried that I was deluding myself, and history might repeat." She shakes her head vigorously. "I really, really don't want that."

Any words I might say get stuck in my throat, and a sense of powerlessness overcomes me. I don't know what to say to make it better. It hurts that she's willing to believe everything could play out like it did last time, when we've both grown so much. I don't point out all the ways in which we've changed because I don't want to upset her more than she already is. If I say the wrong thing, that could spell the end of us. I feel like I'm navigating a minefield with no idea where the mines are buried.

"Don't push me away," I plead. "You are strong. You took care of this all by yourself. *You* did that."

She shakes her head again, the denial immediate. "I was overwhelmed."

Don't leave me.

My brain screams at me to do whatever it takes to make sure she won't suddenly decide she's had enough of me, the way she did last time.

"But you managed."

"Barely." The tears continue, and I ache for them to stop. How can I make her see that I won't let her down again? That she and I are in this for good? "I called a freaking ambulance. I could have asked one of my colleagues for a ride to the hospital or called a friend but I couldn't even handle the idea of it. God knows how much it will cost when I get the bill."

"Don't worry, I'll cover it. I always, *always* want you to be safe, no matter the price. You're the most important thing."

She makes a miserable sound that guts me.

"I love you, Ash," I tell her. "What do you need right now? I want to help." When she doesn't say anything, my desperation grows. "What if I promise you'll never be alone again?" Inspiration strikes, and I reach into my pocket and pull out the box I've been carrying around since she told me she loves me. Popping it open, I show her my wedding ring. The one I never let go of no matter how much I told myself it was over. "Let's make it official. Marry me again."

Her lips part, and her eyes widen with shock. She looks from me to the ring and back. "Seth..."

"Say yes." The seconds drag out and I feel like a fool, but I was going to do this eventually anyway, so why not now?

"Have you been listening to a word I said?" she demands, her voice shaking with emotion. "I can't do this with you right now. I need time to think."

Panic seizes me. She's saying no. Fuck, she's saying no.

"You can have however much time you need," I promise. "We don't have to get married tomorrow."

She blinks rapidly, and wipes her eyes with the backs of her hands. "Put it away. We can't have this conversation when our emotions are running high."

"But we can have it later?" I clarify, because if she's trying to blow me off, I won't let it go so easily.

"Yes."

"Okay." She isn't ready now. I accept that. "Can I hold you at least?"

"I guess."

Her disinterest is a blade to my heart. I pull her into my embrace, but even though I can feel the warmth of her skin, she's a million miles away, and I'm not sure I can close the distance between us.

My instincts rage at me to put distance between Seth and I. To say whatever it takes to make him leave. There's so much going on inside my head that I don't have the energy to withstand both him and my own negative thoughts. But even with all of that, I recognize that I'm not being fair to him. He's had as much of a scare as I have, and it's not his fault that I haven't come as far as I believed I had. My emotional breakdown isn't on him.

"Are you hungry?" he asks after a while.

My stomach churns with a combination of nausea and fear. Hunger is pretty much impossible, but I know I need to feed our baby.

"Maybe for something small."

"Okay. You stay right here. I'll be back." He disentangles himself from me and kisses my forehead before leaving. That gentle caress nearly starts the waterworks again. Ugh, I hate feeling like this. So out of control. I forgot the havoc pregnancy wreaks on my hormones.

I'm not sure how long I stay alone for, but eventually Seth returns, bringing with him something that smells amazing. Suddenly, I'm ravenous.

"What's that?"

He smiles. "Potato and gravy. From a packet, I'm afraid."

My eyes well up all over again. Potato and gravy is what I craved last time I was pregnant. He remembered. "Thank you."

"You eat, I'll cuddle." He slips into bed beside me and places an arm around my shoulders. My instincts tell me to let him take care of everything. It would be so easy. But I can't. I need to depend on myself, right?

I grab the spoon and dig into the potato. Meanwhile, Seth's silent presence is simultaneously comforting and discomfiting.

"I don't know what I'd have done if something happened to

you or the baby," he says eventually. "I've loved you since the day we met, and I've already grown to love the little guy too."

I continue with the potato, unsure how to respond.

"It's okay if you don't feel like talking." He rubs his palm up and down my back. "I'm trying to be a better communicator than I used to be. The truth is, I loved you when we were apart, and I believe I'll love you until the day I die."

My gaze snaps to him, temper flaring. "You'd better not be planning to die anytime soon."

He chuckles. "I'm not. But even if something were to happen to the baby, I'd want to be with you." His hand stops moving and rests on the small of my back. "You may think you're weak, but not seeing you for three years nearly destroyed me. There was nothing in my life worth coming home to at the end of the day. If anything, I'm the weak one. If you need a kid to be happy and the worst were to come about, we could try again, or choose to adopt or foster instead. I love you, Ashlin. Unconditionally. And I'm here for you when you want to talk."

The last mouthful of potato nearly sticks in my throat, which is so clogged with emotion that I struggle to swallow. When I manage it, I set the bowl aside and nestle into the crook of his shoulder. Then the tears come again. He's so perfect. Saying all the right things. But I feel like I'm about to crack into a thousand pieces. I love him with every fiber of my being, but for some reason, I just can't bring myself to say it tonight. Admitting my feelings doesn't feel safe. It's as though my subconscious believes I'll be able to hold myself together— come what may—as long as I don't verbalize anything.

25

SETH

My fist slams into a punching bag and I grunt with the effort, then draw back and let fly with the other fist. Left, right. Left, right. My knuckles scream in pain, not used to this treatment after years of taking it easy. Still, it's not enough. I kick the bag. Again. And again. Around me, the gym is oddly quiet. Rap plays over the speakers, but the usual chatter is absent.

Punch. Kick.

A timer squeals, but I don't stop. It's like there's a demon I need to exorcise. I woke up angry and left the house before Ashlin got out of bed, leaving a note and breakfast for her on the counter. I was afraid that if we were in the same room at the same time, I'd snap at her, when it's not her I'm angry at. It's myself.

I hate to think what she went through yesterday, and how scared she must have been when she couldn't get in touch with me. All because I was on a stupid work-related phone call, trying to schmooze my way into getting Leo his first fight at my gym. She needed me, and I wasn't there for her. Once again, I let her down.

But that's not the only thing causing me pain. I proposed,

and she didn't accept. Perhaps it was shitty timing, but I meant it with my whole being.

Punch. Kick.

"Seth!" A voice calls from behind me.

Jase.

"Chill out, man," comes another.

Devon.

Spinning around, I pin them both with a glare for daring to interrupt. Devon holds his hands up in a gesture of peace, but Jase stares right back at me, then jerks his thumb toward the office.

"I'm busy."

He repeats the motion, eyes becoming flinty. "I don't think you want me airing your dirty laundry out here."

"You wouldn't."

He crosses his tattooed arms over his chest. "I don't want to, but if it's the only way I can talk to you, then I might have to."

I glance at Devon. "You're in on this?"

He shrugs. "Jase is the closest thing you have to a best friend. Someone needed to tell him."

I sigh, and glance longingly at the bag. This is what you get for befriending your fighters. "Fine."

I lead the way to my office and sink into my usual chair, leaving them to decide who gets the other one. Jase sits. Devon leans against the wall.

"I'm sorry," Jase says, watching me with a degree of caution that's completely warranted. "Yesterday must have been hard for you."

I raise a brow as if to say, 'you think?'

He cocks his head. That's the trouble with Jase. He knows me well. "How's Ash?"

"Recovering." When I left this morning, she was smiling in her sleep. Peaceful, and so fucking beautiful, but even though she was right there, it felt like she was miles out of my reach. "She and the baby are both okay, although she got a fright."

"And you guys are all right?"

I swallow, and glance at Devon, wondering just how much he's told Jase. "I proposed. She didn't answer. So I don't really know what we are."

Devon face-palmed. "Dude, why would you propose?"

My eyes narrow. "You saw how she started pulling away from me. I couldn't lose her again."

"But Seth," Jase says, drawing my attention back to him. "She was freaked out. From what Dev has told me, she felt out of control. We both know you meant well, but trying to get a lifelong commitment from someone who's in an emotional tailspin is a crappy idea. You probably made it worse."

I scowl, but he has a point. Something he said lingers in my mind. *Out of control.* Ashlin confessed to feeling powerless and overwhelmed. I'd been thinking of myself when I tried to lock her down, but that's not what she needed. I should have handed her the reins and stepped back. Perhaps that would have given her confidence, rather than me barging in and stomping all over her emotions with my clumsy feet.

"Maybe I went about it wrong," I admit.

"You acted like a dumbass in love," Jase confirms, his expression turning wry. "Trust me, I know what that looks like. The question is: how are you going to fix it?"

"I don't know." But I'm sure as fuck not going to give up. "Thanks, man. I needed a pep talk."

Jase nods, and Devon presses his lips together so firmly that I'm sure he's biting back some kind of smartass remark. For the first time all day, my lips twitch into a half-smile.

"You've got our backs, we've got yours." Jase holds out a fist, and I bump it. "You've got this."

———

ASHLIN

When I roll over and encounter an empty spot where Seth slept, memories of loneliness and grief flood my mind.

He's gone.

After assuring me he'd be here for me, he left. And for what? Work.

Whoa, hold on, girl.

Sensing that I'm traveling a dangerous path, I call a halt to those slippery negative thoughts.

"I'm a strong woman who can take care of herself." I repeat the affirmation I've said hundreds of times before. "I choose to have people in my life, but I don't depend on them."

Calmness descends. The first time my therapist had me say affirmations, I felt ridiculous and thought they were a load of hocus pocus, but I found that the more I said them, the truer they felt, until suddenly, I couldn't distinguish them from truth anymore and they became my truth.

"He had to work," I tell myself. "That doesn't mean it's the start of a pattern. Yesterday was a difficult day for both of us."

So what am I going to do to deal with it?

Call my support team.

Thirty minutes later, I've showered, dressed, and have pancake batter in the skillet when I hear a knock on the door followed by the sound of a key in the lock. A moment later, Paige bounds into the room. Her gaze settles on me, then she rushes over and hauls me into a hug. The breath gusts from my lungs.

"Oh, baby girl." She squeezes me tighter, and I meet Jessica's eyes over her shoulder, mouthing "help me." She smirks, and shrugs. "Are you okay?" Paige doesn't wait for me to answer. "Of course you're not. No one would be. But the baby is fine, and you're healthy, and I don't need to kick the universe's ass on your behalf." She draws back, searching my face, and what-ever she sees there must reassure her because she kisses my cheek and lets me go. "I can't believe you didn't call me."

"Paige." Jessica's hand lands on her shoulder. "You know

exactly why she didn't call us. She was being the thoughtful, loving friend she is and trying to protect us from sharing her pain." Gently, she moves Paige to the side and scoops me into a hug so tender I'm afraid I'll cry. "Don't do it again," she whispers in my ear. "We can handle it." She stands back and swipes at invisible moisture under her eyes. "Love you."

"Love you, too." My eyes prickle. "Damn you." I laugh, despite myself. "You're setting me off again."

"Sorry."

Paige grabs each of us. "Group hug."

For a brief moment, I let them sweep me into their arms, but then I extricate myself. Too much of that and I'll start bawling. The scent of pancakes reminds me of the skillet, and I busy myself dishing one onto a plate and loading another into the pan.

"What's on your mind?" Jessica asks as she pours juice into three glasses on the breakfast bar.

"Give me five minutes." I finish cooking our breakfast and we sit together at the bar. I drag in a deep breath, not sure where to start, just knowing that I need to launch into it. "Yesterday, when I started bleeding, I felt so overwhelmed. I panicked. Didn't know what to do. I called an ambulance, for God's sake. I'm scared that I'm going to fall into old habits if I stay with Seth. I can't go back to that dark mental place I was in before our divorce."

"Okay, let's break this down." Jessica carves off a piece of her pancake, her table manners meticulous, and finishes it before continuing. "You started bleeding. You panicked. What happened next?"

Even the memory makes my mouth dry, so I sip my juice. "I called Seth."

"And when he didn't answer?"

"I called 911. Probably an overreaction, in hindsight, but the operator told me what to do."

214

"So, you managed to organize an ambulance, and for Seth's sister to support you, all on your own?"

"No." Hasn't she been listening? "The emergency services operator told me what to do."

"Okay." She nods but there's a stubborn set to her jaw. "And who told you to call emergency services?"

"Common sense." My frustration grows. She's making out as though I didn't have a breakdown.

"Whose common sense?" she persists.

I roll my eyes. "Mine, obviously. But I'm beginning to wonder if it was even that sensible to call 911 considering the price tag."

Her expression softens. "You're safe, and you have a wealthy man who—unless I'm mistaken—is probably happy to pay the fee if it gives you peace of mind. Isn't that right?"

"Um, I guess so."

"I *know* so." She smiles sweetly. "So just to sum it up, it was *your* common sense that got emergency services coming to you—which is well within your means—and that put you in touch with the person who helped you navigate the situation successfully."

Now it's my turn to pause. I hadn't thought of it that way.

"I… guess so."

"Good." She smiles with satisfaction.

"You handled yourself well," Paige adds. "Anyone would have been upset in the circumstances, but you did what you needed to make sure you and the baby were safe."

"But I felt overwhelmed," I protest weakly. "Scared."

Paige scratches her chin and turns to Jessica. "What's that famous quote? Courage isn't the absence of fear, but feeling the fear and doing it anyway?"

"Something like that," Jessica confirms. "The point is, Ash, however you felt inside, you took the actions you needed to. Honestly, if you're asking more of yourself than that, then I'm not on board with it."

A weight on my chest lightens. When they put it like that, I can see where they're coming from. For the first time since yesterday, I experience a flicker of pride. They're right. I did do what was needed. Maybe my instincts made me want to play dead, but I didn't let the fear win. I'm stronger than that. But I can't ask myself to be perfect.

"Thank you." I extend my hands to grab theirs. "I love you guys so much."

I *have* changed. And this version of me is capable of being in a relationship with a man like Seth, even when he gets bossy. Hopefully I haven't pushed him away.

26

SETH

The next day, fighters circle me warily at the gym, as though they saw me letting loose on the bag yesterday and are afraid to get in my way. They don't need to worry. When I went home last night, half afraid of what I'd find, Ashlin was up and about. She hadn't gone to work, which meant I didn't need to remind her of the importance of taking care of herself. She'd also had her friends over. Whatever they said to her had worked magic because she was almost unrecognizable from the previous day. I owe those women my gratitude.

Still, something was off this morning. As I watch Harley and Enya work on pads—each of whom seem thrilled to have the opportunity to train with another female at their level—my mind is on the way Ashlin hustled me out the door, almost as though she was trying to get rid of me. I'm not used to that, and I didn't like it.

Several rounds pass while I offer suggestions, and when they finish, I direct Enya to the weight bench. For somebody with flawless technique, her strength leaves a lot to be desired. I suspect she's only come as far as she has because of her speed and tenacity.

I wander the gym floor, correcting strikes and offering advice, but after a while, the place begins to empty. It's not until I head into my office and return to find Jimmy dashing for the exit, the gym completely abandoned, that I realize I'm not imagining it.

"Oy," I shout, and startle him into stopping.

"Oh, man." His cheeks flush the color of beets. "I'm just doing what I'm told."

"By who?"

He glances at the exit, all jittery. Then, before I can reach him, he darts outside.

"Damn." I stride across the floor, not in the mood for games. What the fuck is going on? I'm only halfway there when Bruno Mars' song, *Marry You,* blasts over the speakers.

What. The. Fuck.

The door opens, and I put my hands on my hips and glare, but then Ashlin appears and all I can think is that she's walking around in a belly-baring top where anyone could see. It takes me a moment to realize what she's actually wearing. *Fight gear.* Her crop top stops above her stomach, which isn't curved yet. If I didn't know about the pregnancy, I wouldn't be able to tell. Her slender legs extend beneath a pair of shorts with the gym's logo printed on the front. Fuck, it feels right to see her in something that shows her allegiance to me. But the costume doesn't stop there. Someone has given her the fighter's jacket, and it hangs from her shoulders. I glance at the wall where it usually stays and find the spot empty. Who'd have dared to remove it?

My gaze journeys down her bare arms to her hands, which are clad in knuckle wraps that leave her fingers free to move. I meet her gaze, and she smiles tremulously, as though unsure of her reception. She moves across the floor toward me, freeing space in the doorway, and Harley appears behind her, followed by Jase, Devon, and Gabe. Harley has a bucket clasped in her grip. That's when it hits me. They're role playing. Acting as

218

though Ashlin is about to enter the ring, and they're in her corner. The song echoes in my head, the words bouncing around.

What the hell is going on here?

I stay exactly where I am, curious to see where this little act is going. Ashlin stops in front of me, and the music cuts out.

"Hi, Seth."

"Hey, baby. Want to tell me what's happening?"

Her lips curve up. "Can't you guess? I'm fighting for us." There's so much to unload in that statement, but before I have a chance, she continues. "I was worried I wasn't strong enough to be with you. That I'd fall back into the dark place I was before. The other day, I thought I'd confirmed all of my fears."

Unable to help myself, I brush a loose strand of hair from her forehead and tuck it behind her ear, letting my fingers linger on her skin.

"I was blind," she says. "I expected things to go badly, so that's how I interpreted them. My friends helped me realize that I am strong. Maybe I don't always feel it, but nobody does. It's my actions that matter."

"You're so strong," I tell her. "Most people wouldn't be brave enough to approach their ex for help."

"You're right." Her lips curve in a slight smile, and her dark eyes search mine. "I'm sorry if I hurt you when I pulled away. I can't guarantee I won't do it again if I get overwhelmed, but I can promise I'll always come around because I love you, and our relationship is worth everything."

She turns to Harley, who reaches into the bucket and passes her something—it happens so quickly I don't see what it is—but then Ashlin sinks to one knee and opens her palm to reveal a jewelry box. She pops the lid open and a pair of rings sparkle up at me. Ones that are very familiar, because she used to wear them every day.

"I'm sorry I haven't got yours," she says. "I tried to find it in your condo, but I didn't have any luck." She sucks in a breath, her expression giving away her nerves. "Will you marry me again?"

Oh, my God. Is this actually happening?

My pregnant ex-wife is down on one knee, proposing.

"Isn't that my job?" I ask.

She shrugs. "Technically, you already asked, but your timing wasn't ideal. I'm just hoping the offer still stands."

She doesn't seem bothered that I haven't answered yet. It's like now that she's put everything on the line, she's not afraid anymore. Fuck, that's hot.

"The reason you couldn't find my ring is because it's in my pocket." I draw the box out and open it, then drop to one knee, so we're both kneeling on the ground, more or less at eye level if you ignore the fact she's several inches shorter than me. "I've been carrying it around, waiting for the moment I can put it back on."

Her face lights up, and my heart grows wings. I want to make her smile like that every day for the rest of our lives.

"Yes, sweetheart. I'll marry you again." I slot the ring onto my finger, and she slips her rings as far up her finger as the knuckle covers allow, then we edge closer to each other and I capture her mouth in a kiss meant to show her we belong together always.

ASHLIN

Thank God.

While I know for certain that I'd have survived if Seth said no, I can unequivocally say I'm happy he agreed. He angles his head, taking the kiss deeper, and someone wolf-whistles. I pull back, blushing. I don't shy away from public affection, but I'm not used to being the center of attention either. Seth gets to his feet, then offers me a hand. I slip mine into his, loving how calloused and huge it is. He's always made me feel delicate and feminine just by existing, and the contrast between us emphasizes it.

Then, without warning, he scoops me into his arms.

"Hey!" I exclaim, clinging to his chest. Not that I'm afraid he'll drop me. It's just a really excellent chest. Broad, solid, sexy as all get-out.

He nuzzles the top of my head. "I'm taking you home, wife."

I giggle. "I'm not your wife yet."

He smirks. "You will be soon."

I don't argue with that. "Take me home, future husband."

His eyes gleam with love, and he kisses me once before addressing Jase. "Lock up behind you. Don't leave a mess. Call if there's an emergency, but only then."

He nods. "You got it."

Still holding me, Seth carries me outside. "Where's your car?"

"Not here. Devon brought me."

"They were all in on this, huh?"

I smooth a hand up his chest. "Don't be annoyed with them."

"I'm not, baby. I'm so fucking grateful."

He takes me to his car and somehow manages to support me with one arm while unlocking it with the other, then lowers me gently into the passenger seat. He gets in, and we hold hands for the entire duration of the drive to my place. When we arrive, he sweeps me off the ground again, and I laugh. My first instinct is to protest that I'm an independent woman and don't need him to carry me, but to be honest, I like it, so if he wants to, where's the harm? I'm strong enough to give us something we both want.

Instead of taking me to the bedroom, he goes to the living room, where he deposits me on the beanbag, flops beside me, and holds me firmly to him.

"We need to talk about a few things."

I sigh, knowing he's right.

"First off, I want you to know that I recognize how strong you are, and if I ever do anything to suggest otherwise, let me know." His lips press together, and he rubs a hand along his jaw. "I know I can be bossy, and I'll try to rein it in, but you've got to tell me how you're feeling, too."

"Deal." I snuggle into his shoulder. "But that goes both ways. You can't just bury yourself in work or a project and hope a problem goes away. We need to communicate. Promise?"

"Promise." His hand slides between us and finds mine. They intertwine, and something inside me flutters, almost as though the baby senses the importance of what's happening and wants to encourage us to keep going. I know it's far too early in the pregnancy for that to be realistic, but it's a nice thought. "While we're talking about the future, I'd like to move in so we can be together. I love what you've done with the place, and I want to help make it ours so we can raise our family here."

Hearing the nerves in his voice, I grin. As if I'd say no. "You've practically been living here anyway. I've got no problem making it official."

"Good." He tilts his chin. I could swim in the depths of his ocean eyes forever. "The condo was just a place to crash. This feels like home." He pauses, then swallows, his Adam's apple bobbing. "You feel like home."

A sense of rightness fills me, and a golden glow that seems to come from the inside out. "I love you, Seth."

"Love you too, baby." His eyes tell me it's true. "You're the most important thing in the world to me." He smiles. "You always will be."

27

Ashlin - 3 months later

"Ugh, the sweating won't stop," I groan, wondering why on earth I decided to wear a full-length wedding dress. I should have opted for something shorter, so the air could circulate. "Why does it have to be so hot today?"

"Uh, babe, it's not that hot," Paige says, holding a cold compress to my forehead. "Thank God for waterproof makeup."

"If it helps, you're glowing," Harley chips in from behind her.

"That's because I'm a million degrees."

Paige lowers the compress, and I glance in the mirror of the gorgeous hotel suite we're getting ready in, immediately remembering why I chose this dress. It was one of the few maternity options that left plenty of room for growth but still flattered me.

I turn and kiss Paige's cheek. "Thanks, honey."

She yanks me into a hug and squeezes, heedless of the dress. "It's not every day your bestie marries her ex. I'm happy it's all worked out for you."

"We've given Seth plenty of notice that he'll be in trouble if he doesn't keep you happy," Jessica says, coming to stand alongside Paige. My three best friends—including my future sister-in-law—are stunning in pale green dresses. With their blonde hair and sun-kissed skin, Harley and Jessica could be sisters. Paige has made a couple of comments about being the ugly stepsister, but secretly, I know she likes to stand out and isn't at all concerned with how she looks.

"Are the flowers ready to go?" I ask.

"Yes, and they're beautiful." Harley fidgets with her dress. It's unusual for her to wear something like this, but she's made an exception for me.

"Devon isn't going to be able to keep his hands off you," I whisper, hoping to ease her discomfort.

"He'd better not," she grumbles.

I reapply my lipstick—hopefully for the last time this morning. There's a knock on the door, and we all turn as it sweeps open. Mae steps inside, and her forest green skirt swishes around her knees. She and my mother opted for matching green dresses that are several shades darker, so they're distinct from the bridesmaids but in keeping with the theme. She pauses, takes us all in, and then her gaze settles on me.

She smiles. "Have we been here before?"

I laugh. "It does feel familiar."

She crosses the room and her hands settle on my shoulders. We're much the same height, but unfortunately, my feet are swollen and my ankles are beginning to disappear, so flats are a must for the wedding.

"I'm so glad to have you back in the family." Her eyes shine with joy, and I know it isn't all for me. With the way she and Rick have been looking at each other lately, I can't help but wonder if there might be another Isles family wedding in the near future. She deserves happiness. "As far as I'm concerned, you never left."

"Thank you, Mae. That means a lot. I'd kiss you, but..." I gesture at my lipstick.

"He won't know what hit him." She runs a hand over my shoulder. "I'd better go and make sure he hasn't passed out from the anticipation. I'll see you after."

"Bye, Mae." I watch her leave, thinking what a wonderful grandmother she's going to make.

"Five minutes," Jessica says. "The celebrant just messaged. Any last things we need to do?"

"I think we're good," I tell her.

"Good?" Paige asks. "We're gorgeous. None of us can hold a candle to you, but this one," she pokes Harley's toned arm, "could be mistaken for an Amazon goddess."

I hide a smile. Paige seems to have really taken to Harley, who's not quite sure how to handle her. There's another knock at the door.

"Really?" Jessica huffs in frustration. "It's nearly go-time, people."

My brother and father step into the room, expressions sheepish.

"Sorry, Jess," Liam says. "We'll just be a minute."

She narrows her eyes and makes the universal gesture for 'I'm watching you'.

Liam slings an arm around my shoulders and kisses the top of my elaborately arranged hair. "Congratulations, Ash. I know I wasn't exactly supportive of your plan at first, but I'm glad it ended up here."

"Thanks, Liam."

Dad crowds in on the other side and they sandwich me between them.

"Careful of the dress," Jessica warns. She's appointed herself protector of my big day, and I love her for it.

Dad winks at me. "I always knew you'd find your way back to him. Couldn't be prouder of you, darling." He kisses my cheek lightly so he doesn't smudge the makeup. "Now go put that boy out of his misery. He's afraid you won't turn up."

SETH

I adjust my silk tie, which seems to constrict tighter around my neck with each breath I take.

Please let her show.

I've been standing at the end of the aisle with my groomsmen—Jase, Devon, and Gabe—for several minutes, waiting for my bride to arrive, and I'm starting to sweat. Logically, I know she wouldn't leave me. We're crazy for each other. But on some deep level, my subconscious fears she'll get cold feet. It's one of the reasons I wanted a short engagement, with the other one being that planning a wedding with a newborn to care for sounds like hell.

I glance at the clock. Still two minutes until the ceremony officially begins. We've rented the ballroom of a five-star hotel for the venue, although it's only half full. We've done the big wedding before and wanted to keep it more intimate this time around. Only close friends and family are present.

I turn to Jase. "Do you think there's any chance she won't show?"

He pats my shoulder. "She'll be here."

"But what if—"

"Bro," Devon interrupts. "Ash is a good woman, and she loves you. She'll come."

At that moment, music begins. It's the Bruno Mars song she played when she proposed.

Jessica appears in the doorway. She looks nice, but when her eyes lock on mine, they silently threaten me with all kinds of harm if I fuck up. I nod in return. Message received. I'm glad she has my girl's back.

Paige comes next, practically bouncing along the aisle.

Harley follows, moving carefully as though she's counting her steps. Finally, *finally*, the moment arrives.

I see my bride.

She's a vision. Her hair is pinned up, exposing the elegant length of her neck. My gaze travels along the curve of her shoulder, where the neckline of the dress suddenly plunges. My mouth drops open. Ashlin's tits are always great, but pregnancy has made them spectacular, and now her perfect cleavage is on display for all the guests to see. A growl rumbles from my chest, and I hear Devon smother a chuckle. Forcing my eyes up, I focus on her face, and any jealously quickly dies. She's radiant. Her eyes shine with love and affection. They're drinking me up the same way I just did her, as if she can't get enough. They meet mine, and hold.

My heart gives a whump-whump.

Damn. She's even more stunning than last time, and I'm the luckiest son of a bitch on the planet to be marrying her again. This time, I won't let go. Not ever.

"I love you," I say when she reaches the end of the aisle. The celebrant mutters something, but I ignore him. "You're beautiful."

She smiles almost shyly. "I love you, too. Are we doing this or what?"

I take her hand. "Let's do it."

We turn to the celebrant, who seems to be fighting laughter.

I say my vows with purpose, meaning each and every word of them. I will stand by this woman no matter what. She's mine, and I'm hers. Her lips tremble as she takes her turn, and then we slide rings onto one another's fingers. The same ones we used to wear. We discussed buying new rings for a fresh start, but decided our history is part of what makes us strong, and we want to honor it going forward.

The celebrant gets to the part I've been waiting for. "You may now kiss your bride."

My hands go to Ashlin's hips and I draw her as close as her

baby bump allows. Then I kiss her with everything I have and everything I am. Her lips part, and I take the kiss deeper, trying to tell her with my actions everything I just said with my words. This is our forever, and I'm going to hold onto our second chance with my entire heart and soul.

"I love you," I say, drawing back. "And I will never, ever let you go."

EPILOGUE – BABY'S FIRST BIRTHDAY

Ashlin

"Peek-a-boo!" Mae uncovers her face to smile at the baby in my arms. "I see you."

Baby Noah gurgles happily. The three of us are in the nursery, temporarily escaping the madness of the living area.

"Do you want to hold him?" I ask. "He's getting heavy."

"Of course." We engage in a pass-the-baby shuffle that I've perfected over the last year, and she sits him on her hip. I kiss the tip of my little boy's nose, and his vibrant blue-green eyes flick to me. My heart melts.

"Happy birthday, baby," I murmur, emotion threatening to choke me. A couple of years ago, I'd never have dared to hope I'd end up here. Not only do I have a healthy son, but my marriage is pretty wonderful too.

A pair of arms wrap around me from behind. "How's my wife?"

I smile and tilt my chin to look up at Seth. He loves calling me that and takes every opportunity to do it.

"Perfect." I kiss his chin because it's the only part of him I can reach from here. "How's my handsome husband?"

His lips curve. "Better now that I'm here with you." He lowers his voice. "How do we know so many people with babies, and did we have to invite them all?"

I cover my mouth to hide a smile. "Noah needs his friends here."

"He's one." Seth kisses my temple, and I go boneless against him. "He won't remember it."

"But his mommy will," Mae cuts in, leveling him with a look. "She needs to know she threw the best first birthday party she could."

He grumbles. "Fine, but when they all go, I'm going to need to join Noah for a nap."

Footsteps sound in the hall, and two more faces appear in the doorway. Harley and Devon.

"Nobody told us the party was moving," Devon complains, his gaze settling on Mae and Noah. "Oh, don't mind if I do." He stops at Mae's side, and Noah reaches for him. Devon takes him from Mae just as the baby grabs a handful of his shirt. He grins down fondly. "You've got good taste, kid." He glances at me. "Some of the babies are getting antsy, and the parents want to say their goodbyes to the birthday boy before they go."

"Okay." I nod. "I guess we'd better head back out there."

"I'll make a start." He carries Noah out of the room, and Harley follows behind. Mae sends us a smile and does the same, leaving us alone temporarily.

I turn in Seth's arms. "Can you believe this is our life?"

He rests his cheek on the top of my head. "It's pretty incredible. Have I told you lately how grateful I am that you came to me with your crazy pregnancy plan?"

I smile into his chest. "Not as grateful as I am that you decided you wanted me as well as a baby."

"God, I love you."

Drawing back, I gaze up at the man I can't get enough of. His ruggedly handsome face, and the gorgeous eyes our son inherited.

"The universe gave us a second chance, and I'll always be thankful for that." I step back and clasp our hands together. "Come on. Let's go see our family."

THE END

FIGHTER'S FRENEMY EXCERPT

Leo - A month after he switched gyms

I grit my teeth as the throb of a bass rattles the nightclub floor. Parties are not my scene. Especially not alcohol-fueled messes like this one. I don't have the patience for this crap, but unfortunately, I have to be here. It's the official after-party for my first professional fight since I shifted from City Fight Center to Crown MMA Gym. I lean against the bar, watching a mass of people writhe on the dance floor. Once upon a time, I'd have been in the thick of it, but I've been involved in the MMA circuit for long enough that fights don't have the same hype they used to. I'm certainly glad my new coach, Seth Isles, worked so hard to get me back in the cage, but I wish all I had to do was win and go home. As it is, my being absent would set tongues wagging. Many people still wonder whether I was complicit in the cheating operation my previous coach and fellow fighters were arrested for.

I wasn't.

Did it surprise me when I found out? Hell, no. There are some seriously dodgy people in this business. But I hadn't heard a whisper about it until the police showed up during a training session and started cuffing people.

My eye twitches. My opponent got a good shot in and I've already got a hell of a shiner. It'll be worse come morning. If I could've gone home, I'd have iced it, but at the moment, I'm the dude who has to do what he's told and go where his manager wants him.

Voices to the side catch my attention, the words "drugs," "cheater," and "fat skank" passing through the general noise and pricking my psyche. Straightening, I seek out the offending parties. I level my gaze on the backs of three guys who are facing a woman. I can't see who she is from here, but they've obviously cornered her.

"What in the actual fuck makes you think you can show your ugly face here tonight?" one of the men demands.

My jaw grinds. Whoever she is, no woman deserves to be spoken to like that.

"Is there a problem here?" I snap, shoving my way over to them.

All three men spin around, and when I spot their victim for the first time, I nearly roll my eyes.

Camile Hayes.

I should have known.

Her wide blue eyes land on me, silently begging to be rescued. Her full pink lips tremble as though she's on the verge of tears, and she hugs herself, emphasizing the way her tits nearly spill out the top of her dress. I swallow past an instantaneous gut-punch of lust. Yeah, Camile is sexy, with thick curves and an ass that's practically pleading for a man's hand to grip it, but she's a princess who doesn't think for herself. She lives in the shadow of her twin brother, Karson, one of the fighters who was recently arrested, and seems to be dependent on him for her confidence and sense of self.

"You." Their leader's eyes narrow. "You're as bad as her. Probably in on it. Fucking cheats."

Oh, fuck no. He did not just say that. My jaw locks and I shove up the sleeves of my button-down shirt, revealing tattooed forearms. "Look, I already beat the crap out of one guy tonight, and I'd rather not do it again. Leave the poor girl alone and pick on someone who can fight back."

One of the guy's friends steps toward me as though he wants to take a shot, but the leader stops him with a gesture.

"Fine." He holds up his hands. "She's all yours." He sends her a scathing look. "She's probably been passed around by half the men here anyway."

My fists curl tighter, but I resist the urge to plant one in his face. That's the last thing I need right now. When they've disappeared into the crowd, I turn to Camile. "Go home, Cami. Get your beauty sleep. There's nothing for you here."

To my surprise, temper sparks in her eyes. "You don't get to decide that," she snaps, dropping her arms from her waist and advancing on me. This close, I catch a hint of a subtle fragrance that makes me want to lick her until I find the source of it. "I'm sick and tired of men thinking they know what's best for me."

My jaw drops. Honestly, I've never heard Camile string more than a couple of words together, and certainly nothing as assertive as this. It shocks me. Especially given how she reacted to those bullies.

Raising her chin, she pivots, then sashays away, heading in a direction that isn't toward the exit. I stare after her. What the hell was that? Is there more to the princess than meets the eye?

And why do I want to follow her and find out?

ACKNOWLEDGMENTS

Thank you to Brittany and Sheridan for getting real with me about a range of emotions I haven't personally experienced before. I wanted this story to be as authentic as possible and you helped with that. Thank you for being so open and generous with your time and knowledge.

Thank you to Serena for, as usual, adding detail to give the story depth, and making sure everything happens where it ought to and that no body parts randomly go missing. Kate, I appreciate your enthusiasm for this series and for my writing so much. Some days, I really need that support, but you always help make me better as well as building me up. Thank you Maria for your ongoing supply of badass covers. You've pretty much single-handedly created the branding for this series.

Thank you to my family and friends for your support, and to my mastermind buddies for talking me down from so many metaphorical ledges. Finally, thank you from the bottom of my heart to my husband. You are my biggest cheerleader every single day, even when I don't feel like cheering for myself. Thank you for being there. For believing in me. I will never, ever take that for granted.

ABOUT THE AUTHOR

Alexa (A.) Rivers writes romance with strong heroes and heroines who kick butt and take names. She loves MMA fighters, investigators, military men, bodyguards, and the protective guy next door who isn't afraid to fight the odds for love.

Printed in Great Britain
by Amazon

30774779R00138